TICKET TO
TOMORROW

TICKET TO
TOMORROW

a romance mystery by
CAROL COX

BARBOUR
PUBLISHING

ISBN 1-59310-948-2

This book is a work of fiction. Names, characters, places, and incidents are either products of the author's imagination or used fictitiously. Any similarity to actual people, organizations, and/or events is purely coincidental.

Scripture quotations are taken from the King James Version of the Bible.

For more information about Carol Cox, please access the author's Web site at the following Internet address: www.CarolCoxBooks.com

Cover & Interior Design by Müllerhaus Publishing Arts, Inc., mhpubarts.com

Published by Barbour Publishing, Inc., P.O. Box 719, Uhrichsville, Ohio 44683, www.barbourbooks.com

Our mission is to publish and distribute inspirational products offering exceptional value and biblical encouragement to the masses.

 Member of the
Evangelical Christian
Publishers Association

Printed in the United States of America.
5 4 3 2 1

Dear Reader,

Some time ago I came across a history of the United States printed in the 1940s. Intrigued, I thumbed through its pages and found my attention caught by a passage on the World's Columbian Exposition, held in Chicago in 1893. Those brief paragraphs sparked my interest and set me off on a trail of research where I discovered a fascinating moment in America's history.

After winning the honor of hosting the great fair, Chicago opened its doors to the world and invited people from every nation to come to the White City. And come they did! Over twenty-seven million visitors passed through the gates during the fair's six-month duration.

By the time it was all over, America had established its position as a forward-thinking, cultured nation, and innovations such as the Ferris wheel and the midway, hamburgers and carbonated soda, Cracker Jack and ragtime music had become American institutions.

Thank you for joining me in reliving the moment that ushered in the twentieth century in America. I hope you will enjoy it as much as I have. Please visit my Web site at www.CarolCoxBooks.com. I'd love to hear from you!

Blessings,
Carol Cox

Dedication

To LeRoy and Lometa,
your love of Chicago has rubbed off on me,
and I will always be grateful!

Acknowledgments

My heartfelt thanks go to:

LeRoy and Lometa Cox, for extending their hospitality
and providing personalized tours of Chicago

Cheryl Hammock, whose knowledge of the area around Jackson Park
helped me find the perfect location for Mrs. Purvis's boardinghouse

and

Kristin Standaert, Assistant Dean, Bibliographic Systems at the
Paul V. Galvin Library, Illinois Institute of Technology, who graciously
provided me with floor plans of several of the exposition's buildings

CHAPTER I

June 1893

Annie Trenton lowered her knitting to her lap and stared out the train window, watching the farmland give way—first to a scattering of houses, then to an ever-increasing number of brick buildings. Silas Crockett dozed in the adjoining seat. Gentle snores emanated from his lips.

A flock of gray and white birds wheeled overhead. Annie nudged Silas. "Are those sea gulls? We must be getting quite close to Lake Michigan." Chicago and its mighty sprawl couldn't be far away now.

Roused from his doze, Silas rubbed the palm of his hand across his hair, leaving wisps of gray sticking out in all directions. "Michigan? No, Annie. Chicago is in Illinois."

Annie shook her head and picked up the mass of soft gray yarn lying in her lap. She resumed knitting, her fingers slipping the yarn from one needle to the other without conscious thought.

Beside her, Silas dug first in one pocket, then another.

Coming up empty-handed, he squirmed to one side and shoved his hand into the crevice between the seat and seat back. A frown rippled his brow, and his lips moved soundlessly. Annie watched with mild amusement as Silas curled forward and dragged his satchel out from under his seat. He unlatched the clasp and pawed through the contents with his head between his knees and his posterior angled toward the ceiling.

One corner of Annie's lips quirked upward. If the Crockett-Trenton Horseless Carriage didn't draw the interest they hoped for at the World's Columbian Exposition, Silas could always hire himself out as a contortionist on the Midway Plaisance.

She leaned forward and rested her arms on her knees. "What are you looking for?"

"My notebook." Silas twisted to one side and looked up at her, his face dark red from the rush of blood to his head. "It's gone. I wanted to make a quick sketch of an idea I just had." He straightened and peered at her over his wire-rimmed spectacles with a plaintive expression.

Annie reached out and pushed his spectacles back up on the bridge of his nose. "It isn't gone. You just aren't looking in the right place. Think back. Where did you see it last?"

A blank expression settled over Silas's features.

"You had it in the dining car," Annie prompted.

Silas brightened. "Ah, yes. I was jotting down some notes about gear ratios during lunch."

Annie remembered. His complete absorption with his task and resulting inattention to their meal had drawn their waiter's marked displeasure. Fortunately Silas hadn't noticed. "Why don't you go back and see if it's still there?"

Silas wandered off obediently in the direction of the dining car. Annie watched him push through the door at the rear of their car and hoped he would remember how to find his way there and back.

She shifted her position on the uncomfortable seat and tried to smooth some of the wrinkles from her dark blue gored skirt. Travel in the confines of a railcar didn't do a thing to help keep a person looking presentable.

Picking up her yarn again, she continued knitting down the row. Early June might seem an odd time to be working on a Christmas present for Silas, but it kept her fingers busy and her mind focused on safe thoughts.

Normally one wouldn't think of making a gift while sitting next to the intended recipient, but with Silas, it didn't matter a bit. If he noticed it at all, he would never put two and two together. The man might be a genius when it came to things mechanical, but he seldom showed the least bit of interest in the everyday world around him. Her fingers looped the yarn around the needles in practiced rhythm.

A scarf for Silas. Annie's fingers slowed. She once expected to be knitting an array of tiny garments in preparation for motherhood at this point in her life. Instead. . .she pressed her lips together and increased her speed again. Maybe she should make a whole series of scarves after finishing this one. Silas probably wouldn't manage to keep any one of them more than a couple of months at best. The one she made him last Christmas hadn't lasted two weeks before he went off and left it who knew where.

The front door of the car swung open, admitting the conductor. "End of the line in ten minutes, folks. Next stop, the World's Columbian Exposition. Make sure you have all your belongings before you leave the train."

Annie completed the row of knitting, then rolled her work into a loose ball before tucking it back into her valise.

Someone nudged her left elbow, and she shifted to let Silas resume his seat. Instead of her companion, a sharp-faced woman slid in beside her.

Annie eyed the woman. She had noticed her before in a group already on the train when she and Silas had boarded in Bloomington, Indiana. Their curious stares and spates of cackling reminded her of a flock of hens. The woman's beaklike nose did nothing to dispel the resemblance at close range.

"We haven't had a chance to visit during the trip. I am Mrs. Peter Tompkins, president of the Bedford Ladies Club. We plan to spend next week touring the fair. And you are. . . ?"

"Annie Trenton."

"And the gentleman you are traveling with. . .your father?"

"Silas?" Annie shook her head. "No, he isn't my father."

"Oh. Your husband then."

A heaviness settled in Annie's chest. "No. We aren't related."

"Oh?" Mrs. Tompkins's eyebrows soared up near her hairline. "Oh!" She swept back down the aisle to report to her wide-eyed followers. A collective gasp hissed through the car, followed by barnyardlike twittering.

Annie closed her eyes and considered. She could spend the final moments of her journey explaining her relationship with Silas to the ladies of Bedford, but why bother? Their narrow minds were already made up about her, and nothing she could do would be likely to change that.

Instead, she busied herself gathering her belongings and tried to convince herself it didn't matter. To be sure, the two of them traveling together was more than a bit unconventional, hardly the norm for a respectable young woman. But normalcy had flown out of her life a year ago and didn't seem ready to make a return appearance anytime soon.

Silas hurried up the aisle and brandished his notebook triumphantly. "You were right. It was in the dining car." He settled into his seat and tucked the notebook inside his satchel. "I believe I'll take a short nap."

"No time for that. We're pulling into the station now." Annie scooped up her reticule and adjusted her hat pin to hold her new straw skimmer firmly in place. "Do you have everything—your hat, your walking stick?"

The train slowed and came to a stop. Annie braced herself against the seat in front as the slack in the couplings was taken up, and tried to quell the nervous flutter in her stomach. "All right then. We're here."

She slid past Silas and waited for an opportunity to move into the packed aisle. From the determined set on the other passengers' faces, it looked to be a long wait. A lighthearted, fair-going holiday mood would come later. For now, they appeared every bit as eager as she to get off the train and escape the confines of the hard, narrow seats.

Annie glanced out the window. Her spirits plummeted when she saw the jostling mass of people. Surely the fairgrounds wouldn't be this crowded all the time. She squared her shoulders and lifted her chin. If they were, she would just have to get used to it. She knew when she decided to come it might not always be easy.

Spotting a gap in the shuffling procession, she inserted herself into it, creating a buffer so Silas could get out. "Let's go."

Silas settled his bowler atop his shock of gray hair and stepped into the aisle. "Ready, my dear." The gap filled in again

11

the moment he moved next to her.

"Where's your satchel?"

"Oh, dear me." He dove back toward the seat he had just vacated, worming his way through the irritated passengers in a manner that reminded Annie of a salmon swimming upstream. He emerged again, satchel in hand, oblivious to the outraged sputters of their fellow travelers.

Ah, well. Annie turned and let the flow of the crowd move her toward the outer door. Life would never be dull with Silas around.

CHAPTER 2

Once outside, Annie paused to draw a breath of air. Not the pure, sweet air she was used to at home, but at least it wasn't the train's cooped-up atmosphere laced with the smells of food, sweat, and stale tobacco. She eyed the teeming mass of humanity inching its way toward Terminal Station like grain flowing into a hopper and felt a quiver of expectation creep up her backbone.

Silas forged ahead, and Annie reached out to grip his arm. It wouldn't do to become separated in this crush. Silas would never find his way to the exhibit building on his own. More likely, he'd wind up wandering the streets of Chicago. A stout woman—one of the Bedford ladies, if memory served—bumped up hard against her. Annie scrambled to regain her balance and jutted out her elbows, hoping to prevent another collision.

Outside the train, its former passengers now seemed ready to give their exuberance free rein. Snippets of conversation chased each other through the air:

"I'm heading to the stock pavilion first. There's supposed to be a new breed of cattle on display. . . ."

"Have you heard about the giant wheel that fellow Ferris is building? They say it's going to take people up off the ground in compartments the size of Pullman cars."

"Ha! Sounds like a fool notion to me. I'm glad we came before they finished setting it up. What's to keep the thing from getting loose and rolling right across the grounds? Why, something that large would crush everything in its path."

Annie leaned close to Silas and raised her voice to be heard over the hubbub. "We need to find someone to help us with the carriage. Do you know where we're supposed to take it once it's unloaded? And what about the rest of our luggage? We'll need to find out where they're unloading the baggage and where we can store it while we set up the exhibit."

Silas blinked like a startled owl. "Didn't I tell you? I wired my nephew. He's going to meet us here."

It was Annie's turn to blink. "I didn't know you had family in Chicago."

"I don't." Silas stopped in his tracks and craned his neck to scan the crowd.

Annie resisted the impulse to shake him. She knew all too well that while many of Silas's comments thoroughly confused the hearer, some vestige of logic lay underneath, in Silas's mind at least. With a forbearance borne of long experience, she accepted the existence of the hitherto-unknown nephew. . .for the moment.

Silas continued to peer about, a dam blocking the flow of traffic. "I do hope I recognize him. I haven't seen him since he was a lad in knickers."

"Then how will we manage to know him?"

"It shouldn't be too difficult to spot him. People always said he reminded them of me." Silas gave a modest chuckle.

Annie stifled a groan. Much as she loved Silas, his dithering ways could be maddening. One muddle-headed genius to tend to was quite enough. The prospect of having two on her hands. . . No, it didn't bear thinking about.

She set her valise down by her feet and scanned the crowd but didn't see anyone who appeared to be searching for them. "What's his name?"

"His name?" Silas's face assumed a blank expression that made her want to grind her teeth. But why should she expect him to remember? If they had been discussing a design for some new mechanism, every detail would be at the forefront of his mind, but the name of a mere nephew. . .no.

His eyes took on the light of knowledge. "Nicholas. That's it. Yes, Nicholas. After my late brother, you know."

Annie didn't, but she chose to keep that to herself. Getting Silas sidetracked was all too easy at the best of times, and this moment hardly qualified as one of them.

A portly man with a large family in tow pushed past them, sending Annie teetering off balance. One of the younger children tripped over her valise and set up a wail. The father shot a sharp glare at Annie, scooped up the youngster, and continued on his way, muttering about inconsiderate people who left belongings lying about.

Annie scooted the valise closer to her. She needed to get them out of this crush. Where was the nephew? She searched the crowd again, trying to pick out anyone who looked like her companion. Knowing Silas, though, he could easily have gotten his nephew's location confused before blithely sending the wire telling him to appear at the station at a certain time. Even now, a younger version of Silas Crockett might be waiting on a platform in New York or Baltimore, watching in vain for a glimpse of his uncle.

Silas exhibited none of the anxiety that plagued Annie. He bounced on his toes, seeming to enjoy himself thoroughly. "It's hard to believe we're here at last. Wouldn't Will have been excited to see this day come?"

Grief plunged a dagger into Annie's heart, and tears blurred the crowd into a confusion of shifting colors. For a moment, the depot receded, and she was aware of nothing but her pain. Then Silas's voice broke through the fog.

"Annie. Annie?"

She fumbled in her reticule for her handkerchief and dabbed at her eyes. Silas hovered next to her, remorse evident in his crinkled brow. "I didn't mean to cause you pain, my dear. I just couldn't help thinking how pleased Will would have been. He would, wouldn't he?"

Annie blinked the last of the tears away and forced a tiny smile. She gave Silas's shoulder a reassuring squeeze. "Of course, he would. That's the reason I'm here, remember?"

He flashed a relieved smile; then his gaze darted toward the door. "Perhaps he's waiting for us inside." Without another word, he hoisted his satchel and plunged into the maelstrom of people jostling to enter Terminal Station.

"Wait!" Panic-stricken at the thought of being separated, Annie picked up her valise and was swept up in the current. Once inside, the flow opened as most fairgoers headed straight for the outer doors and the wonders of the exposition. Annie ducked into a sheltered spot beside one of the thick, white columns. From there, she spotted Silas. . .just as he collided with a dapper man hurrying toward the exit.

The impact knocked both men to the ground. Hats, satchels, and walking sticks scattered across the pavement. The incident barely caused a ripple in the river of people. They continued their rush past, stepping over the fallen men and their strewn belongings. Annie launched herself toward Silas.

"Are you all right?" She tugged at his arm and helped him to his feet.

"Good heavens!" He wobbled in a tight circle. "Did I run into a wall?"

"No, that man over there." Annie brushed at his coat. "Are you hurt?"

He passed his hand over his eyes. "My vision is blurry. I must have hit my head on something."

Annie rescued his spectacles from where they dangled off his left ear and settled them back onto his nose. "How is that?"

"Ah, much better. And now I must see to the poor fellow I knocked down." He picked his way across the litter of scattered belongings and bent over the well-dressed, mustachioed man. "My apologies, sir. It seems to have been entirely my fault."

"Indeed it was."

"I'm terribly sorry." Silas reached out to assist his victim.

"Then perhaps you will be more careful in the future." The man brushed Silas's hand away, struggled to his feet, and began to gather his things. Still looking penitent, Silas handed him his satchel. The man snatched it away with a cold stare. "I have business here myself, but you don't see me bowling people over."

Silas wrung his hands. "It truly was an accident. I humbly beg your forgiveness."

"Consider yourself forgiven then. I must be on my way." The man tucked his walking stick under his arm and disappeared into the throng.

Annie gathered Silas's things and carried them to him. "He didn't seem like a very sympathetic man."

Silas relieved her of the satchel and set his hat atop his head. "He didn't, did he?" He stared at a point over Annie's right shoulder, and his face brightened. "There's Nicholas!" Turning back to Annie, he confided, "The family resemblance is still there. I'd know him anywhere." He started across the station, a smile lighting his face.

Annie stared in the direction he headed and tried to pick out someone with Silas's vague eyes and distracted air. She spotted a weedy, bespectacled man on the fringe of the crowd over near the station entrance.

Sure enough, Silas spread his arms wide as he approached the little man, then proceeded to walk right past him.

Annie picked up her valise once more and dogged Silas's steps. *What now?*

"Uncle Silas!" The cry came from up ahead. Annie picked up her pace and saw Silas enveloped in a bear hug from a robust man in a fringed buckskin jacket.

Silas dropped his satchel and pounded the brawny man on the back. "It's been a long time, my boy. How is life on the wild frontier?"

"Couldn't be better. Joining up with Bill Cody's Wild West Show is one of the best things that ever happened to me." He smiled down at his uncle and clapped him on the shoulder. "I can't tell you how pleased I was to get your wire. So one of your inventions has found success at last, has it?"

"It has indeed, even more than I hoped for. So true that two heads are better than one. I should have joined forces with a partner years ago."

Annie shifted from one foot to the other and studied Nicholas while she waited for an introduction. Where was the family resemblance Silas had spoken of?

Nicholas looked around at the rushing crowd. "Ah, yes. You said something about your partner coming with you."

Annie cleared her throat gently.

Silas chuckled. "Wait until you see the carriage. It's going to make horses obsolete one day."

Annie cleared her throat again.

Nicholas turned a warm, brown gaze upon her. "May I help you, ma'am?"

Silas glanced her way; then his gaze sharpened. "Annie! There you are. Allow me to introduce you to my nephew, Nicholas." He made a sweeping gesture. "Nicholas, this is Annie. . .Mrs. Trenton," he amended.

Annie stared into the dark brown eyes and discarded the mental image she had created of Silas's relative. This tall, broad-shouldered cowboy looked like he would be more at home atop a horse on a windswept prairie than here. She extended her hand. "I'm pleased to meet you. Thank you for coming to meet us, Mr. Crockett."

Nicholas's hand enveloped hers in a strong grip. "My pleasure. But it's Rutherford. Nick Rutherford." He pushed back a wave of chestnut hair that seemed determined to fall across his forehead.

"But. . ." Annie turned to Silas. "I thought you said he was named after your brother."

Silas beamed. "That's right."

Nick threw back his head and laughed. "I get the feeling Uncle Silas's way of explaining things is still as bewildering as ever. He's quite correct that I'm named after his brother, Nicholas. But his brother is my other uncle. My mother is their sister, thus the difference in our last names." He smiled down at Annie. "Are you thoroughly confused?"

Annie sighed and smiled back. "I'm used to it by now."

"Let's get out of this crowd," Nick suggested. "You're probably wanting to get your exhibit set up."

Silas's features twisted into a comical look of dismay. "But we can't go without the carriage. Where is the baggage car? I need to make sure they don't damage it while unloading."

"All taken care of." Nick patted his uncle's shoulder and pointed outside. "That's what made me late in finding you. She's sitting right outside. I wanted to supervise the unloading myself."

Annie followed the two men through the station doors and stopped still at the grand sight before her.

Nick turned back and seemed to recognize her sense of awe. "It takes your breath away, doesn't it?"

Annie could only nod. A broad plaza opened out in front of her. On the far side, a massive white building stretched across the width of the open area. Above the enormous arched doorway, she could see a second level surrounded by columns. And atop it all, a golden dome soared high above the teeming activity of the fair.

"And that's only the Administration Building," Nick said.

"Wait until you see the rest of the place."

Annie looked up at him, feeling dazed. "There's more, isn't there?"

A low chuckle rumbled from Nick's throat. "Much more." He glanced over his shoulder. "This way, Uncle! She's right over there, ready to move and already attracting a crowd of admirers."

Annie looked in the direction he pointed and saw the small knot of people clustered around the Crockett-Trenton Horseless Carriage, its finely polished body gleaming in the sunlight. A surge of pride mingled with pain shot through her as it always did at the sight of the vehicle.

Forgetting Nick Rutherford, the curious crowd, and even Silas, she crossed the short distance and ran her hand along the carriage's smooth sides. Silas was right. Will would have rejoiced this day, seeing the culmination of his hopes and dreams. For now, that would have to suffice.

CHAPTER 3

Nick watched Annie stroke her fingers along the side of the carriage with a touch as tender as a caress. He shook his head. This day was turning out to be full of surprises. First, seeing his uncle again after so long, then realizing he had actually come up with a useful invention, something the gatekeepers of the fair deemed important enough to display at this lavish international event.

And what an event! The fair directors had enticed entries from every corner of the world.

Granted, those same directors had been too snooty to allow Buffalo Bill's Wild West Show and Congress of Rough Riders of the World to put up their arena on the fairgrounds. But true to form, Bill Cody rose to the occasion and set up his headquarters just outside the gates.

Nick grinned. If he didn't miss his guess, the show would bring in enough income to make the fair board rue the day they turned away Cody's business—and the resulting commission from its proceeds.

As for Uncle Silas and his grand invention, Nick had kept up on news about this most recent project through the family grapevine. Speculation ran rife as to whether this was truly a stroke of genius or another harebrained scheme destined to join the likes of the contraption he'd come up with a few years before, designed to mechanically saddle a horse.

From the reaction of the people hovering over the shining vehicle, it just might fall more into the realm of genius. Nick smiled. *Good for Uncle Silas.* Nice to know one of his brainstorms actually produced something worthwhile.

Whispers about a partner in the enterprise circulated along with the rest of the family gossip. Nick suspected the success of the horseless carriage could be attributed to this. Uncle Silas needed someone to keep things on a practical footing and prevent his ideas from spiraling off into the absurd. Nick grinned at the childhood memory of the combination cheese maker and cream separator that flew apart in his grandmother's kitchen, flinging a stream of curds that covered the walls as well as his outraged female relatives.

But in his wildest imaginings, he never dreamed of a partner like Annie Trenton. He studied her now, noting the way the sunlight glinted on the ash blond curls peeping out from under the brim of her straw hat. She didn't seem flustered by the gawkers, but her calm, sea blue eyes and grave expression gave Nick the impression that nothing much ruffled her air of tranquility.

A woman her age ought to be home tending her children. What could she possibly know about designing a vehicle? And how did she come to be working with his uncle? Nothing about the situation—or Annie Trenton—made sense.

Mrs. Trenton, he reminded himself. Nick had to admit to the shock of disappointment he felt on learning she was married.

But that only added to the mystery. Where on earth was her husband? What kind of man let his wife traipse around the country in the company of another man, even one as harmless as his uncle?

He turned his attention back to the carriage. The knot of onlookers pressed closer, drawing a squawk of dismay from Silas, who hurried over to wipe any smudges away with his handkerchief. Annie Trenton stepped back and allowed him to field the onslaught of questions. Nick moved closer so he could hear.

"Where's the tongue?" a young man asked.

"There's no need to hitch horses to this carriage," Silas explained. "It's self-propelled."

"You mean the thing moves on its own? Are you sure it runs?"

"Of course it runs." An aggrieved note tinged Silas's voice. "It has been thoroughly tested, I assure you."

"Let's see how it works," the eager man suggested. "How about showing us right now?"

Silas wadded his handkerchief into a ball and mopped his brow. "I'm afraid we can't do that. It's high time we were on our way to. . ." His voice trailed off, and he threw a desperate look at Nick and Annie. "Where is it we're supposed to be going?"

"The Manufactures and Liberal Arts Building," Nick supplied.

"The Crockett-Trenton Horseless Carriage will be on display in the Manufactures and Liberal Arts Building shortly," Silas told the crowd. "Please stop by and examine it there at your leisure. I will be most happy to answer any questions you may have."

With the help of a couple of stalwart young lads recruited by Nick, Silas guided the carriage around to the left of the Administration Building and followed the walkway east.

Annie trailed along behind with Nick close at hand, already feeling the effects of their long day. If she could persuade Silas to part from his beloved masterpiece long enough to get settled in their lodgings, perhaps they could get some rest. She rounded the corner of the Administration Building.

For the second time that day, Annie stopped dead in her tracks and simply stared. Points of light sparkled across a long pool of water that stretched out toward the shore of Lake Michigan. And surrounding the pool. . .

She caught her breath at the panorama of colonnaded buildings, each a pristine white that glittered in the late afternoon sun.

Annie felt the sting of tears, and her throat thickened. The sight seemed too much for the mind to take in all at once. She struggled for words to describe the scene. "It's. . .it's. . ."

"They call it the White City. A bit overwhelming, isn't it?" Nick's gentle voice sounded like it came from a distance. "Come on, there will be plenty of time for you to see it later and give it all the attention it deserves. For now, we'd better keep moving if we don't want to lose sight of Uncle Silas."

"Silas!" Annie snapped to attention and hurried after him, with Nick bringing up the rear.

"I can't thank you enough for your kindness in seeing to all these details." Annie smiled at Nick and leaned against the small table at the back of their exhibit booth, a shelter from the constant press of onlookers. Silas, in his element, stood beside the carriage, explaining its workings to anyone who would slow down long enough to listen.

Nick chuckled. "You're very welcome. But I'll confess it wasn't so much my sterling character as knowing what would happen if my uncle were left to take care of it all on his own."

Annie's mouth stretched wide in an unexpected yawn. "Excuse me. It isn't suppertime yet, and I'm already drooping. I don't think even the prospect of seeing more of the White City could make me move much farther today."

"In that case. . ." Nick stepped over to Silas and managed to pry him away from the carriage. "It's time you got settled for the evening, Uncle."

"Is it getting late? I hadn't noticed."

"Left to yourself, you'd probably stand here answering questions all night."

"Nick's right," Annie said. "We need to be on our way." She clapped her hand to her lips. "Our luggage! I never thought to look for it once we met you at the station."

Nick gave a half bow. "Already taken care of. I gave the baggage carriers instructions for your things to be sent on to your boardinghouse ahead of you."

"Oh, my. Is there nothing you haven't thought of?"

Nick grinned his appreciation. He pulled an envelope from his pocket. "I'd take you there myself, but I have to get ready for tonight's show. Don't worry, though. I've written down instructions on the best way to get there. Your exhibitors' passes and a map of the fairgrounds are in here, as well." He started to hand the envelope to Silas, then pulled it back. "Perhaps Mrs.

Trenton should be in charge of this."

"Quite so," Silas agreed. "Annie is a marvel at keeping track of things."

Nick gave Annie a conspiratorial wink and handed her the envelope.

The hansom cab deposited Annie and Silas in front of a neat redbrick house with bay windows on either side of the front door and limestone arches outlining the windows upstairs. Without waiting for Silas, Annie toted her valise up the front steps and banged the knocker against the door.

It swung open almost immediately to reveal a bright-eyed, middle-aged woman. She nodded a smiling welcome, and her iron gray curls bobbed merrily.

"You must be Mrs. Trenton and Mr. Crockett," she said, stepping back to allow them entry. "I'm Ethelinda Purvis. Come right in. I've been expecting you."

She pointed to her left as she sailed through the neat parlor with Annie and Silas in tow. "The dining room is through there. That is where we'll take our meals each evening. Your rooms are right upstairs."

Mrs. Purvis mounted the steps and continued without pausing for breath. "Your bags are all ready and waiting in your rooms. I had the delivery man take them up when he brought them."

"Thank you," Annie panted, struggling to keep up with their landlady. Behind her, she heard Silas's heavy puffing.

Mrs. Purvis hesitated halfway up the flight and tapped on the wall in a slow circle. She listened intently, then shook her head and went on. "I thought maybe—" she called back over her shoulder. "But I don't know why it should be. I've checked that very spot a dozen times already."

Annie's steps lagged until Silas bumped into her; then she hastened to catch up to their hostess, her tired mind trying to make sense of that last comment. All she needed now was a mentally unsound landlady to deal with.

It didn't matter, she decided, trudging up the last few steps. She could always shove a piece of furniture in front of her door during the night. Nothing was going to keep her from unpacking and falling into bed at the earliest opportunity.

Annie said a silent prayer of thanks when they reached her room first and Mrs. Purvis continued down the hall to Silas's quarters, dispensing a nonstop commentary on the exposition, Chicago, and life in general.

Annie shut her door and looked on the small but tidy room with approval. She eyed the bed with longing. More than anything, she yearned to sink onto its welcoming mattress. But if she did, she would probably sleep right through until morning.

With a sigh, she dragged her trunk across the floor to the dresser and set about unpacking. She had nearly finished when she heard a tap at her door.

She opened it to find Silas, holding up a shirt obviously too small for him and looking utterly bewildered.

Annie looked from Silas to the shirt and back again. "Did the last tenant leave something behind in your room?"

"No, I found it while I was unpacking."

She pressed her hand to her forehead, hoping to stave off the headache she felt coming on. "I must be more tired than I thought. I don't understand what you're saying."

"I was taking things out of my satchel. Only it isn't."

The throbbing in her head increased. "What isn't what?"

Silas assumed a patient expression as if explaining something to a small child. "The satchel, Annie. It isn't mine."

CHAPTER 4

Annie slid a stack of neatly folded camisoles into the top dresser drawer and pushed it closed. Her fingers traced the crack that spanned the cherry finish from side to side and came to rest on top of a circular watermark, apparently left when a previous boarder neglected to use a saucer under his teacup.

The hem of the white lace curtains fluttered. She moved across the room to push the window up farther to capture more of the night breeze. Squeezing past the solitary wooden chair, she caught sight of the satchel Silas had left in her keeping. She wrinkled her nose at the offending piece of luggage. What a lot of trouble the irksome thing had caused! At some point, she would have to determine how to exchange it for Silas's, but not tonight. All she wanted at this moment was to finish her bedtime preparations and fall onto that inviting mattress.

Thanks to the summer humidity, the window stuck fast. Annie braced her shoulder against the frame and shoved, finally gaining enough leverage to force it upward. Cool night air, heavy with moisture from the nearby lake, flowed into the room.

She edged past the balloon-back chair again, wishing she could find a more convenient spot for it. Not likely in this tiny room, though. It held little enough space for the bed, the dresser, and a dressing table, let alone an additional piece of furniture.

Longing for the comfortable room she left behind in Indiana washed over her, and she gripped the chair back. Through the open window came strange noises and pungent smells, far different from the chirp of crickets and scent of new-mown hay. Another reminder she wasn't at home anymore.

Annie fought back the wave of homesickness with an effort and squared her shoulders. This was home now, at least for the duration of their stay in Chicago. She had better get used to the idea.

She crossed to the dressing table and pulled the tortoiseshell hairbrush through her tangled curls. There would be no hundred strokes for her tonight. Tired as she felt, she would be glad to make it to her bed without falling asleep on her feet.

Weaving the ash blond strands into a quick braid, Annie staggered across the room and turned down the bedspread. If that mattress felt half as inviting as it looked. . .

She gave her tired muscles permission to relax and sank blissfully onto the crisp white sheets. The mattress more than lived up to its promise. Its downy softness wrapped her like a mother enfolding a child in her arms.

With a contented sigh, she tucked her feet under the top sheet and pulled the covers up to her waist. What a day it had been! And tomorrow promised to hold just as much excitement.

Annie curled up on her right side and tucked her hand

beneath her cheek. If she had her choice, she would sink into the welcoming pillow and sleep for a week. She levered herself up on her right elbow, ready to blow out the lamp on the bedside table, and caught sight of the satchel again.

What on earth was she going to do with the thing? By now, the reason for its sudden appearance in Silas's possession seemed clear enough. When he collided with the stranger at the station, their belongings had flown everywhere. The satchels looked similar enough at first glance. They must have gotten switched then. It was the only logical explanation.

Easy enough to figure out what happened; less simple to plan a course of action for getting this one back to its owner.

How could she find the ill-tempered man among the masses at the fair? Annie directed a glare at the satchel that should have reduced it to ashes. There were goals aplenty to accomplish during their time in Chicago. She hardly needed one more thing to worry about.

She could simply turn the satchel in to the lost-and-found department. Surely a fair of this size would have such a thing. The owner would realize his loss and be able to retrieve his missing property with no further effort from her. Thus satisfied, she settled back on her pillow and closed her eyes.

But how would that help her get Silas's things back? He was a wonderful man and a dear friend, but he would be hopeless at coming up with a solution on his own.

Annie groaned. Pushing herself off the bed, she reached for the satchel and settled it atop her sheets. She started loosening the straps that held it closed, then paused, hesitant at the thought of going through someone else's things.

But Silas had already looked inside it, or he would never

have realized it wasn't his. Tamping down her distaste, she unfastened the buckles and pulled the top flaps apart.

Gingerly she reached inside and drew out the contents one by one, setting them on the bed: a shirt; a pair of cuff links; a bulging manila folder; a kit containing a razor, soap, and shaving brush; a small square envelope; and a pair of socks.

Annie slipped the shirt and socks back in the satchel right away. Handling some unknown man's clothing went far beyond the lengths she was willing to go to in order to find the owner.

With increasing reluctance at the violation of privacy, she picked up the cuff links and turned them over in her hands. Both were engraved with an *F* in flowing script but bore no further clue to their owner's identity. Annie dropped them back inside the satchel with the clothes.

She saw nothing unique about the shaving things. They followed the cuff links and clothing.

There has to be something in here. Annie opened the folder. The papers within proved to be letters to and from a Mr. Frost of the Pan-American Sugar & Rum Company. The address used was in Philadelphia. That wouldn't help her here in Chicago. She wrinkled her nose and put the file away.

The square envelope still lay on the bed. Annie picked it up and held it between her thumb and forefinger, her sense of intrusion growing stronger. The flap of the envelope was sealed, but the top had been slit open. She reached in and pulled out a single sheet of paper.

Feeling like the worst sort of snoop, Annie shook the paper open and stared at the bold lines scrawled across the surface. Only a few words appeared on the page—not even words, really. Certainly nothing she could make sense of.

She turned the note—if it was a note—over, but the back of the paper was empty. Mystified, she held the page closer to the lamp and peered at the writing.

In the flickering light, she could make out: *MT 10a; TH J8; STAT REP.*

Annie rubbed her forehead. It made no sense at all. Could it be some kind of shorthand? She thought back to the notes she had made for Will in his work. She routinely shortened words when writing quickly; perhaps this was some sort of abbreviation or code.

She stared at the page as if she could make its meaning clear by sheer concentration. *MT 10a.* She had no idea what that might mean. Her mouth stretched wide in a yawn, and she blinked to clear her vision. What about the next group of figures?

Annie traced the writing with her forefinger. *TH J8.* She often used TH as an abbreviation for Thursday. Could this be a date? Closing her burning eyelids, she tried to force her tired mind to concentrate. Today was Wednesday, June 7.

Her eyes flew open. Maybe the note indicated Thursday, June 8. Heartened, she continued. What about *MT 10a*? The name of a place, perhaps? But what could it be? Her mind sifted through several prospects: mountain, metal, material. She shook her head. Too many possibilities.

Wait a minute. Could *MT* indicate "meeting"? If that was the case, then perhaps *MT 10a* meant a meeting at 10:00 a.m. *Ten o'clock tomorrow morning.*

Further encouraged, she went on to the last group of letters. She had the possibility, at least, of a meeting time and date. Maybe this would give her the place.

STAT REP. Annie stared at the letters, willing them to mean something. Her mind drew a complete blank.

Her shoulders drooped. Who was she trying to fool? With a sense of defeat, she replaced the paper in the envelope, then stuffed both back inside the satchel and buckled the straps. She needed to get some sleep, not waste her time playing detective.

But sleep refused to come. Thoughts chased through her mind. This might be the only chance to find out where Silas's satchel could be. She heaved herself back up on her elbow and lit the lamp again.

She propped herself up against the headboard and cradled her head in her hands. *All right, think!* Someone was apparently planning to meet at ten tomorrow morning. But where? *STAT REP.*

Annie ordered her mind to dredge up any words that might fit, muttering them as they came to mind. "Statistics of report?" No, that wouldn't name a place. "State representative?" That might give her a *who*, but she still needed a *where*.

*Statutory. . .*no. *Statute?* Or maybe *statue. . .* Annie's heart beat faster. A statue would make a good meeting place, but which statue could it be? There must be dozens scattered throughout the city of Chicago.

Think, Annie, think! She closed her eyes and massaged her temples with her fingers, trying to remember whether she had packed a headache powder. There had to be a logical way to approach the problem.

She went over the few facts she had. The collision occurred at Terminal Station, entrance to the exposition. Wouldn't that indicate that the satchel's owner might have an interest in the fairgrounds specifically, rather than in Chicago in general? He had arrived in the afternoon along with her and Silas, too late to do much in the way of sightseeing. A person would need days, maybe weeks, to see the whole fair.

Her eyelids flew open again. In that case, tomorrow's meeting—if there was one—might be located there, right on the fairgrounds.

She remembered the papers Nick handed her earlier. Hadn't there been a map of the fairgrounds among them? She sorted through the envelope, giving a soft cry of triumph when she located it.

She unfolded the map and peered at it closely, trying to make out the tiny print in the dim light. She would approach the task with the same tenacity she had used when she and Will tried to work out a problem. Order and logic had served her well in the past. There was no reason to suppose they wouldn't now. Starting with Terminal Station, Annie worked her way east toward the lake.

The Machinery Hall and its annex, and across from it, the Agriculture Building. A stock pavilion and exhibit halls for leather and forestry. Nothing there that would fit the bill.

She moved her finger along the shoreline, noting the long pier, the Music Hall, and an assortment of exhibits dotting the east side of the Manufactures Building. The certainty of being on the right track faded. With more than six hundred acres and what looked like dozens, maybe hundreds, of buildings, she would never be able to find every detail. But she couldn't give up. Not yet. Just a few minutes more, and she would go back to bed.

The map became a blur of meaningless lines and shapes. Maybe if she went back over the tiny segment of the grounds she had already seen to reorient herself. . .

She planted the tip of her finger on the rectangle that

marked Terminal Station, locating the spot where the collision occurred, then finding the place where they had met Nick.

From there, they had walked past the Administration Building. Annie traced their path across the plaza, recalling the shock of delight she felt when she first glimpsed the huge reflecting pool beyond.

What was it called? She peered closely at the tiny lettering. Ah, the Grand Basin. She ran her finger along its length.

Her eyelids snapped open when her fingernail reached a dot at the farthest end of the basin. The map labeled the spot the Statue of the Republic.

Annie sat bolt upright, her heart racing. She held the map up to the light to be sure. Yes, that was the statue's name. But was it the location of the meeting, assuming there was one?

It had to be. It all fit. She blew out the light, then settled against her pillow, ready at last to get some rest.

CHAPTER 5

"Come on, Ranger, let's give it a try." Nick nudged the stallion with his heels.

Ranger didn't need further urging. Nick sat loose in the saddle and let the horse's long, smooth stride speed them around the horseshoe-shaped arena.

In the evening, silver conchos on the performers' saddles and costumes would catch the spotlights, sending glittering flashes dancing across the faces in the audience. Eighteen thousand spectators would alternately gasp and cheer at the feats of derring-do as the troupe recreated scenes of life on the frontier.

This morning, Nick heard only the steady *thrum, thrum* of Ranger's hooves on the packed earth as they completed their circuit. At the top of the arc, he nudged the horse with his left knee. Ranger wheeled to the left and shot straight down the center of the arena like an arrow loosed from a bow.

Dead ahead, a large hoop hung suspended seven feet above the arena floor. Nick stood in his stirrups, then brought his right foot up to the saddle seat. Shifting his weight to his right leg, he pushed himself upright, bringing his left foot to the seat as he did so.

Balancing atop the saddle, Nick flexed his knees to absorb the roll of the horse's gait and narrowed his vision to focus on the hoop.

In another twenty yards. . .ten. . .five. . . Now!

As the horse's head passed under the hoop, Nick bunched his muscles and sprang into the air. Tucking his knees and bending his body forward, he let the momentum of Ranger's speed carry him through the hoop, ready to land back on the saddle on the other side.

At the top of his leap, he realized things weren't going to work out according to plan. His position was off. Only by a matter of inches, but that was enough. Nick made a valiant effort, twisting his body to try to regain the correct placement, but it was too little, too late. Instead of his boots reconnecting with the saddle, they scraped against Ranger's flank. Nick plummeted downward and landed on the dust of the arena in an ungainly heap.

He lay still for several long moments, waiting for breath to return to his lungs. Then he wiggled his fingers and toes. When nothing appeared to be broken, he tested his wrists and elbows, ankles and knees, working up each extremity to his torso.

Everything seemed to be intact, if his joints did feel a bit looser than before. He gingerly moved his jaw from side to side and ran his tongue around the inside of his mouth. Not even a broken tooth. *Amazing!* Nick gathered his knees under himself and managed to stagger to his feet, grateful that his only injury appeared to be to his dignity.

Ranger came to a stop thirty yards away. Now he whickered

and trotted over to Nick, wearing a curious expression, as if wondering what had gone wrong.

"You and me both, fella." Grateful no one besides his horse had seen his humiliating fall, Nick leaned against the stallion's shoulder for balance while he bent to retrieve his hat and used it to swat the dust from his clothes.

"I take it you won't be performing that particular stunt at tonight's performance?"

Nick whirled around and grimaced when he saw a tall, slender man step out of the shadows of the grandstand. *Bill Cody. Great.* Of all the people in the world, his boss was the last he would have chosen to witness his disgrace.

He managed a rueful smile. "Looks like it's going to take a little more time to work the kinks out of it."

Cody's silver goatee trembled with suppressed mirth. "From the way you hit the dirt, I'd wager you're going to have some pretty big kinks to work out of your shoulders, too." His face split in a wide grin. "You keep working like this, and I'll have to give you star billing." He dropped Nick a wink and strode off.

Nick caught up Ranger's reins and led him back to the stables, where he brushed his coat to a glossy finish. One of them, at least, would look his best for tonight's crowd.

Had Bill been serious about his comment on stardom? He ran his hands down Ranger's legs, checking for hot spots. Based on what Nick knew of the man's character, there was a good chance Bill meant exactly what he had said. Nick pulled a hoof pick from his hip pocket and went to work on Ranger's feet.

Back when Nick had joined the show, he'd been little more than a willing learner, barely able to believe his good fortune at the chance to spend his days working around the legendary Buffalo Bill.

He would have been content to remain just one of the background performers, but Bill had seen potential and given him the chance to advance. Now it looked like he might go even further.

He leaned against Ranger's flank and bent to pick up the animal's near hind hoof. Nick winced. Bill wasn't kidding about the kinks in his shoulders. He needed to do something to make sure he'd be fit for the evening's performance. Rolling his shoulders cautiously, he went back over the practice in his mind. What had gone wrong? He'd tried that move before, and it had gone without a hitch. He knew the moves, knew the timing. All it really required from him now was a high level of concentration. . . . And immediately, he knew where the problem lay.

He'd felt a little off-kilter ever since his uncle wandered back into his life. Nick's lips parted in a fond smile. Crazy old Uncle Silas.

Or maybe not so crazy. From what he'd seen yesterday, the Crockett-Trenton Horseless Carriage just might have the makings of a viable invention. He patted Ranger on the neck, then turned him over to one of the stable hands and headed back toward his tent, trying to ignore the stiffness in his muscles that increased with every step he took.

Good for Uncle Silas! After all those years of dreaming, to think he'd finally come up with something that really worked. Nick well remembered the jokes that flew around the family while he was growing up—the sly nudges, the winks.

He'd always felt a sympathy for his uncle. It was nice to

think the old boy might have turned the tables on the rest of the relatives and be getting the last laugh after all these years. He and that partner of his.

Nick reached his tent and sailed his hat onto the small table in the corner. He felt the muscles catch in his shoulder. He needed to do something about that, and soon, or he'd never be able to pull himself onto the top of the coach during the rescue of the Deadwood Stagecoach in tonight's program.

He took off his jacket and pulled his shirt over his head, then took a bottle of horse liniment out of his foot locker and stared at it thoughtfully. It seemed to do all right by Ranger.

He poured a dollop into his palm and massaged it into his shoulder. Warmth spread through his muscles, and his nostrils tingled at the scent of menthol and oil of wintergreen.

And speaking of Uncle Silas's partner, where was the man? He'd half expected him to come striding out of the station behind his uncle and Mrs. Trenton, but both of them went off to set up the carriage without any mention of him. Maybe he'd been delayed back in Indiana.

Nick pulled his shirt back over his head and buttoned the front. What kind of delay would keep a man behind yet allow his wife to travel on ahead of him to take care of business? Especially a wife as attractive as this one.

Attractive? The word didn't do her justice. A picture of her pensive face and delicate features sprang into his mind. What kind of man let a woman like that out of his sight? And with only his uncle for protection, no less. Nick stretched out on his cot with a sigh and pillowed his head on his folded arms. Uncle Silas was the best-hearted man he knew, but he had all the protective instincts of a kitten.

Maybe he ought to step in and lend a hand. Other than an occasional rehearsal, he didn't have much to occupy him outside of performance times. With several hours a day to call his own, he could take it upon himself to keep an eye on both of them until Mr. Trenton showed up.

Finding the idea appealing, Nick pushed himself up off his bed. He wouldn't mind spending more time with Uncle Silas at all. He could go right now, as a matter of fact. He slicked his hair and pulled his jacket on.

Maybe Mr. Trenton had arrived. If so, it wouldn't hurt to have a chat with the man on the difference between life in the city and in the Indiana countryside.

Sunlight glinted off the immense white buildings. In the morning light, the White City appeared even more breathtaking than it had the previous evening.

Annie squinted her eyes, dazzled by the brilliance. She took a firmer hold on the handle of the errant satchel and set off along the walkway that ran the length of the Manufactures Building.

With Silas safely tucked away in their booth, she should have plenty of time to complete her errand. If only she could be sure he would still be there when she returned.

A momentary flicker of concern marred the beauty of the morning. No, surely he wouldn't leave his beloved carriage. Not while he had an appreciative audience, and there had been a constant stream of spectators since the first wave of fairgoers poured into the grounds. It wouldn't take long to return the satchel to its rightful owner and make her way back.

Minutes later, Annie decided her assessment of the time her errand would take might have been overly optimistic. She hadn't traversed even half the length of the Manufactures Building yet. The night before, she had thought it looked big enough to swallow her uncle's hay field back home. At the time, she attributed her reaction to sheer exhaustion, but seen in the full light of day, the building was even bigger than she remembered.

She shifted the satchel to her other hand and kept on walking. On the opposite side of the walkway, a light breeze ruffled the waters of a lagoon. Annie strode along briskly, skirting knots of fairgoers stopping to stare openmouthed at the massive building with its sea green roof.

Wait until they got their first glimpse of the exhibits it held! Just the sampling she had seen so far made her mind reel. She could have stayed inside and followed the broad avenue that bisected the building lengthwise, but she would never have made it to the other end in time. Not with so many people jammed together. A sense of wonder, almost a reverent hush, seemed to overtake them as soon as they walked through the doorway and slowed them to a snail's pace. No, she never would have gotten to the meeting place in time.

If there was a meeting. Annie switched the satchel back to her other hand, assailed by a niggling sense of doubt. The whole thing could turn out to be a fool's errand, the product of her imagination.

She dodged a young man pushing a rolling chair and thumped the satchel squarely into a bewhiskered man standing near the water's edge.

"Excuse me," she murmured.

She glared at her troublesome burden. If she didn't find its owner by that statue, she would be tempted to pitch the satchel into Lake Michigan, right then and there.

Annie rounded the corner of the Manufactures Building at last and came face to face with the Grand Basin. She set the satchel down long enough to catch her breath and get her bearings. According to the map, the Administration Building should be on her right. Yes, there it was, even more imposing than before, with its golden dome gleaming in the sunlight.

The Statue of the Republic, then, should be off to her left. Annie swiveled her head and saw it, a gilded figure with upraised arms, standing on its pedestal at the end of the Grand Basin nearest the lake.

She picked up the satchel again and headed toward the statue, wondering suddenly how she would ever find its owner in this crowd. The thought prompted a quick prayer. *Please let him be there. And help me to recognize him.*

And there he was, looking just like he had the day before in the station but without the angry scowl creasing his face. Her quarry was deep in conversation with a stocky man with swarthy skin.

Two other men, rough-looking types, flanked them. One, with a nose that looked like it had been flattened in a fistfight, gave Annie a look of hostility that made her steps falter.

He pointed to the satchel. "Where'd you get that?"

The man she sought turned at the interruption. He followed the direction of his companion's gaze, taking in Annie and the satchel with a single glance. His dark eyes gleamed, and a pleased smile split his face.

He stepped toward Annie and inclined his head. The other

men moved back, but Annie could see them darting curious glances her way. The one who had questioned her didn't bother to pretend to look elsewhere but stared straight at her with a boldness that made her feel exposed.

Turning her back to the group, Annie focused her gaze on the man before her and lifted the satchel slightly. "I believe this belongs to you."

"It does indeed. I had lost hope of ever seeing it again. I certainly never expected it to be returned by such a charming courier."

Annie searched his face, finding no vestige of the peevish man who had snapped at Silas the day before. "The man you bumped into at the station is my companion. Your satchels are remarkably similar. I believe they were switched in all the confusion."

Please, just take it and let me be on my way. She didn't have to look to know the flat-nosed man still stared at her. She could feel his burning gaze between her shoulder blades.

The satchel's owner reached for the bag with his left hand and took Annie's fingers in his right. He brushed the back of her hand with his lips. "Amazing that I could have missed noticing such a lovely lady, even in the midst of all that chaos. Allow me to introduce myself. John James Frost, at your service, and eternally grateful for the return of my property."

Annie tugged gently and freed her fingers from his grasp. Clasping both hands against her waist, she curved her lips in what she hoped would pass for a pleasant smile.

"I'm glad I was able to find you, Mr. Frost. I suppose it would be too much to hope that you might have the other satchel with you?"

46

"Alas, I'm afraid I left it behind in my lodgings. I had no idea I would discover the identity of its owner this morning. But if you'll tell me where I can send it, I will have it delivered posthaste." He produced a scrap of paper and a pencil.

"How did you know where to find me?" he asked, while Annie scribbled down Silas's name and the address of their boardinghouse.

Heat tinged Annie's cheeks. "I'm afraid I was compelled to look through your satchel for some clue as to whom it belonged to. I found a note in an envelope and only hoped I had interpreted it correctly. But I didn't know for sure until I saw you here."

"You figured it out from those scribbles, did you?" Frost's features grew taut. He studied her for a long moment; then his face relaxed, and he favored her with an easy smile. "That was very clever of you, if you don't mind my saying so."

He glanced down at the paper Annie handed him. "I'll have the satchel delivered right away, Mrs. Crockett."

Annie lifted her chin and met his eyes. "It's Mrs. Trenton. Annie Trenton. Mr. Crockett and I are business partners. We have an exhibit on display in the Manufactures Building."

"Ah, I see." Frost eyed her with renewed interest. "You appear to be a woman of many talents, Mrs. Trenton. I must stop by to see your exhibit one day. I'm here on business myself."

Annie nodded and edged back, waiting for an opportune moment to take her leave.

"I'm involved in a number of varied business interests," Frost continued. "Most of my time at the fair will be spent studying the sugar exhibits in the Agricultural Building. The exposition gives an unparalleled opportunity for forward-thinking men to see what is new. One has to stay up-to-date, you know."

"Yes, well. . ." Annie backed up another step. "I'm pleased we've been able to iron out this little mixup. I hope you enjoy your stay at the fair."

"I plan to." Frost smiled. "Perhaps our paths will cross again."

Annie gave a tight smile and turned away. She devoutly hoped not. The man and his companions made her skin crawl.

"Good morning, Uncle. Looks like you've been hard at work." Nick grinned when Silas took a moment or two to place him before smiling in response. Last night, they had done little more than park the carriage in its assigned space. This morning, bunting adorned the display area and a placard proudly proclaimed the name of the Crockett-Trenton Horseless Carriage to all who passed by.

"Indeed, indeed." Uncle Silas rubbed his handkerchief across the carriage's gleaming surface. "I'm glad you like it. Annie put the finishing touches on it this morning before she left."

"Left? You mean she's gone back to Indiana?"

"Hardly, dear boy." His uncle chuckled. "She merely had to run an errand here on the fairgrounds. She'll be back shortly."

Nick perused a series of posters describing the concept of internal combustion and outlining the procedure for starting the engine.

"It was nice of her to take such an interest. When is her husband supposed to arrive?"

The question drew a blank stare from his uncle. "Why, he isn't. He couldn't now, could he?"

A skinny fellow with a ginger-haired girl in tow stopped to eye the carriage. "What's going to make me trade in my horse for one of these?" he demanded. The girl giggled.

Uncle Silas bristled. "How long can your horse carry you without getting tired? The Crockett-Trenton Horseless Carriage can run without taking a rest as long as it has fuel."

Nick settled back to wait while his uncle extolled the advantages of motorized travel.

"You don't need to feed it hay twice a day. Moreover, it will never run away. . .and you don't have to clean up after it."

The girl giggled again at her swain's discomfiture. The young man reddened, and they left abruptly.

Nick drew nearer to his uncle. "Why couldn't he come?"

"Who?"

The corners of Nick's mouth twitched upward. "Mr. Trenton. Why isn't he able to come to Chicago?"

"Will? Why, he's been dead for over a year, God rest his soul."

"Dead?" Nick's jaw sagged. "I don't understand. I thought he was your partner."

"He is. . .or was, I should say." Uncle Silas looked out across the crowd that filled the Manufactures Building, but Nick had a feeling his eyes weren't focusing on anything but the past.

"We built the carriage together. It was his brainchild, as a matter of fact. I remember how excited he was when we first talked of bringing it to the fair. He would have been as thrilled as I am to be standing here today."

Uncle Silas pulled his kerchief from his pocket and made a show of polishing his spectacles. "It's a bittersweet thing, to be here without him."

He turned away and leaned over to breathe on one of the wheels and give it a loving polish, then flick an invisible speck of dust off a spoke. "Annie came along to help. She's been a part of things from the very beginning, taking notes on procedures and keeping things in order. She even helped with the mechanical drawings. She's very efficient, you know."

Nick smiled, recalling the way she had taken his uncle in hand the night before, with barely a ruffle in her composure. "So she's your partner now?"

"Well, yes, in a manner of speaking. She doesn't do the actual design work, you understand, but she can read specifications nearly as well as I can. And she knows as much about the carriage as either Will or I did. Quite a remarkable woman."

"Yes," Nick said slowly. "I can see that."

A knot of people began to gather at the edge of the display area. One man started asking questions. Nick excused himself and wandered toward the nearest exit.

He made his way outside, lost in thoughts of the young woman with the sea blue eyes. *A widow—and at such an early age.* Such things happened often enough, but that didn't make it any easier for those concerned. He hated to think of someone as lovely and fragile as Annie Trenton having to endure such a loss.

That could account for the hint of sadness in her eyes and her air of vulnerability. She was far too young and beautiful to be left on her own. Dealing with Uncle Silas on a daily basis was challenge enough for anyone. Having to cope with that kind of grief on top of it. . .

His heart ached for her. Trying to keep up with the demands of the exposition would be difficult, especially for someone more used to the slower pace of life in Indiana than to the bustle of a big city. Maybe he would have to watch out for her, as well as his uncle.

Yes, he could do that. He would try to make sure she was comfortable, do what he could to bring a little happiness into her life. In fact, there was something he could do right now.

CHAPTER 6

Annie ducked inside the west door of the Manufactures Building and joined the throng inspecting the exhibits from Great Britain and Germany. Perhaps she couldn't justify taking the time to stroll the full length of the building, but surely she could allow herself the luxury of admiring some of the displays on the way back to the booth.

Without slowing her pace, she let her gaze trail over sections displaying miniature vases, pottery ware by Doulton & Co. of London, even a reproduction of an English banqueting hall. She breathed deeply and let her earlier tension drop away and, along with it, the feeling of revulsion she had carried after her encounter with Frost and his men. With Frost's satchel back in his hands and the return of Silas's assured, she felt free at last to give way to her excitement at being there.

So much to look at; so many things to see! Annie drank in the sights while her feet carried her back toward the booth and Silas. She reached the clock tower that marked the center of the immense building and turned north along the broad central thoroughfare. Columbia Avenue, they called it. Annie smiled at the fanciful name. *Imagine, a street within a building!*

Her steps slowed when she spotted an elegant display. Glancing up, she noted the name: Tiffany & Co. Her breath left her lungs in a *whoosh*. Small wonder it caught her attention.

Casting a look of sheer longing at the glittering array, she forced herself to hasten along the indoor avenue, consoling herself with a promise to come back when she could give the lovely goods her undivided attention.

More displays drew her as she continued on her way. She would have to find snippets of time to see them all. She would *make* the time. It would be a crime to be there, right in the heart of the greatest exposition ever put together, and not savor every aspect of the experience.

The prospect of touring the grounds like any other fairgoer buoyed her spirits. All the months of planning and dreaming; the long days and longer nights spent designing, fabricating, and testing parts; then scrapping those that proved unworkable and coming up with new ones—that was all in the past. They were here at last, she and Silas, a part of this grand world's fair that would draw visitors from every corner of the globe.

But Will isn't. The thought stopped her in her tracks.

With a supreme effort, Annie collected herself and forged ahead. No, Will wasn't here to witness the achievement of his dream, but his genius would be recognized. She would see to that. The carriage would garner all the acclaim it was due.

And please, Lord, an investor or two. A financial backer would keep Crockett-Trenton solvent while she and Silas investigated ways of manufacturing the vehicles on a larger scale. The carriage deserved to be more than a pleasant memory in the minds of fairgoers. It had to be made available to the public. And that took money, far more than either she or Silas could come up with on their own.

Thinking of Silas, Annie picked up her pace, chastising herself for dallying when she saw him standing alone at the back of the booth, looking harried and fretful.

"What's the matter?" she asked the moment she drew near enough to be heard.

"We're in the Manufactures Building." Silas's expression couldn't have been more woebegone.

"Yes?" Annie waited, knowing the rest of the answer would come eventually.

"But we aren't supposed to be here."

"Not supposed. . . No, Silas, this area was marked off for us when we got here last night, remember?"

"I thought it a perfectly wonderful location, but that gentleman over there"—Silas pointed to a stocky man heading toward a collection of vaults and safes—"told me there is a separate building just for transportation exhibits. He said he was surprised we weren't in there.

"They've put us in the wrong building, Annie. Whatever shall we do?"

Startled, Annie turned in a slow circle and studied the exhibits surrounding them. With such a vast array of items on display, she hadn't taken the time to try to sort them into any kind of order before, but Silas was right. There wasn't another vehicle anywhere in sight.

But the fairgoers didn't seem to mind. A steady stream of curious spectators continued to flow past their booth. She tilted her chin and forced a smile. "The wrong building? Hardly! We've been here less than one full day, and look at the interest people have shown already." She nodded at a small group peering intently at the carriage. "I'd hardly consider this a failure, would you?"

Silas followed her gaze and perked up a bit. "I suppose you're right." He drifted over to explain the carriage and answer questions.

Annie's smile remained in place until his back was turned; then she sagged against the small table at the rear of the booth. What if Silas's informant was right? Would all their hard work be for nought if they were in the wrong place and never got a chance to connect with the people who could help them?

How had such an error come about at this meticulously organized fair? She had handled the paperwork herself. . . .

No, she hadn't. She had sent off the initial inquiry about exhibiting and set the process in motion. But that was back when the fair itself was in the planning stages. Once Will's accident shattered her existence, she had been in no condition to handle such matters.

Silas had taken over the paperwork in those dark days following Will's death, when all she could remember was wandering about like one lost in a fog. It would have been all too easy for him to have turned a straightforward entry into a confused jumble.

She took another look around, noting the nearby displays of valises, trunks, canes, and umbrellas—travel items all. It would have been just like Silas to send a letter saying he desired to enter an exhibit related to travel and leave the fair superintendents to draw their own conclusions.

One more thing to straighten out. Annie drew a deep breath and wondered who she should talk to about relocating.

No. All her energy had been spent just getting them there and setting up the display. As it was, they had arrived after the fair's opening, due to Silas's insistence on performing a series of minute adjustments until he was satisfied the carriage was as perfect as he could make it. The thought of having to start all over again. . . *I just can't do it, Lord.* They would stay where they were—misplaced or not—and trust that God would bring the right people their way.

As if in response to her decision, a swell of people moved toward them and clustered near the carriage. Annie stepped to the rear of the booth to allow them a better view.

"Booth" is an appropriate term, she mused. They certainly didn't have a display to compare to some of the more lavish entries. But if the interest this group showed was any indication, maybe that wouldn't matter.

The crowd stirred, and a distinguished-looking man stepped forward. People murmured and moved aside to let him through. Annie's heart quickened, and she focused her attention on the newcomer, obviously a person of some note. She had heard rumors of Chicago's mayor spending a considerable amount of time at the fair. Could that be him? And would it help their cause if he paid special attention to the carriage? She watched the man closely and held her breath.

He cupped his chin in one hand and studied the carriage from end to end. His deep-set eyes seemed to take in every detail. He turned to Silas and appeared to size him up in a single glance. "You're the creator of this vehicle?" he asked in a soft voice.

Silas nodded happily. "I am indeed. Designer and builder. . . along with my late partner."

"I thought so. You have the look of a man who sees things

in a way others don't." Their visitor glanced at the placard. "Are you Crockett or Trenton?"

Silas's chest swelled. "Silas Crockett, at your service. Is there anything you'd like to know about the machine?"

The man leaned closer, bending so he could peer at the engine beneath the seat. "I see you have two cylinders, modeled along Daimler's pattern. Are you using the same type of valve design, as well?"

"In principle." Silas beamed, recognizing a kindred spirit. "I've made some modifications to both the valves and the pistons, though. It gives a better compression ratio. Let me show you." The two knelt while Silas pointed under the carriage and were soon deep in a discussion about pistons and magnetos.

Annie couldn't help but smile. She hadn't seen Silas so animated since he and Will had first fired up the engine and made their successful maiden run.

A stripling stepped to the front of the rapt onlookers and called out, "Hey, Mr. Edison! Do you think this is the coming thing? Are you giving up on the kinetoscope?"

Chuckles rippled through the crowd. The quiet man turned his head long enough to smile acknowledgment of the question but didn't interrupt his talk with Silas.

Annie's lips parted. *Thomas Edison, founder of the General Electric Company?* It must be. And here he was in their booth, talking to Silas as an equal.

She felt the sting of tears. Who would have guessed? But here in this city of marvels, it seemed anything could happen.

"Make way!" called a loud voice behind her.

Annie whirled around and spotted a group of people moving at a stately pace a short distance down the broad avenue. *What now?*

A blond woman who looked to be only a few years older than Annie walked in the center of the group. The careful distance maintained by her entourage proclaimed her status as someone of importance. The crowds in the aisle stood like frozen statues, gaping at the sight.

Annie watched the woman, mesmerized by her regal bearing and imperious demeanor. She had a walk like no one Annie had ever seen before, proud and with purpose, as though she expected the way to clear before her.

When the group drew even with the booth, the woman looked Annie's way. Her cool blue gaze swept past as if Annie were invisible; then she came to an abrupt halt. She pointed and raised her voice. "What is that thing?"

A slender, dark-haired man with a neatly trimmed mustache detached himself from the group and studied the placard. "It appears to be a motorized conveyance of some sort, Your Highness."

"Move aside," the woman commanded. "I wish to see for myself."

The crowd parted like the Red Sea before Moses, and the woman strode into the booth, moving with her determined gait even within its narrow confines. Annie glanced at Silas, still talking to Mr. Edison and utterly unaware of the commotion behind him. She stepped toward the visitor and put on her most gracious smile.

"Good morning. I am Annie Trenton, and I would be happy to answer any questions you may have."

"Are you the inventor?" The woman's haughty tone made it clear she already knew the answer.

Annie took a step back. "No, my husband—"

"Is that him over there?"

Annie's smile slipped. "No, that is Silas Crockett. He and my husband are the inventors of—"

"Then he is the one I wish to speak to."

Annie shot a quick glance over her shoulder. "I believe he is almost finished with Mr. Edison. Perhaps while we're waiting, I could tell you a bit about it."

The blond woman looked her up and down. "Why would I waste my time talking to a mere shopgirl? I will speak to Senor Crockett. Now."

Annie looked toward the men again and saw the great inventor stand and shake Silas's hand. "I've toyed with the idea of an electric carriage, but I believe gasoline will be the motive force for the vehicles of the future." He gave the carriage a look filled with admiration. "I think you're on to something, Crockett. The best of luck to you."

Annie gritted her teeth. "It appears Mr. Crockett is free now." She waved him over. "Silas, this is. . ." She trailed off and flinched at the woman's stony stare.

The dark-haired man stepped into the breach. "Her Highness, the Infanta Eulalia of Spain. She has expressed an interest in your horseless carriage and is anxious to speak to you."

Silas all but snapped to attention, then bowed in a courtly fashion. "I would be most pleased to discuss the carriage with Your Highness." The two of them walked toward the back of the booth, leaving Annie standing alone and ignored.

The dark-haired man came up to her. "Allow me to introduce myself. I am Miguel Díaz, her highness's chief of security. You must understand the princess. She is used to royal treatment at home. It will take time for her to become accustomed to American ideas of equal status for all." He smiled in an engaging manner.

Annie pressed her lips together and nodded. She saw no point in taking out her frustration on him. Maybe he was only an inconsequential minion. Like herself.

"I know it doesn't look like much, Mr. Frost, but it's the best I could come up with." The tall man fidgeted in the doorway.

John James Frost stepped inside the small building and surveyed the dimly lit interior. A small desk, several wooden chairs, and a set of shelves nearly filled the available space.

The flat-nosed man at his side snickered. "How hard did you look, Burns?"

The tall man shuffled his feet. "They set it up as an office at first, then decided to use another building instead. My friend—the one who let us use the place—says no one ever comes here.

Frost pursed his lips and counted five slow beats before nodding his approval. Burns relaxed, and Frost smiled inwardly. It always paid to let subordinates worry a little before putting them at ease. Never let them forget who was boss; that was his motto.

He set the leather satchel on the scarred desktop and unbuckled the straps. Reaching inside, he pulled out a shirt and a pair of socks. He frowned.

"What's the matter, Mr. Frost?" The flat-nosed man stepped over to him.

Frost didn't answer but continued to empty the satchel. His shaving kit, the file of correspondence. . .

He felt a tic begin in his left eyelid. "Where is it?" Hearing the frustration in his tone, he lowered his voice. "Where is it?"

he repeated, under his breath.

He rummaged through the remaining items, pulling them out faster and faster. An envelope. A cuff link and its mate.

Frost turned the satchel upside down and shook it. The straps flapped, and the buckles rattled against the desktop. A piece of lint fluttered out and drifted down to land atop his socks.

He pulled the top open wide and peered inside, then ran his hand around the interior. Nothing. He gripped the satchel in both hands, then slammed it down on the desk and stared at it blankly. "It isn't there."

The other two men shifted uneasily. "Maybe it just fell out somewhere, Boss," Burns said.

"That's right," the other chimed in. "No one has to connect it with you."

Frost sent them a withering glance that shut them up quickly. He hadn't come this far by settling for easy assumptions and not attending to every last detail.

Think, now. Think. He closed his eyes and tried to calm his breathing. The satchel had been strapped shut. Nothing could have fallen out on its own. It must have happened when that old fool started to unpack, then realized he had the wrong satchel.

Either that or it had been removed and kept deliberately. *If they have it, they know it belongs to me.* The thought chilled him. This could mean the end of everything.

He wiped his hand over his face. No, things had come too far. He had put in too much effort. Nothing could keep his plans from coming to fruition.

He wouldn't allow it.

CHAPTER 7

Nick spotted Annie when he was still some distance from the booth. He shifted the bags of sandwiches in his arms and slowed his pace, enjoying the opportunity to watch her unobserved.

She stood near one of the explanatory posters, talking to a lantern-jawed woman wearing a hat bedecked with flowers and birds' wings. Listening, rather. Even from a distance, it was obvious the other woman dominated the conversation. Nick drew near enough to eavesdrop, keeping himself out of Annie's line of sight.

"On the sixth round, you double crochet twice, then chain two, then double crochet twice more. All in the same opening, you understand." The woman nodded to emphasize her point. From where Nick stood, he could see her chins wobble. "Then you continue as before until you reach the next corner."

Annie nodded politely. From the glazed look in her eyes, Nick suspected the conversation had been going on for some time. Long enough, anyway, to deserve a break.

He edged to his right so Annie could see him over the other woman's shoulder, and he was rewarded by a smile as radiant as the sun rising over Lake Michigan.

Her companion glanced back at Nick and clucked her tongue. "It appears my husband is ready to leave now, Mrs. Trenton. I enjoyed our discussion. I'm sure we both found it far more interesting than discussing engines and whatnot."

She collected her husband and steered him toward the Star & Crescent Mills Co. booth and their display of Turkish towels and cloakings. Annie sighed, and her eyes lost their hunted expression.

"I didn't mean to interrupt," Nick teased. "I could call her back, if you'd like."

"Don't you dare." Annie emitted a gurgle of laughter that sent a tingle along his nerve endings. "I've been listening to her describe her crochet expertise for half an hour. Far more interesting than that boring discussion the men were carrying on," she added in a parody of her recent visitor.

"Wouldn't she be surprised if she knew the woman she was talking to drew up some of the plans for that boring engine?"

The look of amusement lingered in Annie's eyes. "I suppose she would." Her gaze lit on the paper bags in his hands, and she looked up at him questioningly.

"I figured you and Uncle Silas wouldn't have had time to get your bearings yet, so I took the liberty of picking up some sandwiches from one of the lunch counters."

"What a lovely thing to do!" Annie took the bags from him and set them on the small table at the rear of the booth. "That way, it will be ready whenever Silas decides he's hungry."

Nick frowned. "Aren't you going to eat? I brought plenty for both of you."

63

"I couldn't eat a thing right now." Annie laughed. "I'm too excited, I guess. It's hard to believe we're really here at last. I can't wait to explore it all."

"You haven't had much chance to see any of the rest of it. Would you like to walk around a little and satisfy your curiosity?"

"Oh, I couldn't."

Nick tilted his head. "Why not?"

"I couldn't just go off and leave your uncle."

Nick glanced over at Uncle Silas. "Look at him. He's perfectly happy here, talking to all and sundry about his grand invention. He probably won't even notice you're gone."

Annie bit her lip in a way that made her look like a little girl fighting temptation. "I really do want to see more than just this booth. And I'd probably feel safer if I had someone with me." She paused again, then smiled. "All right, I'll take you up on your invitation."

"Where would you like to start?"

She didn't hesitate. "The Tiffany pavilion." She pointed south along Columbia Avenue. "It's right back this way, down by the clock tower."

Nick chuckled. "In that case, I'll let you lead the way."

They strolled companionably along the concourse, with Annie drinking in all the sights and sounds, and Nick's attention focused on only one sight: Annie. He studied the way she closed her eyes and inhaled the heady scents wafting from the Lundborg perfumery exhibit, and watched a tiny dimple form in her right cheek when a whimsical wooden toy caught her fancy.

"There it is," she breathed.

A lavish pavilion stood before them, an impressive structure in its own right, though dwarfed by the sheer size of the

Manufactures Building. Groups of columns marked each corner, leading the eye upward to the low dome that capped the palatial edifice.

"Are we going to stand here looking at it all day, or would you like to go inside?" Nick's gentle teasing brought Annie out of her trance, and she moved eagerly toward the main entrance.

Inside, she walked among the array of gold and silver ware with the enchanted air of a child in a toy store. Nick tagged along behind, equally entranced by the lovely woman in front of him.

He chuckled when she recoiled from a piece in the form of a coiled rattlesnake, but he had to agree with her reaction. Even the serpent's emerald eyes and pearl rattles couldn't make its appearance a pleasant one.

She settled instead on a tiered display of silver cups and vases. Reaching out, she traced the lines of a delicate silver vase shaped like a woven basket.

A thin-faced attendant stepped toward them, seeming to share neither Annie's delight nor Nick's amusement. "Is there anything I can help you with?"

"Just seeing the sights," Nick told him. "This is quite a place you have here."

His response seemed to mollify the man. He gave a satisfied nod and swept his arm out in a circle that took in the extravagant display. "The pavilion itself cost one hundred thousand dollars," he said. "The display items are valued at more than two million."

Annie drew her hand back as though she'd been burned and gave Nick a startled look. "I had no idea," she whispered. "Maybe we'd better leave."

They left the pavilion and ambled along the avenue that crossed the building from east to west. One of the exhibitors

65

called out, "Hey, Mister, buy your wife a souvenir."

Annie's steps faltered, and she tightened her grip on Nick's arm. Her lips stretched in a taut smile, but he could see tears pooling in her eyes.

He cupped his hand under her elbow. "Let's go outside. I think we could both use some fresh air." She nodded and let him lead her to the east door.

"I'm sorry about that," Nick told her after they exited the building and stood on the promenade separating the Manufactures Building from the lakeshore. "Are you all right?"

Annie stepped across the walkway and leaned against a lamppost. She gulped in a deep breath and nodded. "It just caught me off guard, that's all." She glanced up at Nick, a shadow in her eyes. "I hope you weren't offended."

"Not at all." Nick moved closer beside her, searching for the right words. "Uncle Silas told me about your husband. I'm very sorry."

Crystal droplets sparkled on her lower lids. "It was all so sudden."

Curiosity overcame Nick's reluctance to intrude. "Was it. . . an illness?"

Annie shook her head. "No. That would have provided some warning at least." She clasped her hands around the lamppost and stared out at the teal waters of the lake. "He and Silas had finished testing the first working model of the carriage and were ready to go into production, but we needed a backer.

"Someone Will met put him in touch with a prospective investor. Will set up a meeting with him in Indianapolis." Her voice dropped to a whisper. "From what we gathered later, Will was crossing a busy street on his way to the meeting place, hurrying to get across ahead of a streetcar. A woman with several children was walking on the opposite side of the road. One of the little ones darted toward the street. She picked that one up, but another little boy ducked past her and ran out into the path of the streetcar."

She traced the filigree pattern on the lamppost. "Will saw what was happening. He scooped up the little boy and tossed him out of harm's way. . .but he wasn't able to get clear himself."

Her fingers gripped the post until her knuckles whitened. "By the time we heard about it, everything was all over. The child was safe. But Will was gone."

"I'm sorry," Nick said again, wishing he had more to offer than empty words.

Silence settled over them once more, but this time of a comfortable sort, as though no words needed to be spoken between them.

Finally Annie pushed away from the lamppost and turned to him. "I must apologize. I'm afraid I'm not very pleasant company right now."

"Not at all. I'm glad you felt you could tell me. So the investor. . . ?"

Annie shook her head. "He must have thought Will just didn't keep the appointment. With everything else I had to see to right then, we lost contact with him."

"So that's why you're here in Chicago—looking for a backer?"

"That, and to make sure the world recognizes what a genius Will was." The tilt of her chin left Nick with no doubt she had the determination to make that happen. "It's the least I can do for him. That and. . ."

"And?"

Sadness settled over her face. "I need to visit Will's family while I'm here."

"I see. Were you very close?"

Annie shook her head. "I've never met them. They didn't even come to the funeral."

"Their own son? Then why. . . ?"

Her mouth set in a firm line. "There's some unfinished business I need to attend to." She squared her shoulders and managed a tiny smile. "I don't mean to take up too much of your time. I'm sure you didn't plan to spend all day playing tour guide."

"I didn't mind a bit." He would be happy to spend days on end doing just that, but he could take a hint. "Would you like me to escort you back to the booth?"

Annie shook her head. "Thank you, but I need to learn my way. I appreciate you showing me around. I enjoyed it very much."

"It was my pleasure." He started to walk away, then turned back. "I'd be glad to do it again another time, but in the meantime, don't be afraid to wander about on your own. One of the things the fair board is touting is their commitment to provide a safe environment here, and they've done well on that score."

Annie smiled a farewell, and Nick went on his way, weaving through crowds of fairgoers while thinking about the woman with blond hair and eyes the color of the lake. He had plenty of time to daydream while he skirted the Manufactures Building and crossed the lagoon. Then there was the mile-long walk down the Midway Plaisance before he got back to the Wild West encampment.

Had he just cut the ground out from under himself by suggesting she go sightseeing on her own? He looked around and chuckled. No fear of that; the fairgrounds were huge. She couldn't possibly cover all that territory on her own. There should be plenty of opportunities for him to show her around again. He would see to that.

"Did you see how many people stopped by today, Annie? Did you see how interested they were?"

"Yes, it's wonderful, isn't it?" Annie paid the cabdriver and joined Silas at the foot of Mrs. Purvis's front steps.

"I do believe we're going to find success here," Silas said. "I feel it in my bones."

Annie gave a distracted nod. What she wanted most at the moment was a comfortable place to sit and relax after a long day spent on her feet. Didn't Silas feel the strain at all? He hadn't stopped bubbling since they left the booth.

And the days to follow would be even more draining since they would be walking to and from the fairgrounds from now on. Her aching limbs would protest, but it had to be done. Today's use of a hansom cab had been a delicious luxury, but they needed to start thinking about cutting costs. No telling how long they would remain in Chicago, and they would have to make their money last.

Annie eyed the steps and tried to summon up the energy to mount them. After all, she told herself sternly, the boarding-house lay less than a mile from the fairgrounds. Hardly an extreme distance by any means.

Stiffening her resolve, she set her foot on the first step and climbed to the porch. She would do anything she had to, endure any hardship necessary to see Will get the recognition he deserved. And to take care of the other business that awaited her.

Mrs. Purvis threw open the door before they reached the top of the steps. "Oh good, you're back." She held the door wide to let them enter.

Annie stepped into the entry hall, giving the landlady a second glance when she passed her in the doorway. Were Mrs. Purvis's eyes giving her trouble? Her lashes fluttered like laundry flapping on a clothesline.

Curiosity made her forget her exhaustion, and she turned to study the woman more closely. The blinking continued, increasing in speed when Silas drew near. Still rattling on in his excitement, he walked right past her.

As Annie watched, a look of disappointment crossed Mrs. Purvis's face and the blinking miraculously stopped.

Oh dear. Annie pressed her lips together to suppress her mirth.

Mrs. Purvis followed Silas into the parlor and gave him a coy smile. "A man delivered your satchel this morning, Mr. Crockett. I put it up in your room."

"Wonderful!" He started for the stairs.

Annie scooted after him and grabbed his sleeve. "Not until you've had dinner."

"But I want to go through it and make sure all my papers are intact."

"First things first. If I know you, you'll get so wrapped up in what you're doing, you'll forget all about eating."

"It's ready to set on the table now," Mrs. Purvis joined in. "You don't want to let my pot roast get cold, do you?" She batted her eyelashes again.

Silas's face lit up. "Pot roast? Very well, I suppose I can spare a few minutes." He allowed Annie to tow him to the dining room.

Mrs. Purvis darted ahead of them and soon appeared in the doorway bearing a platter of succulent beef. The savory smells made Annie's stomach rumble, and she pressed her hand to her stomach, hoping no one had noticed.

"With only the two of you boarding here right now, this seems almost like a family meal, doesn't it?" Mrs. Purvis simpered in Silas's direction. "Please sit here, Mr. Crockett." She indicated the chair next to hers and set the platter in front of him.

"And why don't you take that seat, my dear?" She pointed to a chair opposite her own.

Annie circled the table, trying to hide her amusement at the widow's blatant attempts to beguile Silas.

Mrs. Purvis stiffened. "Stop right there!"

Annie froze. What had she done?

"Take two steps back, then walk to the chair again, will you?"

Baffled, Annie complied.

Mrs. Purvis narrowed her eyes. "Would you say the floor sounds different nearer the middle of the room? Listen." She pushed her chair back and stood, then thumped her heel against the floorboards.

Annie shook her head slowly. "No. . .no, it sounds about the same to me."

Mrs. Purvis sank back into her chair and picked up her napkin. "Ah, well. You never know, do you? Shall we say grace?"

Annie shot a look at Silas, who stared hungrily at the platter. She shrugged. After spending so much time with him, she could deal with a few additional eccentricities.

She bowed her head and waited for Mrs. Purvis to ask the blessing.

CHAPTER 8

Annie opened the door on a brilliant blue morning, feeling as radiant as the sunshine. Amazing what a difference a good night's sleep could make! After dinner, she had retreated to her room and drifted into a dreamless slumber that left her feeling fit and ready to face the day.

She lifted her face to catch the sun's warmth while Silas retrieved his walking stick from the walnut hall tree and joined her on the little porch. Even the walk to the fairgrounds couldn't daunt her this morning.

"Wait!" Mrs. Purvis hurried from the kitchen, a paper sack in her hands. She held the sack out to Annie but directed her words to Silas. "I thought you might want some fruit and biscuits to munch on during the day. I know how hungry a hardworking man can get."

"Thank you." Silas nodded his approval. "Are you ready, Annie?" He descended the steps, swinging his stick with a jaunty air.

Annie took the proffered sack and gave Mrs. Purvis a quick hug. "That was very thoughtful of you. I'm sure we'll enjoy it."

"Take good care of him today, will you?"

"I'll do that." Annie grinned and hurried to join Silas, waiting impatiently on the sidewalk. Nothing could dampen her mood today. Silas had his satchel back, and the carriage had already drawn a significant amount of attention on its very first day of display. She couldn't imagine a more promising beginning for their stay.

She caught up to Silas and glanced back to see Mrs. Purvis waving from the doorway. Annie returned the wave and chuckled, remembering the coquettish looks their landlady had cast Silas's way during dinner the night before.

Would it be kinder to put her out of her misery right away and tell her she'd stand more chance of catching his attention if she were a set of mechanical drawings? Annie smiled at the notion.

Movement stirred off to their left. Annie jumped when she spotted a thin man in a slouch hat standing in the narrow space between Mrs. Purvis's house and the one next door. As if in response to her startled glance, the man stepped forward and stared at her boldly. Annie looked away and quickened her steps. At the corner, she cast a quick glance over her shoulder to find him still standing there, looking after them.

Another resident of South Blackstone Avenue? *Surely not.* He didn't seem to fit into this neighborhood. Perhaps he was looking for a place to lodge and someone had directed him to Mrs. Purvis.

A shudder rippled across Annie's shoulders. She hoped not. If he did, perhaps Mrs. Purvis would turn him away. Or would she? Annie realized she had no idea of her landlady's financial situation or how badly she might need the income an extra boarder would bring.

Even so, Annie hoped she wouldn't have to stay under the same roof as that man. The very thought unsettled her. How would she deal with a situation like that?

No. She shook off her gloomy thoughts. She wouldn't worry about such things right now, not on this day full of promise. She kept pace with Silas, more than ready to reach the exposition where the Columbian Guards assured the safety of those on the fairgrounds.

"How fast will it go?"

"And how far before you have to put more fuel in it?"

"There's an electric cart running around the fairgrounds already. What makes this any better?"

Silas held up his hands. "Please, ladies and gentlemen. One at a time. I'll be glad to answer your questions in an orderly manner."

Annie watched from the farthest corner of the booth, observing the crowd's interest. Silas looked happier and more carefree than she'd seen him in a long time. Seeing his focused, confident air now, one would never know she'd had to send him back twice that morning to change his socks until he came up with a matching pair. Able to hold forth on his favorite topic, he was totally in his element here, a situation that made Annie feel at loose ends.

She stirred restlessly, then brightened. Silas would be perfectly all right on his own as long as he had an audience. And from the looks of it, there would be no worries on that score. Her excitement mounted. With no need to play nursemaid, she now had an opportunity to tour the grounds, and she might as well make the most of it.

Reaching into her reticule, she unfolded the map of the fairgrounds. Where should she begin? The Woman's Building, she decided. Mrs. Purvis had extolled its wonders the night before. "Some of the most exquisite laces and embroideries I've ever seen. You simply must pay it a visit." Very well, then. That's exactly what she would do.

After spending so much time inside, it felt good to get outdoors and move around a bit. Annie strolled along the edge of the calm lagoon, feeling every inch the tourist. The breeze from the lake ruffled her curls, pulling loose strands free from the combs that held them off her face.

She meandered around the north end of the lagoon, across the bridge that spanned the strip of water connecting the lagoon and the North Pond, and saw the Woman's Building straight ahead. Though smaller by far than the Manufactures Building, it would have dwarfed any edifice back home.

Annie started toward the building. If today's expedition went without mishap, there were other worlds to conquer. Plans for future excursions danced through her mind. On another day, she could visit the Horticulture Building, then perhaps the Palace of Fine Arts. . . .

She stopped short and looked behind her. Had someone called her name? She glanced around, then gave a little shrug and started off again. She must have imagined it. Who would know her in this crowd?

"Annie!"

She heard it clearly that time. Stopping once more, she scanned the crowd. She smiled at the sight of a broad-shouldered man coming her way.

Nick Rutherford strode toward her, looking as unconcerned as if he were crossing a meadow instead of moving through the bustle of people. Annie couldn't help but admire the way he seemed right at home here, even though his fringed buckskin jacket stood out in marked contrast to the sea of coats and ties.

Ignoring the curious stares he drew from the passersby, he covered the remaining distance in a few quick strides.

"I thought it was you," he said when he reached her. "I'm glad I was right." A warm grin split his face.

An answering smile sprang to her lips. "I'm surprised you noticed me in all this mob." Stunned might be a better word. No one could miss Nick in his western garb, but she certainly didn't stand out from the crowd in any special way.

Nick shook his head, dispelling the notion. "If you set your mind to it, you can always spot what you want to see. You get a picture of one pretty face in your mind, and you can find it in a mass of confusion even if you only catch a glance."

Confusion mingled with pleasure and sent a wave of heat washing over Annie's cheeks. "I decided to take your advice and see a bit of the fair on my own."

"Good for you! Would you mind some company? I have some time on my hands, and I'd be glad to escort you again. Where were you heading?"

Annie glanced over his shoulder at the Woman's Building.

Something told her Nick Rutherford would not be thrilled at the idea of oohing and aahing over displays of tatting and handmade lace. But what would appeal to a rugged man like this?

She stared about at the maze of buildings, then smiled up at him. "I chose yesterday. Why don't you decide today?"

He offered his arm. After a moment's hesitation, Annie slipped her hand into the crook of his elbow. The buckskin felt as soft as velvet under her fingers.

"In that case, I recommend a relaxing stroll along the lagoon. It'll give you a view of the overall setting and a better idea of where you'd like to spend your time."

They ambled beside the water's edge, enjoying the light breeze that swept the mugginess from the air. Walking along with no set destination, Annie felt the pressures of recent days lift from her shoulders. With a sense of release, she allowed herself to begin to relax and enjoy herself.

She could feel the strength of the man beside her and appreciated the small courtesies he showed, like the way he shortened his stride so she would have no trouble keeping pace with him. This was her idea of a true gentleman, even though he wore the garb of a rough frontiersman.

A long boat with upswept ends skimmed past them, its single occupant using a long pole to push it forward. Annie stared. "Is that a gondola?"

Nick's laugh rumbled from deep in his chest. "A little bit of Venice right here in the Windy City."

Annie stared in wonder as the graceful craft plied the waters. A sudden gust of wind set rows of flags snapping atop the nearby buildings, adding to the festive air.

Nick bent down to pick up a scrap of bread some careless

picnicker had tossed aside on the grass. He tore off a small chunk and flipped it into the water, where a group of ducks converged on the morsel.

Nick handed the rest to Annie, who crumbled the bread into bits and sprinkled them on the grass at their feet, laughing when a parade of waterfowl came waddling up on the bank to claim their prize. For the first time in many months, she felt as carefree as a girl.

They followed the edge of the lagoon until they came to a stop in front of the Mines and Mining Building. Nick glanced at Annie, then looked out at the sparkling water. "Are you planning to stay until the fair closes in October?"

Annie shook her head. "That's doubtful, though it's a possibility, I suppose. The whole point of our being here is to promote the carriage and acquire financial backing. Once we've accomplished that, we'll head back to Indiana and start working out the details on production."

Nick seemed to turn her answer over in his mind. "In that case, you need to make the most of the time you have here." He turned and nodded toward the long building behind him. "That's Transportation."

"So that's where Silas thinks we ought to be." Annie took in the arched, golden doorway and the profusion of reds, oranges, and yellows in the stonework that made up the exterior. The contrast between its autumn hues and the pristine white of the buildings that formed the Court of Honor couldn't be more pronounced. *I hope we made the right choice in staying where we are.*

Nick led the way back toward the north, where they passed the building that housed the horticultural exhibits. Annie started

78

to suggest going inside but instead made a mental note of its location for future reference. She could visit it on her own another time. Today was hers to enjoy the beautiful weather outdoors and the company of this intriguing man.

"That bridge leads to the Wooded Island." Nick pointed toward the center of the lagoon. "That's probably my favorite spot on the fairgrounds. It's a good place to get a bit of respite when all the bustle gets to be too much or if you find you need a quiet spot to get away and think."

"Or pray," Annie murmured. Her eyes lingered on the island, feeling its air of peace call to her. It was good to know a place existed where she could escape when she needed seclusion. She would have to take advantage of its sanctuary from time to time.

"And straight ahead is the Woman's Building." Nick glanced at her doubtfully. "I don't suppose you want to go inside and look around?" Annie shook her head and held back a smile when she saw his barely veiled look of relief.

Nick continued in his office as tour guide. "That big dome you see farther along is on the top of the Illinois Building. And beyond that, on the other side of the North Pond, is the Palace of Fine Arts. There are even more buildings past that, put up by the various states and some foreign countries.

"But now. . ." His eyes twinkled. "How would you like to travel the world. . .without ever leaving the fairgrounds?"

Annie's mouth dropped open. "And how do you propose to do that?"

Nick winked. "Come with me and find out." He turned left, and they headed toward an area away from the Court of Honor.

Annie glanced up at a white building on their right and came to a halt in the middle of the walkway. "Am I seeing things, or are there children playing up there on the roof?"

Nick laughed and pointed out the fence around the roof's edge. "Believe it or not, it's a playground. This is the Children's Building. Parents can drop their children off there while they see the fair and know they're in competent hands. Not a bad idea, actually. I probably would have enjoyed that more myself as a youngster than traipsing around through all these buildings for hours on end." He pursed his lips and regarded the rooftop play yard. "Although I probably would have been inclined to scale the fence and see if I could shinny down the side of the building."

Annie broke into a smile. "I can believe that." Nick's love of adventure seemed an integral part of him. She looked straight ahead and drew back when she realized where they were headed. "Isn't that the Midway?"

"That's it." Nick's eyes glowed. "Gateway to adventure." Something in her expression must have given away her apprehension. His eyebrows drew together. "What's wrong?"

"I've, uh, heard stories about. . ." She broke off, too embarrassed to continue.

Nick's frown disappeared. "You're worried about its respectability." A look of understanding shone in his eyes. "First of all, let me assure you that perfectly respectable women go through the Midway every day. And secondly—" His deep brown eyes grew even darker. "I would never take you anywhere that would compromise your reputation."

Annie studied his face a long moment, then nodded. She could read the truth in his eyes. This was a man she could trust. With a lighter heart, she looked again at the entrance to the

Midway Plaisance. A sense of girlish excitement bubbled up within her. "Is this where they're building the Ferris wheel? Could we see that?"

Nick threw back his head and laughed. "That, and a great deal more. This way. . ."

Annie followed, letting him thread their way through the chattering throng. A profusion of voices rose up around them: flat Midwestern twangs and soft Southern drawls mingled with languages she didn't recognize.

They slid past a group of people and forged on ahead. Off to her right, Annie spotted a man in a slouch hat leaning against a pillar. He paid no attention to the tumult around them but stared directly at her.

She caught her breath in a quick gasp and averted her eyes. Was that the man she'd seen outside Mrs. Purvis's earlier? She looked back, but the man was gone.

Annie tried to control her breathing, not wanting Nick to see her sudden tumult of fear. Surely it couldn't have been the same man. Then again, why couldn't it be? Reason reasserted itself. Thousands of people thronged the fairgrounds daily. Why shouldn't that man—if it was the same one—choose to do the same? It was merely a coincidence, nothing more.

Determined to recapture her lighthearted mood, she turned her attention back to Nick, who was pointing out sights of interest. "We're passing the Irish Village now. Across the way is Hagenbeck's Animal Show.

"And there—" He pulled her to one side and pointed straight ahead.

Annie saw it then: a great steel skeleton rising to the sky, its spokes sticking out like a giant spider's legs. And people were planning to ride to the very top of the monster! She drew in a shuddering breath. "Oh my!"

"Quite the feat of engineering, isn't she? Ferris has done himself proud. What do you say? Would you like to take a spin on her when she's finished?"

Her eyes traveled upward, trying to imagine what it would be like to sail high above the buildings, the fair, the city itself. "I don't think so." Her voice came out in a tiny squeak.

Nick shook with laughter. "In that case, let's focus on something a little more down to earth. How about some lunch?"

Annie tore her gaze from the mammoth wheel. "Is it lunchtime already? Oh dear. Silas—"

"Is undoubtedly so busy demonstrating the carriage that he has no interest whatsoever in food right now. Come on." He gestured toward a point farther along the Midway. "I hear the German Village turns out a wonderful schnitzel."

"Mm. Delicious." Annie took another bite of schnitzel and savored the veal cutlet's spicy flavor.

"I'm glad you think so." Nick swiped at his mouth with his napkin and gazed around the outdoor eating area with a look of pleasure. "I acquired a taste for them when I was in Stuttgart."

"You've been to Germany?"

"The show toured Europe last year—Germany, Belgium, England, and Scotland."

"That must have been exciting." She hid a grin and added in a casual tone, "The only contact I ever had with Europe was meeting the Spanish Infanta."

Nick's fork stopped halfway to his mouth. "You met the princess?"

Laughter bubbled out despite her attempts to stop it. "If you could call it that. She stopped by the booth." Annie took a long sip of carbonated soda. "She seemed quite taken with the carriage and Silas, but I'm afraid she didn't find me of any interest whatsoever."

A slow smile spread across Nick's face. "That just goes to prove what they say about most royalty being nothing more than half-wits."

Annie laughed again, her earlier irritation with the woman's overbearing manner slipping away. "She certainly made me feel like one." She toyed with her food, hoping Nick didn't notice the flush she felt creeping up her neck. She wasn't used to receiving such open compliments.

"Maybe I didn't show the proper amount of awe. It was obvious she was used to everyone in her retinue bowing and scraping every time she lifted her finger." She regretted the caustic note in her voice as soon as the words were out.

"What did she think of—"

Annie laid her hand on his arm. "There she is now!"

Nick glanced over his shoulder. "Who?"

"Her. The Infanta. See her? The blond woman right over there, walking to that table on the far side of the seating area."

Nick swiveled around in his chair. He watched for a moment, then looked back at Annie, his eyebrows raised.

"So where are all the bowers and scrapers? All I see is a woman having lunch alone." He smiled and picked up his fork again. "It must be someone with a passing resemblance."

Annie focused on the woman intently, watching her every

move. "It's her. Did you see the way she carried herself, as though she owned the fairgrounds and everyone on them? I'd recognize her anywhere."

Nick tilted his head to one side. "But why would a princess be out here alone on the Midway? That doesn't make sense."

Annie bristled at his obvious disbelief. "I'll prove it to you." She scooted her chair back and moved away from the table.

Nick caught her arm. "What are you doing? You can't just waltz up to a perfect stranger and ask if she's the princess of Spain."

"If she isn't, the worst she can do is think I'm mentally unbalanced. But it *is* her. I'll show you." She pulled away from his grasp and wove her way through the tables. Behind her, she heard Nick's chair scrape back and the sound of his footsteps following. *Good.* In just a moment, he would find out she was right.

Halfway to her goal, a man stepped into her path. "Ah, Senora Trenton."

Annie stopped short, trying to place the dark-haired stranger. Recognition came, and her face brightened. "Senor Díaz, isn't it?"

A smile wreathed his face. "It seems we both have a good memory for faces. Speaking of which. . ." He nodded in the direction Annie was headed. "Am I mistaken, or was it your intention to approach the Infanta?"

"So it is her?" Annie cast a smug look at Nick, now standing beside her.

Díaz inclined his head. "*Sí.* But as impolite as it seems, I beg you not to do so." He beckoned to Annie and drew both her and Nick aside to the shelter of an overhanging roof draped

84

with vines. He lowered his voice to a whisper. "You saw the entourage who attended the Infanta?" Annie nodded.

"There are times when so much ceremony becomes very tiring for her highness. She longs for the freedom to move about on her own, the freedom you yourself enjoy. As you have perhaps already guessed, the Infanta is a woman of strong personality." His apologetic smile told Annie he hadn't forgotten the slight she received at the Infanta's hands earlier.

"Even back in Spain, she embraced the idea of going around incognito, able to experience the simple pleasures without being recognized. You can sympathize, I am sure."

Annie nodded slowly, responding to his earnest entreaty. "Yes, of course. I'd never thought about it before, but I'm sure that must be very difficult."

Díaz spread his hands. "And so I am sure we can count on you both to respect her privacy and not give her little secret away?"

Annie returned his smile. She had accomplished her goal of proving herself right. No need to disturb the Infanta.

Nick tugged at her arm. "We'll be happy to oblige. It's a good thing the princess has you around to keep an eye on things."

"I do my best." Díaz bowed from the waist and drifted back into the shadows.

Annie followed Nick back to their table and began gathering up the remains of their meal. She slanted a triumphant smile his way.

"All right." Nick's genial tone showed no offense. "I admit it: You have an amazing eye for detail, and I'll never doubt you again. How's that for an apology? Is that good enough, or shall I go back to the counter and see if the menu here runs to a helping of crow?"

Annie laughed and abandoned her pretended hauteur. "That will do nicely, thank you. No need to eat crow."

"In that case, what do you want to see next? It appears the Infanta is off-limits, so what would you say to a look at Hagenbeck's trained animals?"

CHAPTER 9

"Mrs. Purvis!" Annie stared through her bedroom door in disbelief. Backing into the hallway, she hurried to the stairwell and leaned over the railing. "Mrs. Purvis!"

The landlady bustled into the parlor and looked up at her. "What is it, child? You nearly gave me apoplexy."

Annie pointed toward her door with a shaking finger. "Someone has been in my room. What happened?"

Unperturbed, Mrs. Purvis made her way up the stairs. "I was in there this morning as usual. Just tidying things up, you know. I'm sure I didn't disturb anything." She reached the landing and went down the hallway to the open doorway. "After all, it's a landlady's job to—" Her eyes widened, and her mouth formed a circle when she looked inside. "Oh. Oh my!"

She took a cautious step inside the room. "I assure you, my dear, this was none of my doing."

"I never thought it was." Annie joined her, standing trans- fixed at the utter devastation that met her eyes: clothes strewn everywhere and drawers upended, then tossed carelessly on the floor.

"But who could have—" She was cut off by Silas bleating from his doorway.

"Annie," he called, "something has happened. Come and see."

Oh, no. Not his room, too! Annie flew down the hallway with Mrs. Purvis puffing in her wake. They skidded to a stop at Silas's door. His belongings had been subjected to the same upheaval as Annie's.

Mrs. Purvis clapped her hands to her face. Her words came out from between her splayed fingers. "It looks like we've had a burglar." She turned and ran back to the stairway. "I'll check downstairs and find out what's missing," she called over her shoulder. "Oh! My mother's silver!"

She returned moments later, a puzzled expression creasing her face. "Nothing has been taken. The downstairs is just as I left it."

Annie looked up from where she knelt in the midst of debris littering her floor. "Nothing of ours has been taken as far as I can tell."

"How very curious. What kind of burglar turns two rooms inside out, then doesn't take anything?" The landlady turned to Silas, who hovered in Annie's doorway, and clasped her hands beneath her chin. "Oh, Mr. Crockett, whatever shall we do?"

He shot a pleading look over her head, but Annie was too distracted to take charge of Silas's problem.

"I don't understand it." She stood up and prodded a pile of clothing with the toe of her shoe. "Should we call the police?"

Mrs. Purvis turned from Silas and patted her hair into place. Her curls dangled around her face like tiny sausages. "They won't be very interested, I'm afraid, seeing as how nothing was stolen. I guess the only thing for it is to clean things up and hope it never happens again."

Annie nodded absently, already weary at the prospect of spending her evening bringing order from this chaos. A thought struck her. "How did they do all this without you hearing them?"

Mrs. Purvis knitted her brows. "I went out early this afternoon to do some shopping. It must have happened then." She shook her head slightly. "But how did they get in? None of the windows are broken. I checked while I was downstairs."

Years of dealing with Silas prompted Annie to ask, "Did you lock the door when you left?"

"Well, of course I—" A pink flush tinged Mrs. Purvis's cheeks. "At least, I think I did."

"Maybe we should all make an effort to see that it's kept locked from now on," Annie said gently.

"You're quite right." Mrs. Purvis nodded as though she had come to the same conclusion. "And now I ought to be seeing to our supper." She paused a moment in the doorway. "Maybe they know something I don't. Do you suppose I've been looking in the wrong places all these years?" Without waiting for an answer, she hurried downstairs.

CHAPTER 10

*F*ifty-first and Indiana. Annie folded the paper containing Mrs. Purvis's written directions and mounted the steps to the elevated platform.

Five minutes later, a northbound train rumbled into the station, and Annie boarded, taking care to select a seat by herself to keep her clothes as wrinkle free as possible. She straightened her lace-trimmed, shirred bodice and box pleated skirt, both of the same deep blue hue. Today she needed every detail of her appearance to be as perfect as possible.

The train started up, hesitated, then surged ahead with a burst of speed. Annie swayed with the rocking of the car and fixed her gaze outside the window. She noted details of the scenery as they passed, wanting to focus her attention on anything but the ordeal ahead.

Clickety-clack, clickety-clack. The sound of the wheels marked off their progress with relentless rhythm. Annie's thoughts turned at an equally rapid pace. What kind of reception would she get from the in-laws she had never met? Were the Trentons really as well-off as Will had described?

Trees lined sections of the track, their leafy crowns even with the elevated railway. Annie watched them flit by and tried to pretend she was taking a pleasant drive through a wood instead of speeding through the midst of a great city. That notion was dispelled as soon as the leaves and branches gave way to rows of brick apartment buildings. Annie alternated between looking down on rooftops and staring straight into third-floor flats.

The train jolted again, and Annie braced her hand against the seat back in front of her as they slowed for another station.

In the building opposite the platform, a little girl sat in the window of her flat. Her golden curls hung in ringlets along her plump, rosy cheeks. She watched the approaching cars, making eye contact with Annie when the train ground to a halt. She seemed so close Annie felt she could reach out and touch her.

She stared back, captivated by the child's calm acceptance of this noisy intrusion into her world. The little girl raised her hand and curled her fingers into a shy wave.

Annie smiled and waved back, trying to ignore the twinge of longing even that brief contact brought. If she and Will had had children, would they have looked like that? She knotted her fingers in her lap and tried to regain her composure as the train pulled out again, bringing her ever closer to her destination.

Could this be the right place? Polished columns flanked the entry, and a turret dominated the right front corner, giving a castlelike effect to the three-story brownstone. Annie's heart sank. She expected something nice, but this went far beyond her wildest imaginings.

Lord, give me strength. I have to do this for Will. She pushed open the wrought iron gate and climbed the stone steps.

A man dressed in somber black answered her tentative knock and stared coolly when she gave her name. Looking as though he would like nothing better than to close the door in her face, he stepped back and allowed her entry, then ushered her into a drawing room that opened off the central hallway.

"Please wait here." The condescending note in his voice nullified the courteous words. He glared at Annie as though expecting her to make off with the silver the moment his back was turned, then disappeared into the recesses of the house.

Annie took advantage of the respite to catch her breath and study her surroundings. The rich furnishings reflected the elegance of the house's exterior. She made a slow circuit of the room, careful not to jostle the numerous tables filled to overflowing with bric-a-brac and objets d'art.

Something flashed in the sunlight that streamed in through the bay window. Annie stepped closer to investigate and gasped when she recognized a near duplicate of the basket-shaped vase she had admired in the Tiffany pavilion.

She reached out to touch the delicate latticework, then pulled back, remembering the butler's suspicious attitude. Closing her eyes, the better to concentrate, she listened intently but heard no approaching footsteps. With her pulse pounding in her throat, she stretched out her hand again. Turning the vase over, she quickly looked for the maker's stamp. There it was: Tiffany & Co.

Annie clutched the little vessel in both hands and set it back in its place with infinite care. The cost of the items on display at the fair was still fresh in her mind. Turning around, she scanned the room again with a new appreciation of its contents.

"Oh, Will." She barely breathed the words. "It's more than you said. So much more." For the first time, she began to understand just what kind of life he had given up to follow his dream.

And to marry her. The revelation made today's mission even more important.

The heavy oak door swung open on silent hinges. They came in together, showing a united front, she supposed. Or was it meant as a show of force against a common enemy? Side by side, they faced her: Will's parents.

Richard Trenton stood as straight as though he had a poker rammed up the back of his tailored coat. Tall and hollow-cheeked, he peered at Annie down the length of his aquiline nose.

His wife huddled next to his side, a matronly figure with fair hair shot through with threads of silver. Her lips pressed together, deepening the harsh lines that splayed out from the corners of her mouth.

Annie looked in vain to find any resemblance to Will in either of them.

The butler appeared in the doorway. "Will you need anything, sir?"

"No, Blevins. That will be all." Mr. Trenton never took his gaze off Annie while he spoke. The Trentons stayed at a distance on the other side of the room, regarding her coldly without uttering a word of welcome.

Annie broke the silence. "Thank you for receiving me. When I didn't receive an answer to my letter, I wasn't sure it had reached you."

Mrs. Trenton pinched her lips even more tightly. Her husband cleared his throat. "State your business, young woman. We can only give you a limited amount of time."

Annie's breath caught in a quick gasp. This was going to be even worse than she had imagined. She looked from one to the other, seeing not even a speck of encouragement in their faces. "I'm here on Will's behalf," she began. His parents' faces closed even more at the mention of his name. Annie gripped her hands together and plunged ahead. "He wanted to be here himself."

The door swung open, and a man of about thirty burst into the room. "Mother, I—" He broke off when he saw the tableau. "Excuse me. I didn't realize we had a guest."

He smiled at Annie, and the room seemed to whirl around her. She reached out and clutched at a nearby table for support, fearing that, without it, she might faint dead away.

Here was the family resemblance she sought. The same blond hair, the same features. It was almost as though Will himself stood before her. She stared, a familiar long-ing welling up inside her.

When he crossed the room, he moved with an easy grace. "I apologize for my rudeness. I'm Graham Trenton."

Annie stretched out a hand that trembled. Would the touch of Graham's fingers be anything like Will's? "I'm Annie," she said.

Graham's whole body stiffened, and his hand froze in midair, a fraction of an inch from Annie's fingertips. His face hardened, and he pulled away.

Annie drew her hand back. The spell was broken. This was not Will.

Graham Trenton stepped back toward his parents, forming a family group that excluded her. A sunbeam shot through the window and struck the silver basket, scattering shards of light around the room.

"Let's get this over with," Will's father said. "Say whatever you've come to say."

Annie flinched but stood her ground. "I won't take up much of your time. I wanted you to know that Will was very happy in his work, and we were very happy together. His one regret was the rift that existed between you and him."

She paused to study their faces, hoping for some signs of softening but finding none. Her hands twisted together, slippery with perspiration. More than anything, she wanted to bolt from the room and leave this nightmare behind, but Will would have done this if he had been able. She had to see it through for his sake.

Gathering her courage, she went on. "It's important that you understand. Will was a true genius."

Mr. Trenton snorted. "If he had shown even a fraction of the sense he was born with, he would have stayed with the family business where he was meant to be instead of gallivanting off to waste his life on all that foolishness."

Annie bristled. "You can hardly call it foolishness. Will was a brilliant man. If you had ever taken the time to see some of the ideas he came up with—"

"Preposterous daydreams, every one!"

"How can you say that? Did you ever show the slightest interest in anything he did? Care about his dreams instead of your own?" Annie realized the words would inflame rather than soothe the situation, but she was too upset to care. "Maybe if you'd bothered to put your money behind some of those ideas, more of his inventions would be on the market already."

"So at last we come to the reason for this visit." Richard Trenton's face could have been carved from granite. "I will say this one time, and one time only: We have no intention of giving any money to the likes of you."

Annie stared at the three facing her and struggled for breath. "You think I came here to ask for a handout? You can't mean that." One look at their shuttered faces showed her they did. She felt a tremor run through her body and fought back tears. She had come to make peace, but they saw her as nothing but a gold-digging opportunist. How had this scene turned into such a disaster?

Summoning all the dignity she could muster, she lifted her chin and held her head high. When she reached the door, she turned to address them once more.

"You are wrong. I realize there is nothing I can do to alter your opinion of me, but believe me when I tell you that Will loved you all dearly and wanted more than anything to heal the breach between you. One thing, at least, you can see for yourselves. The horseless carriage is set up in the Manufactures Building at the fairgrounds. Come see it. See what a genius your son was." Looking directly at Mr. Trenton, she added, "You don't owe me anything, but you owe Will that much."

Without waiting for Blevins to show her out, she walked out the front door and down the steps. Her heels clicked an angry tattoo along the walk as she marched back to the station. A woman holding a round-faced little boy by the hand passed her and murmured a greeting. Annie was too distraught to reply. *I failed you, Will. Forgive me.*

Across the street, a man sauntered along, keeping pace with her. Something about him seemed familiar. She ducked her head and peered his way from beneath lowered lashes. Where had she seen him before?

Her blood chilled when she made the connection. He reminded her of the man she had seen outside Mrs. Purvis's and again on the Midway. He didn't wear a slouch hat today, but his gait, his narrow face, the fluid way he moved along. . .

You're being ridiculous! She tried her best to shake off her rising fear. Chicago was a huge city full of people. She had to stop imagining she saw the same menacing person every time she turned around. It must be a product of the disastrous meeting with Will's family and her own black mood.

Even so, the encounter left her shaken. She hurried the rest of the way to the station without looking back.

CHAPTER 11

T hanks for stopping by." Bill Cody waved Nick toward a chair on the opposite side of his desk. "I have some things I want to talk over with you."

Nick settled into the leather camp chair and tried to hide his amusement. Cody's invitation to visit him in his office tent might seem casual enough, but he recognized it as a summons not to be ignored.

Cody flipped open the lid of an ornately carved wooden humidor and held it out to Nick. "Cigar? They're the finest I've had in a while. I order them directly from Havana."

Nick smiled but shook his head. "No, thanks. I've never developed a taste for them."

"That's right. I forgot you don't indulge." He selected one for himself and returned the humidor to the desk. Biting off one end of the rolled tobacco leaf, he lit the other and drew in the smoke, his eyes half closed.

"Aah." He let the smoke trickle out between his lips with

a sigh of pure satisfaction.

Nick watched the performance, fascinated. Cody imbued even so small an act with the same air of showmanship that commanded the adoration of audiences on both sides of the Atlantic. The silence lengthened, but Nick waited without speaking. Cody would get around to whatever it was he wanted to discuss in his own good time.

Sure enough, Cody picked up the conversation as though there had been no interruption. "Not as far as tobacco or liquor anyway." He leaned forward and stroked his goatee. "But who's that pretty lady you've been squiring around the fairgrounds lately?"

The question took Nick off guard. He shifted in his chair and grinned. "I take it you've been spending a considerable amount of time over there yourself. Your eyesight is just as good as ever." He hesitated, not wanting to give his employer the wrong impression. "I've only escorted her a few times."

Cody took another pull on the cigar and gave Nick a long, measuring look through the haze of smoke that encircled his head. "Is she anybody special?"

Nick's lips curved upward. *Special?* Everything about Annie Trenton was special. But in the way Cody meant? He chose his words with care. "Her late husband was my uncle's partner. She came along to help my uncle set up an exhibit at the fair. As it turns out, she doesn't have a lot to do now that that part is done, so she has some time on her hands. I thought I'd show her around a bit, keep her from being lonely."

Cody slitted his eyes and stared up at the tent ceiling. "I understand completely. I've always felt it wasn't right for a lovely lady to lack for companionship."

Nick kept his expression impassive. He had known the show-man long enough to be sure Cody's definition of companionship differed markedly from his own. He also knew that pointing it out wasn't about to change his boss's mind.

Cody gave him a sly wink and sat up straight. "So much for the pleasantries. Let's get down to business. You've been with me how long now? Three years?"

"Five. I joined the show just before it moved from Staten Island to Philadelphia."

"Five, then. You've done a good job with the show over that time. You've come a long way from the green kid who couldn't do much but ride a bronc and toss a loop when you first started."

Nick grinned, remembering the awe he'd felt at first, just to be taken on as part of the troupe on Hugh Smith's recommendation.

Cody rolled the cigar to the other corner of his mouth and clamped it between his teeth while he spoke. "You have a lot of drive. It shows in your dependability and your willingness to develop ideas on your own. That new stunt you were working on the other day—how is it coming along?"

"It still needs some work," Nick admitted. "But I almost have it down." He crossed his arms, wondering if he'd stepped on one of the other performers' toes with his new idea. Was Bill getting ready to tell him to stick to his assigned routine or pack it in?

Cody knocked an inch of ash off the end of the cigar and took his time balancing the stogie on a heavy glass ashtray to his right. "It looks like I may be losing one or two of my star performers over the next few months." He laughed at Nick's openmouthed surprise. "Don't expect me to say which ones either. I don't want rumors getting started."

100

His expression turned serious again. "You have the makings of a star, Nick. You've got the looks; you've got the ability and the determination to make it happen. I'd like to start promoting you now, move you up in the billing. We'll make it a gradual process, build it up so you'll be ready to step into a lead spot when the time comes. . .if you're interested, that is."

He leaned over and rapped his knuckles gently on the desk. "Think about it. Next year in New York, the posters could have your picture on them." He placed the cigar back in his mouth and waited for Nick's response.

Nick worked his jaw, trying to get the words to come forth. "I don't know what to say. That. . .that's everything I've dreamed about. It's like you're handing it to me on a silver platter."

Cody's weathered cheeks creased in a broad smile. "That's what I wanted to hear. You start working up some new ideas to add to that stunt, and we'll do some talking later about how we're going to pull all this together."

He rose and slapped Nick on the back. "Mark my words, son. You're going to be a star."

"What was that, my boy?" Silas turned back from the rooftop railing. "I must have been woolgathering."

Nick opened his mouth as if to repeat himself, then shook his head resignedly. "I was just going over something Bill Cody and I were talking about." The half smile didn't quite mask the disappointment on his face.

Annie watched the byplay with a twinge of sympathy. She had been in Nick's position often enough to know how frustrating it felt to be ignored. Perhaps she could steer the conversation back to Colonel Cody later.

"Would you like another sandwich?" She held a hamburger out to Silas, who accepted it eagerly. There was a bit of wind today, she noted gratefully. And nothing to block them from it, up here on the observation deck. She closed her eyes and savored the cooling breeze. Nick's idea to lunch atop the Manufactures Building had been a stroke of genius. Just what they needed to clear their minds and refresh their spirits.

Silas crunched away at a pickle spear. "Speaking of strange doings. . ."

Nick looked at Annie, who shrugged in reply. That topic hadn't come into their lunchtime conversation at all.

"What was that woman up to last night?"

The light of understanding dawned. "That woman," Annie repeated. "You mean Mrs. Purvis?"

Silas nodded. "I was sound asleep when I was awakened by a strange tapping sound. I sat up and looked around my room but couldn't find anything, so I got up to see what it could be. It took me some time to track it down, but there she was."

"There who was?" Nick looked thoroughly lost.

"That woman. Our landlady, knocking on the wall in the room next to mine." He shook his head. "Doesn't that strike you as odd, Annie? Normal people don't go knocking on walls in the middle of the night, do they?"

Annie gurgled with laughter at Nick's bewildered expression. "Maybe I can have a talk with her and make sure she knows you need your rest." She promised herself she would fill Nick in later.

Mollified, Silas went back to munching on his pickle. He gazed at the lakeshore, watching the breakers lap gently against the sand. "A lovely spot, this."

Annie murmured agreement. She tilted her head back, letting the breeze cool her neck. She took another bite of the hamburger sandwich Nick had picked up at one of the lunch counters. It had been worth the effort it cost them to persuade Silas he could leave the booth long enough to eat a meal at his leisure.

Now that he was up on the roof, he seemed quite content to stay. Annie couldn't blame him. It would be hard to find a grander view. From their lofty perch, they could turn to the east and gaze across Lake Michigan or look to the south and take in the peristyle, the Grand Basin, and the glistening white Agriculture Building.

And no masses of fairgoers to share it with. Several small groups occupied the benches spread along the deck, but nothing like the pressing crowds inside the building or on the walkways below.

Up here, they seemed to exist in a world apart, one that felt calm, serene. . .safe. A world where people weren't followed by strange men and didn't find their rooms turned topsy-turvy for no reason.

Delightful as the setting was, they couldn't stay indefinitely. She knew it but couldn't bring herself to be the one to put an end to this moment of peace. How thoughtful of Nick to suggest this spot.

But that didn't come as a surprise. Every time he dropped by the booth, he showed a consideration for Silas and his needs that warmed her heart. And she appreciated the way he included her, almost to the point she felt like one of the family. She looked at the way the three of them sat in a comfortable circle. *Yes, very like a family.*

Goodness, she thought with wry amusement, *I'm starting to sound like Mrs. Purvis.*

Silas got to his feet. "I'd love to stay and chat with you young people, but I must get back to the booth. Will I see you there later today, Nicholas?"

Nick glanced at the sun's position. "If you need me for something special, I'll be glad to stop by. Otherwise, I need to get back to the arena a little early this afternoon."

"No, that's all right. I'll look forward to seeing you again then. Tomorrow, perhaps?"

Nick smiled and nodded. "You can count on it."

Silas meandered toward the stairway, and Annie began to clear away the wrappers and crumbs from their impromptu picnic. "What were you saying earlier about Colonel Cody?" She watched Nick's face light up while he recounted the conversation and Cody's offer.

"That sounds like a wonderful opportunity." She walked to the railing and stood with her back to Nick, not wanting him to guess at the conflicting emotions that chased through her mind.

He wouldn't understand her disappointment. How could he, when she didn't understand it herself? She ought to be happy for him at this chance to achieve his life's ambition.

But there had to be more productive things for Nick to do than ride a horse and crack a whip. Yes, that must be what was bothering her. Feeling on safer ground, she turned to face him.

"Is being a performer all you want to do with your life?"

Nick's brows drew together, and he straightened in his chair.

I didn't phrase that very well. Annie hurried to make amends. "I mean, is that the sum of what God has in store for you?" *Oh dear, that didn't come out right either.*

104

"Tell me why you joined the show in the first place." She smiled, hoping to smooth his ruffled feathers. "It isn't every young man who achieves something like this."

The lines of strain in Nick's face softened, and he settled more comfortably into his chair. "That's easy to answer. Like most boys my age, I grew up with a fascination with the building of the railroad and the taming of the frontier. I lived to get my hands on all the books I could find that had anything to do with cowboys or the West. . .any of the things Bill Cody did in his younger days."

Annie could well understand the draw. . .for any youngster. But what did it accomplish? How did it make the world a better place?

"And is that reason enough to stay, to make this your life's work? Have you thought about doing anything more with your life than just performing stunts and entertaining the crowds?"

"But that's just it; it's so much more than mere entertainment." Nick leaned forward. His eyes glowed. "This is a way to bring the West to people—thousands of them—and let them see what life was like. I've lived a part of that myself, and I don't want it to be lost. Without something like this, it could be gone like the buffalo."

Annie nodded slowly, trying her best to see his point of view.

"And it isn't just a matter of keeping that heritage alive for people in this country. You should have seen how the show was received in Europe. During a private performance in London, we had four kings and the Prince of Wales aboard the Deadwood Stagecoach! We're doing something here that no textbook could ever hope to accomplish—we're bringing the frontier to life. Next year, we'll be playing in New York, and after that, who knows?

There's a wealth of opportunity ahead. Just developing my part is going to be enough to keep me occupied for a long time."

Annie nodded. "I understand now. It does have value, and you certainly have a passion for it." She scattered the last of the crumbs to a group of grateful sparrows.

Nick stood beside her. "Now what's all this about your landlady?"

"Oh, that." Annie laughed at Nick's frown of concern.

"When Uncle Silas wired me and I met her to make the arrangements for your stay, I thought she seemed respectable enough."

"Oh, she's respectable, never fear. She just appears to be a bit. . .eccentric, that's all. And I think she may have set her cap for your uncle," she added impishly.

"Uncle Silas?" Nick threw back his head and roared. Still chuckling, he added, "But tapping on walls in the middle of the night?"

"She does seem to do a lot of that," Annie admitted. "Not always in the middle of the night, though. But really, she's a dear. You don't have a thing to be concerned about. We're quite happy there."

But as she preceded Nick down the staircase, she couldn't help but wonder what could have possessed Mrs. Purvis to embark on that midnight foray.

A whimsical thought struck her: Knowing Silas's scientific bent, could Mrs. Purvis have been trying to win his affection by tapping out a message in Morse code?

She was still shaking with laughter at the notion when she reached the bottom of the steps. Silas Crockett and Ethelinda Purvis—what a pair they would make!

After the respite of the observation deck, it took a moment for Nick to adjust to the press of the crowd. Streams of new arrivals at Terminal Station rounded the Administration Building and halted in stunned disbelief at their first view of the mighty Columbian Fountain and the Court of Honor. *Just the way Annie looked when she first saw it.* He smiled at the memory.

Annie matched him stride for stride as they strolled past the arches and columns that bordered the Manufactures Building, stepping from shade to light and back again. Gondolas and electric launches skimmed along the surface of the canal.

It looked even cooler on the water than up on the observation deck. Nick made a mental note to take Annie for a gondola ride some day. Uncle Silas, too, of course. Assuming they could pry him away from his beloved exhibit long enough to engage in such frivolity.

He turned to Annie. "I didn't get a chance to tell you yet about one of the ideas I've come up with for a new act for the show. It all hinges on whether Bill approves, of course, but—"

"Do you see that man?" Annie's voice was low and tense. She stared past him toward the bridge that marked the joining of the canal and the lagoon.

Nick followed her gaze to where a large group strolled along the south end of the lagoon. "Which man? There must be at least fifty over there."

"The one with the flat nose and the sour expression. Just behind that couple walking next to the water—the man in the gray suit and the woman in the flowered hat. I've seen him before."

"You're not going to tell me that's the Infanta in disguise, are you?"

Annie shot an indignant glare his way, then turned her attention back to the lagoon. "I'm serious. See the way he's keeping pace with the man in front of him?"

Nick watched a moment. "What else can he do in a crowd that size?"

"But he's acting so suspiciously. Watch him!"

It can't hurt to humor her. He watched the man in the gray suit bend his head attentively to listen to his slender companion. Behind them walked the fellow Annie was watching.

Nick noted the man's appearance. He looked like he might have gotten his nose broken a time or two. His general air was of one more accustomed to a barroom brawl than to an afternoon stroll along a grassy bank. Nick had to admit he stayed closer to the couple than the flow of the crowd demanded.

While Nick watched, the man picked up speed and collided with the gentleman in front of him. "What was that all about? It almost looked deliberate."

Annie quivered like a hound on scent. "Look at his hands!"

Nick shifted his gaze in time to see the flat-nosed man's hand reach under the tail of the other man's coat and reappear holding a wallet, which he swiftly placed into his own pocket. When the man he bumped into turned, he nodded apologetically, then melded into the stream of fairgoers moving in the opposite direction.

"Stop! Thief!" The voice was Annie's.

Her cry galvanized Nick into action. He pushed his way through the sea of startled faces, not taking time to explain. *I'm going to look a right fool if this doesn't turn out to be what we thought.*

The flat-nosed man glanced casually over his shoulder

and saw Nick's approach. Without a second's hesitation, he shoved past the people in front of him and sprinted south in the direction of the Grand Basin.

Sure of himself now, Nick pursued his quarry. His boots pounded along the walkway. When they drew even with the end of the Manufactures Building, the pickpocket veered to the right, running all out across the bridge that spanned the north canal.

He's going to try to cut between Mines and Electricity and lose himself in the crowd. Nick knew it as surely as if he had read the other man's thoughts. *If he gets that far, I've lost him.* He redoubled his speed, his breath coming in heavy gasps. His efforts were rewarded; he was gaining on his target. In a moment, he'd have him.

The man looked back, panic twisting his features when he saw Nick drawing nearer. He stumbled, caught himself, and ran on, arms and legs churning wildly.

He's getting tired. The thought gave Nick the impetus he needed to put on a final burst of speed to close the distance between them. Just before they reached the bandstand, he grabbed the other man around the waist, and they rolled across the pavement. Panting, Nick pinned him to the ground, pressing one knee into the small of his back.

Even after their wild chase, the flat-nosed man tried to brazen it out. "What's the matter with you? Get off me!"

Nick gasped for air, trying to maintain his hold while the other man struggled. A circle of onlookers formed around them. Nick could hear their voices over the other man's shouts.

"What's going on?"

"I don't know. That wild-looking fellow just ran up and knocked him to the ground."

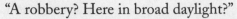

"A robbery? Here in broad daylight?"

A stout gentleman with a walrus mustache stepped forward. "See here, what do you think you're doing?"

"This fellow's a pickpocket." Nick's chest heaved. "I saw him take someone's wallet."

"That's a lie!" The fellow under Nick's knee scrabbled around, trying to regain his footing. "I was just walking along, minding my own business, when this big ox started chasing me. Somebody get him off me!"

The mustachioed man gripped Nick's shoulder. "We don't take matters into our own hands here, like you may be used to doing out West. Why don't you let him up, and we'll sort it all out." He pulled at Nick, throwing him off balance.

"Don't let him go. He's a pickpocket!" Annie pushed her way through the onlookers. She turned to the man behind her, dressed in the uniform of the Columbian Guards. "That's the man we saw. He put the wallet in his right front pocket."

The guard stepped forward. Nick removed his knee from the other man's back and stood, lifting the fellow by the back of his shirt as he did so. "That will be easy enough to prove." He held the wriggling man by the collar and one arm while the guard fished into the suspect's pocket and pulled out a fine leather wallet.

"That's mine," the accused man snarled. "It doesn't prove a thing."

The Columbian Guard riffled through the wallet and pulled out several slips of pasteboard. "Is that so? Then whose name should I find on these calling cards?"

The flat-nosed man sagged. The guard went on, his voice sharp. "Come now, what's your name?"

110

The man licked his lips and darted quick glances from side to side.

Nick tightened his grip. "Oh, no, you don't." He turned to the guard. "What do you want to do with him?"

The guard nodded toward the nearby Administration Building. "We'll hold him there at the guard headquarters until we can turn him over to the Chicago police." He took the thief from Nick and gave him a shake. "Maybe we'll get his name out of him by then."

Annie looked up at Nick. "I don't know his name, but I know who he works for. I told you I'd seen him before. It was when I was returning the satchel Silas picked up by mistake." She turned to the guard. "He was with a man named Frost. Mr. Frost told me he would be spending a lot of time at the fair, mainly in the Agriculture Building."

The guard eyed the pickpocket narrowly. "If he's part of a group, I'd like to check this out and make sure we aren't dealing with a whole ring of riffraff here." He looked back at Annie. "Would you be willing to go over there with me and point out this fellow, Frost, assuming we can spot him?"

Annie's eyes widened. "I suppose I could do that."

Nick sensed her reluctance and moved closer to her. "You don't have to."

"Yes, I do." Her voice wobbled, but the set of her jaw made her determination clear. "If people don't do their part to stand up for the right, what's to keep evil from taking over?"

He considered her words, then smiled. "I can't argue with that. All right. I'll go with you."

"No." Annie put her hand on his arm. "You said you needed to be back at the arena early today, and I've already made you late." She turned back to the guard and eyed his captive with a look of distaste. "He won't be going with us, will he?"

"No, ma'am, he won't." The guard handed his prisoner over to two fellow officers who ran up, drawn by the commotion. "We can be on our way right now."

"Are you sure?" Nick looked from the guard back to Annie. The guard tilted his hat back on his head. "I'll take good care of her, never fear." He extended his hand. "I'm Stephen Bridger, by the way."

"Nick Rutherford." Nick approved of the other man's firm grip. He turned to Annie once more. "I'll go along if you want me to."

She shook her head and glanced at Bridger. "I'll be all right."

Nick felt his hackles rise, but he kept his tone even. "I'm sure you'll be in good hands."

John James Frost watched Annie Trenton walk away in the company of the stalwart Columbian Guard, crossing the rotunda, then disappearing through the doorway that faced onto the Grand Basin. He hoped his performance had been convincing.

He smiled, remembering his display of outrage—the righteous indignation, the protestations of innocence. "I had no idea Miller was of a criminal bent. I assure you, the man will be dismissed immediately."

His brow creased as he went back over the interview, re-membering every nuance. Had his display of injured dignity been strong enough? Had he channeled the fury that churned inside him to show the proper degree of affront?

He rubbed his temple. If only they had let him know before they turned Miller over to the police. He might have persuaded the guard to release him into his custody. As it stood now, it meant sending someone to bail him out, someone who wouldn't give them any reason to draw a connection between him and Miller.

Frost ground his teeth. That meant more time wasted. More importantly, it drew attention to his little group, the last thing he wanted at this critical juncture. At the very least, he would have to keep Miller at a distance, make sure the two of them weren't seen together.

Could he trust the man out of his sight? His frustration mounted. He didn't need this unexpected complication.

The stupid fool! For pocket change, he had been willing to destroy everything they had worked for. Priorities—it all came down to that. He would have to find a way to get Miller and the rest of them back on track.

He turned over the possibilities in his mind. Maybe he really should fire the man. If it hadn't been for him and his greed. . .

And the stupidity to get himself caught! What kind of idiocy overtook him, to allow himself to be seen in the act like that? And by the Trenton woman, of all people.

She didn't appear dangerous on the surface, at least. But maybe there was more to her than met the eye.

Maybe the woman would require more than mere watching.

CHAPTER 12

And you say the gears let you drive at different speeds?"

"Yes." Annie pointed out the lever on the gearbox to the two men examining the carriage, feeling better than she had in days. Silas had been busy all morning with a steady stream of inquirers.

Nothing unusual in that, but today some of them showed a willingness to seek information from her instead of waiting until Silas was free. She continued her explanation, telling the men about the different-sized gears and how the lever allowed them to be engaged. So much nicer than discussing crochet patterns!

One of the men tugged at his mustache. "So you think this will be the mode of transportation for the future?"

"We do indeed." She nodded, refusing to let her smile waver. *Given the money to make it all possible.*

The second man ran his hand along the rear wheel. "If this catches on, it will be big." He leaned toward his companion. "We might have to look into putting some money into this before everyone else jumps on the bandwagon, eh?"

Both men chuckled. The speaker held a pasteboard rectangle out to Annie. "My card. We'll have to come back and talk to both you and your partner when he isn't so busy."

The two nodded to Annie and walked away, casting glances back at the carriage before they disappeared in the crowd.

Annie pressed the card tightly between her fingers before tucking it safely into her reticule. *I can't take any chances on losing that!* They had made the right choice, coming to the exposition. It was the step they needed to take if they wanted to move ahead.

If those two men decided to invest in the carriage and perhaps spread the word to others who would follow suit. . . Enticing possibilities danced through her mind. The noisy throng faded into the distance, replaced in Annie's mind by visions of city streets filled with horseless carriages, all bearing the name Crockett-Trenton.

She pressed her hands together and laughed out loud, drawing startled glances from several people nearby. Could it really be happening—the fruition of all their hard work, hopes, and dreams? She wanted to spin around, to cheer at the top of her lungs, but she couldn't very well do that now. Not here.

She contented herself with taking a position at the corner of the booth, ready to field more questions. Someone cleared his throat behind her. Eagerly Annie turned around. At the sight of the grim-faced pair standing there, she felt as if someone had doused her with cold water.

Graham Trenton looked stiff and uncomfortable, as though he'd rather be anywhere but there. "We came to see the carriage."

Beside him, Mrs. Trenton stood still as a statue, regarding

the carriage with a hungry gaze. "Is that it? Is that what my son created?"

Responding to the longing in her voice, Annie answered softly, "Yes, that's Will's invention." She stepped forward, determined to play the part of a gracious hostess. "Thank you so much for coming. Won't you step closer and let me show it to you?"

At first she thought they would refuse; then she saw the steely glint in their eyes soften. With the air of making a great sacrifice, they stepped inside the booth's perimeter and followed her to the carriage.

"Here it is," she said without elaboration.

Graham circled the carriage slowly, running his hands along the leather seat, bending down for a closer view of the engine. He completed his circuit, then stood back and regarded it thoughtfully, his hands on his hips. "Maybe old Will wasn't so crazy after all."

Mrs. Trenton didn't respond. She stood with her hands pressed against her waist. "May I touch it?"

"Of course."

Will's mother trailed her fingers along the side of the carriage. Annie heard the catch in her breath when she leaned forward and pressed her palm against the polished metal, holding it there as though doing so could bring back some connection with her dead son.

Annie looked on, her throat aching in sympathy. How many times had she done just that—clasped something of Will's to her as though the physical contact could create a link that would somehow bring him back?

Silas strolled over, looking highly pleased with himself. "I just had a most interesting conversation with that fellow Díaz.

116

You remember him, Annie—the one who was here with the Infanta?"

Graham's head whipped around. "The Infanta?"

Annie lifted her chin proudly. Silas's timing couldn't have been better. "Infanta Eulalia, princess of Spain. She stopped by the other day and was most impressed." She couldn't resist adding, "And I was speaking to a couple of potential investors just before you arrived. They said they would be back to discuss matters further."

The Trentons exchanged glances. "Father will want to hear about this," Graham said.

His mother blinked and pressed her lips together. "Indeed."

Annie wanted to wave her hands in the air. At last. *At last!* Maybe she was finally seeing the beginnings of a crack in the wall that existed between her and Will's family.

Graham turned to Silas. "So tell me, Mr.—" He glanced at the placard. "You are Mr. Crockett, I presume?"

Annie's hand flew to her lips. "I'm sorry. I should have introduced you. Yes, this is Silas Crockett, Will's partner and the coinventor of the Crockett-Trenton Horseless Carriage." The name rolled off her tongue with pride. "Silas, this is Graham, Will's brother, and his mother, Mrs. Trenton."

Silas studied them in turn. "Well, bless my soul." He bowed to Will's mother and pumped Graham's hand. "I'm very pleased to meet you. Will was a fine young man. You should be very proud."

A shadow darkened Graham's eyes, and Mrs. Trenton pressed a lace-edged handkerchief to her mouth.

Buoyed by his enthusiasm, Silas didn't appear to notice. "Have you had a chance to look her over?"

Graham nodded. "Quite impressive, I must say. I see you've

117

used a slip belt on the transmission."

Silas beamed. "You'll be pleased to know that was Will's idea." He looked at the carriage with the air of a proud parent. "The initial idea for the carriage was his, as a matter of fact. Between my mechanical experience, Will's creative genius, and Annie's attention to detail—" He gave her a fond smile. "We made quite a team."

Annie didn't miss the look that flashed between the Trentons. She felt she might burst from sheer happiness. "Will's time on earth may have been cut short," she said, "but we can all be very proud that he left such a legacy."

"It would certainly seem so." Graham gave a thoughtful nod. "Well, Mother, we must be leaving. Thank you for your time, Mr. Crockett. . .Annie." The word sounded like he had to force it past his lips. "You've given us a great deal to think about."

Annie's heart overflowed with joy. "Good-bye. Thank you for coming." She waited until they were some distance away, then gripped Silas's arm. "Did you hear that?"

"Yes. They seemed very nice. Not at all what I expected."

A man in a striped vest stepped up to the booth. "What can you tell me about this contraption?"

Silas hurried over to speak with him.

Annie smiled at the obvious happiness on his face, a reflection of her own delight. She waited for more inquirers to stop by; then a happy idea seized her. Let Silas enjoy his moment of triumph by answering yet another stream of questions. She was much too excited to stand still within the confines of the booth. Looping the strings of her reticule over her wrist, she made her way to the northeast archway and headed outside.

Skirting the broad plaza that separated the Manufactures

Building from the U.S. Government Building, she strolled north along the lakeside promenade toward the North Pier. Waves lapped the shore and rolled up onto the beach, sending a pair of seagulls skittering back across the sand.

Annie drew a deep breath, filling her lungs with the fresh, invigorating air. *Does the ocean smell like that?* She and Will had talked about going to the East Coast one day and had looked forward to their first glimpse of the mighty Atlantic.

That wouldn't happen now. That dream had gone the way of so many others, like raising a houseful of children and growing old together.

She left the walkway and stepped out onto the sand. Had Will's desire for fatherhood stemmed from the distance he felt from his own family—a distance both physical and emotional? Annie knew he grieved over the spiritual darkness his family walked in and felt partially to blame because of the rift created when he left Chicago against their wishes.

A scrawny little boy dashed past her on the beach, towing a taut length of string behind him. Looking back over his shoulder, he shouted, "Now!"

Annie turned to see another boy—who looked so much like him they had to be brothers—hold a sunshine yellow kite aloft in his skinny arms and thrust it into the breeze with a mighty heave. The bright paper diamond wobbled and wavered, then caught a puff of air and soared skyward to the cheers of the two youngsters.

Annie stopped to watch, half her mind paying attention to the boys and their kite, the other half remembering the sense of despair she had felt the night she learned of Will's death. It had taken her months to finally find a semblance of renewed purpose in taking it upon herself to see his dreams fulfilled, his unfinished goals accomplished.

It wasn't the same as having Will with her. . .not at all. . .but it gave her a reason to go on.

Given her icy reception at the Trentons' home, she was sure she had failed him in the thing he counted most important. But after today. . .

The kite faltered and started to plummet earthward. "Give it to me!" the older boy commanded, wresting the ball of string from his brother. He tugged on the string, gave it slack, then tugged again, seesawing the kite back up into the heights.

Annie's lips parted in a smile at the boys' triumphant shouts. She felt her own hopes soaring like the kite that danced and bobbed in the air currents over the lake. Maybe she hadn't failed Will after all.

Remembering Silas's reaction, her lips twitched in amusement. She wasn't sure that she would go quite so far as describing Will's family as "nice," but at least they came. At least they listened.

It was a start.

"Mrs. Purvis?" Annie's voice wobbled. She glanced over her shoulder at Nick and Silas. "I'm really not sure springing a visitor on her at mealtime is a good idea."

Nick gave her a wink. "Too late to worry. Here she is now."

Mrs. Purvis bustled into the hallway with a delighted smile. She stretched both hands. "Nicholas, how nice to see you. I've made a pot roast especially for you."

Annie stared wide-eyed. Nick looked at her over the land-lady's shoulder and mouthed, "I told you she wouldn't mind."

"Dinner is almost ready." Mrs. Purvis patted Nick on the arm. "You have just a few minutes to freshen up." She hurried back to the kitchen, humming the tune to "Annie Laurie."

Annie crossed her arms and looked at Nick, demanding an explanation.

He laughed out loud. "I stopped by earlier to pay my respects, and she asked me to come to dinner. He cocked his head. "You didn't really think I'd just show up uninvited, did you?"

Annie tried to glare but found herself laughing along with him. "You went to all the trouble of missing tonight's show just for a free meal?"

"Hey, a man needs home-cooked food every now and then." He stepped nearer to her and lowered his voice. "To tell you the truth, I was a little concerned after hearing about all the midnight tapping. I wanted to check out the situation for myself. Bill didn't have a problem with me taking the evening off."

"I see. And exactly how do you plan to gauge her sanity over a meal?"

"I'll just talk to her a bit." Nick shrugged as though he did this sort of thing every day. "You'd be surprised how much people reveal about themselves in the course of a conversation."

By the end of the meal, Annie had to admit he had a point. Over the soup, their landlady told them about growing up near Pittsburgh as the youngest of four sisters. Between bites of pot roast, Mrs. Purvis talked about moving to Chicago with her late husband just after the War Between the States. And by the time they finished their apple pie, she had filled them in on her theory of what started the Great Fire of '71. . .and all

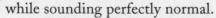

while sounding perfectly normal.

"That was a pretty amazing performance," Annie said when she walked Nick to the door. "Have you ever thought of signing on with Mr. Pinkerton and going into detective work?"

"You never can tell." He smiled. "Life can be funny. One thing leads to another; you never know where you'll end up."

Annie wagged her finger at him. "Be careful what you say. Sometimes your words come back to haunt you."

She continued in the same bantering tone. "So what did you think about Mrs. Purvis? Are we safe spending another night under her roof?"

"That sweet, lovely lady? If I needed a place to stay, I'd move in here at the drop of a hat. I think she likes me, too. Did you hear her ask me to call her Ethelinda?" He dropped Annie a wink. "Besides, the woman makes a delectable pot roast."

Annie laughed. "She keeps telling me the way to a man's heart is through his stomach. Maybe she's right."

Nick pursed his lips. "So that's why she kept pushing extra helpings at Uncle Silas. I was beginning to feel left out."

"You noticed it, too?" Annie sobered a bit. "I keep wondering whether to tell her it's a lost cause. You know your uncle; he doesn't have a clue what's going on."

"No, the poor woman can't help herself. She's been captivated by the irresistible Crockett charm." In a perfect imitation of Silas, he added, "It runs in the family, you know. All the Crockett men are like that."

Annie smiled in spite of her concern. "You're a Rutherford."

Nick dismissed her objection with a wave of his hand. "It's in the bloodline. I can't do anything about it." He broke into laughter, and Annie joined him.

"Thanks for brightening up the evening," she said. "I hope your mind is at rest now."

"About Mrs. P? You were right—she's an old dear." Nick gave her wink. "But I may have to stop in from time to time to sample some more of that pot roast."

"You'll have plenty of opportunities for that if she becomes your aunt by marriage."

Nick laughed even harder. "The only way that will ever happen is if she does the proposing. Uncle Silas would never think of it on his own." He retrieved his hat from the hall tree. "Good night. I'll see you again. Soon, I hope."

Annie closed the door, still smiling, then headed back toward the kitchen. A sense of lightness buoyed her steps. *How long has it been since I laughed like that?*

Memory stirred, and her steps slowed. She knew the answer beyond a shadow of a doubt. It had been the night before Will set off on that fateful trip to Indianapolis. She stopped at the door to the parlor and leaned against the frame.

She had been helping Will pack for his trip, both of them giddy at the prospect of finally getting the investor they needed to move ahead with the development of the carriage. Scene after scene rolled across her mind: the way they laughed, the way Will picked her up and swung her around and around until they were both dizzy.

"We're on our way, Annie." She could hear his voice as clearly as if he stood right there in the parlor with her. "Things are about to change—I can feel it. Haven't I always said we're the golden couple with the golden future? Our lives are never going to be the same."

Stop it! She shoved the painful memories back into the

recesses of her mind and hurried to the kitchen.

"Let me help you with the dishes."

Mrs. Purvis hummed the last bar of "The Missouri Waltz" before answering. "You don't have to do that. Besides, I'm nearly finished."

"I want to." Annie picked up a towel. "You had an extra guest; that means extra work."

Mrs. Purvis dipped a rag in the soapy water and used it to wipe off the stove. "He's an attractive young man, isn't he? Almost as good-looking as his uncle."

Annie turned to set a stack of plates on their shelf so Mrs. Purvis couldn't see the smile that spread across her face. "Yes, I suppose he is good-looking."

"I can see he's attracted to you."

"I hadn't noticed." Annie was glad her back was still turned. She could feel a wave of heat creep up to her hairline.

"Trust me, my dear. I recognize these things." Mrs. Purvis nodded emphatically, setting her springy curls to bobbing. "The man is quite smitten. I'd stake my life on it."

Annie picked up another plate and polished it with vigor. "I'm sure you're wrong. And anyway, he isn't thinking of settling down. He's planning to make a career with the Wild West Show."

Mrs. Purvis shot her a curious look. "You don't sound upset by that."

"I'm not looking for a husband. It's only been a little over a year." *One year, three months, and seventeen days.*

"Oh, I didn't mean to imply you were out hunting. Not at all." Mrs. Purvis scrubbed at the countertop. "It's just that you're young. You need companionship. Our hearts can only

124

stay attached to a departed loved one for so long, you know. Then it's time to move on."

Annie hung the towel in front of the stove and dropped into a chair by the kitchen table. "How long has Mr. Purvis been gone?"

"Dear Randolph." A soft smile played across Mrs. Purvis's lips. "He's been gone ten years now."

"But you haven't remarried." And not for lack of trying, if her efforts with Silas were anything to judge by.

"It isn't so easy at my age. Especially not when this would make my third trip to the altar." She smiled at Annie's look of surprise. "Yes, Randolph was my second husband. I've buried two now."

Annie clapped her hand to her lips. "I'm so sorry. I had no idea." She knew what it felt like to lose a husband. How could anyone bear to have that grief doubled?

She traced a circle on the tabletop with her finger. "After your first husband died, what made you decide to marry Mr. Purvis?"

Mrs. Purvis leaned against the counter and heaved a dreamy sigh. "He swept me off my feet; that's what he did. He always had little surprises for me. Simple things, most of them, but they let me know he was thinking of me all the time. How could I say no to that?" She squeezed out her rag and hung it next to the towel, then sat across the table from Annie. "Even after we married, he would leave little gifts here and there for me to find. It was like going on a treasure hunt."

"You must have been very happy together." Annie spoke softly, hesitant to intrude on the older woman's memories. She understood the solace of reliving moments from a happier time.

But is that all she had to look forward to—living in the past because the present was too painful to be borne?

Panic gripped her at the thought of an unending chain of long, lonely days ahead. "Ten years. How have you managed all this time?"

Mrs. Purvis rested her arms on the table. "I have my memories to keep me going. This house, for instance. My friends told me I should sell it and move into a smaller home, but this place holds so many reminders, I can't make myself leave." Her brow crinkled. "Do you think that's foolish of me?"

Annie swallowed. "Not at all. It makes perfect sense to me."

The cheery smile returned. "I thought you would understand." Mrs. Purvis gazed around the kitchen with a tender expression. "There's so much of Randolph in this house. It was one of his surprises, you know. We lost our first home in the Great Fire of '71, then watched another go up in flames a few years later. We were asleep when that one started; we barely escaped with our lives.

"By the time we were ready to build this house, Randolph swore we would never go through that again. He told me he persuaded the architect to work some rather unusual features into the plan. He said he wanted us to have a safe place to go in case we were ever caught in another fire. And he promised me he had found a way to be sure I would always be provided for."

A shadow crossed her face. "That's one secret I haven't discovered yet."

"And you've been looking all this time?"

Mrs. Purvis shook her head. She reached across the table and patted Annie's hand. "But God has provided for me. He knew I needed people around me in order to be happy, so He gave me this nice big house. It's far larger than anything I need for my own use, but it's just right for having boarders. And that has allowed me to meet some delightful people. . .like you and Mr. Crockett."

Annie nodded, marveling at the courageous way Mrs. Purvis had faced hardship and drawing from it the courage to face her own. God could provide for her as well as Mrs. Purvis. With Him to depend on, she could go on just as she was, with her memories to sustain her.

"But I'm a good bit older than you," Mrs. Purvis added, as though reading Annie's thoughts. "Most of my life is behind me now. But I don't believe God intended for young widows like yourself to stay in that condition. Even the Bible says so. Remember the story of Ruth?"

Annie nodded, wondering where this was headed. She hardly saw herself as a counterpart of the biblical heroine.

"Ruth found a new love and a new life with Boaz," Mrs. Purvis continued. "God hasn't abandoned you, no matter how you may feel at times."

Annie blinked back tears. "Will was such a special man. I don't think I could ever have the same feelings for anyone else."

"When I hear you speak of him, I get the feeling he loved you very much. Is that what he would have wanted for you? Perhaps it's time to look to the future and think of moving on to a life that's fulfilling." Mrs. Purvis patted Annie's hand again. "One day you'll find a man who makes you whole again, or my name isn't Ethelinda Purvis."

Annie nodded, struck by the irony of taking advice from a woman who went around tapping on walls in the middle of the night. "But another husband doesn't have to be the answer. God can take care of me just as He has done for you."

Mrs. Purvis smiled and squeezed her arm. "Trust the Lord to provide but be ready for Him to show you a different way than you may expect." She pushed herself out of her chair and scooted it back under the table. "And now, my dear, I think I'm ready to turn in. It's been a lovely evening, and I thoroughly enjoyed our chat."

Annie stood and gave her a warm hug. "Yes, it was lovely. Thank you."

"And be sure to invite Nicholas for dinner again. Such a nice young man."

Annie smiled. "I'll remember that." She stopped short of promising to go through with extending the invitation. She went upstairs, thinking about their conversation while she changed into her nightgown and brushed her hair.

God has not abandoned you. Mrs. Purvis's words lingered in her mind.

She pondered that thought while she climbed into bed and snuggled against her pillow.

One day you'll find a man who makes you whole again.

Nick? Annie thrust the thought away as quickly as it came. He was a fine man, a good friend. She enjoyed his company immensely, but she wasn't interested in him. . .not in that way.

And even if she was, he was committed to the show, not to settling down.

Richard Trenton toyed with the silver-framed photograph on his desk. "And you say people were actually showing an interest in this folly of Will's?" He ignored his wife's sharp intake of breath at his slighting comment. It never paid to acknowledge weakness.

"That's what I've been trying to tell you, Father." Graham turned from pacing the room. "There was a knot of people clustered around. Mother and I had to wait our turn before either of them were free to talk to us."

Richard Trenton dismissed the comment with a wave of his hand. "Gawkers, that's all. Any new oddity will draw a crowd. That doesn't mean the thing has any staying power."

"I'm afraid I'll have to differ with you on that." Graham took a stance at the center of the Aubusson carpet. "I admit my purpose in going was to sneer at the contraption, but I have to say I came away impressed."

"It's a wonderful invention, Richard." His wife spoke from her spot near the window, her voice quiet but proud. "I'm quite sure it will do well."

Richard Trenton fought back a smile and forced his lips to remain in a stern line. It wouldn't do to let either of them see him soften or realize how pleased he felt when Graham stood up to him. The boy would need plenty of gumption when his turn came to stand at the helm of the family business.

It didn't mean he was right, though. Bad enough the two of them had slipped off to the fair while he was out of town on business overnight. It wouldn't do to encourage further rebellion. "I'm glad it won your approval, but a gaggle of wide-eyed onlookers is hardly a guarantee of success. People go to fairs prepared to look and wonder at anything they may find. It isn't difficult to please them in that setting. Getting the working classes to part with money to buy a product is a different matter altogether."

129

"What about royalty?" His wife faced him, her eyes glowing.

Richard started. "Royalty?"

"That's right." Graham threw his mother a grateful smile. "The Spanish princess seems quite impressed by Will's invention. And she—Will's wife—said she had been talking to some investors just before we arrived."

"According to her." Richard leaned back in his leather chair. "There's no telling what kind of wild tale the woman is capable of concocting. I wouldn't put it past her to have fabricated the whole thing out of thin air, Spanish royalty and all."

"I don't think so," Graham said slowly. "Did you really look at her when she was here? There's something about her. I don't know what to call it exactly, but she seems sincere."

Richard sat bolt upright. "Don't let your common sense be swayed by feigned innocence. A pretty face can mask all sorts of chicanery." He leveled a finger at his son. "If you don't watch out, you'll wind up proving yourself to be just as gullible as your brother was."

"Don't you see? That's just the problem. We've always talked about her as 'that woman' and blamed her for keeping Will away. But seeing her here, seeing her as a real person. . .I don't know, Father. I just don't believe she's making this up."

Richard brought his fist down on the desktop with a crash that tipped the photo on its face. "If Will hadn't married her," he thundered, "do either of you really think he would have defied my orders to come home and take his place in the company?"

His wife put her hand to her throat. "Richard, remember your heart."

Planting his palms on the blotter, he stood and leaned over

the desk. "She encouraged him in his madness. She's the reason he stayed away."

Graham lifted his eyebrows. "You can hardly call it madness, Father, when Will is the one who came up with the notion for the carriage."

Richard settled back into his chair and took a series of deep, calming breaths. He drew his brows together. "It was Will's idea?"

Graham smiled. "That fellow Crockett told me so himself."

Richard picked up the fallen photograph and set it upright. Will's face smiled out at him. He looked up at his remaining son. "And you truly believe this has potential?"

"Definitely." Graham's smile widened. "Wouldn't you say so, Mother?"

"I have no doubt of it."

Richard looked back at the photo and rubbed his thumbs along the edges of the silver frame. "Do you think it will draw investors?"

"Absolutely," Graham said. "It seems Will's wild ideas really did have something to recommend them after all."

Richard stroked his chin. "And Will came up with the idea on his own." He set the photo back in its place and tented his fingers. "That puts things in a different light, doesn't it?" He nodded slowly, thinking it through. "Yes, I'd say we just may have to reconsider our position on this a bit."

Graham stepped over to the desk and helped himself to one of his father's cigars. "I thought you'd see it that way."

CHAPTER 13

Nick dragged the canvas camp chair outside his tent to catch the light of the afternoon sun. He picked up his bullwhip from where he had tossed it on his cot and squinted at the tip. . . or what was left of it.

Unraveling a foot of the braided leather, he began to work in new strands to replace the part that snapped off during last night's performance. Once his fingers established their pattern of movement, his thoughts were free to wander. As they did more and more frequently, they wandered straight to Annie Trenton.

Nick plaited the strips of leather, remembering how Annie had looked when she plunged into the crowd like an avenging Fury intent on capturing the pickpocket.

What would she have done if he hadn't taken the lead and given chase? More than likely, she would have taken off after the miscreant on her own. After all, hadn't she taken the initiative in hunting down the guard Bridger and leading him to the scene of the capture?

Nick chuckled at the mental image of Annie flying along the walkway in hot pursuit of the thief. But she could have been putting herself in danger, going after a criminal like that. What would make anyone go to such lengths to help a total stranger?

He recalled the earnest look in her eyes when she talked of the need to stand for what was right. Her actions had nothing to do with bravado or concern about what anyone else thought. It was just the way Annie did things, living out her faith as a natural part of her existence. She could no more have ignored the incident than she could stop breathing.

Nick continued to ply the leather strands together in a neat braid. Annie and her late husband must have been like two peas in a pod, he mused, willing to put themselves at risk for people they didn't even know, just as a matter of principle.

Would he have done what he did without Annie's headlong flight goading him into action? He'd like to think so, but if he were honest with himself, he couldn't be sure.

Nick trimmed off the protruding ends of the new strips, then finished it off by rolling the new braid between his hands to round it. He looked on his handiwork with satisfaction. It ought to hold this time. He set the chair back inside, clearing a space outdoors so he could try the whip out before the evening show.

He snaked the whip out and tightened his grip on the handle, then drew his arm back over his head and prepared to snap his wrist out.

"Nick! Hey, Nick!" Feet pounded on the packed earth, and a freckle-faced youth appeared from between the tents.

Nick caught himself before he could complete the swing. Deprived of its momentum, the end of the bullwhip swung around

133

and swatted harmlessly against the side of his tent. Exasperated, Nick rounded on the kid. "What's the matter with you, Floyd? You know better than to pop out of nowhere like that. Are you trying to get your eye put out?"

"Sorry." The boy's grin said otherwise. "There's a reporter hanging around. Colonel Cody wants you to talk to him."

"Me? Well, if Bill says so." He tossed the whip on his bunk and followed Floyd to the tent the company used as an office. Inside, he looked in vain for Cody.

The tent's sole occupant, a weedy young man wearing a derby and sporting a sparse mustache, jumped up and greeted him with an eager smile. "You're Nick Rutherford?"

Nick nodded. "That's me. What's all this about?"

The man grinned. "I'm Gil Martin, with the *Tribune*. We're doing a human-interest story on some of the performers here. Colonel Cody said you were the first one I ought to interview."

Nick locked his knees and tried not to let on how stunned he felt. He moved to the leather camp chair and settled into it with what he hoped appeared to be a casual air, then motioned Martin to sit. "All right, what would you like to know?" Cody hadn't wasted any time singling him out for attention.

Martin whipped out a small notebook and licked the end of his pencil. "Let's start at the beginning. Where were you born?"

Nick felt his tension drain away. This was going to be easy. "In Ohio, not far from Canton. My family moved to Indiana when I was five."

The reporter twiddled the pencil in his fingers. "Have you ever been to Wyoming?"

"Sure. I worked on several ranches there. But that was a good deal later."

134

"Of course." Martin scribbled on his pad. "So what took you out West?"

Nick rubbed his palms along the chair arms. He knew well enough what prompted him to make the move, but he'd never had to put it into words before. He started off slowly, trying to feel his way along. "I grew up listening to my grandfather talk about his experiences in the War Between the States. He had quite a time of it, and he could spin stories about his experiences that made you feel like you'd been there right along with him."

Martin listened intently. Nick went on, feeling more confident. "The thing I heard from him over and over was that once you choose to do something, you have to put your heart and soul into it. Halfway measures just wouldn't do. I remember him saying, 'You gotta throw yourself into it. That's what kept me alive. If I hadn't thrown myself into the battle with all my heart, I'd be dead.' Then he'd look me straight in the eye and say, 'You've gotta do that, too, boy. You've gotta go after life the very same way.'"

Martin tapped the pencil against his notebook. "Quite a motivator, your grandfather. So why the West?"

Nick drummed his fingers on his knees. "I wanted a challenge, a way to find out what kind of man I really was." He chuckled. "I didn't see a lot of challenge in growing corn—not the kind I was looking for anyway."

The reporter pursed his lips and nodded. "So where did you go? What did you do?" He leaned forward and planted his elbows on his knees. "Did you know Custer? Hunt any buffalo?"

Nick stared at him. "Seeing as how Custer died when I was eleven years old, that would have been a bit difficult. And the buffalo were pretty much gone by the time I made it out there."

Martin scrawled a rapid note. "Okay, then tell me what you did."

"I'd always been a fair rider, so I was able to find work at ranches in Wyoming and Colorado. That was where I learned to ride rough stock and handle a rope."

"What about this bullwhip you use in your act?"

Nick smiled and leaned back, at ease now. "That came from Hugh Smith. He was an old mule skinner I met in Wyoming. He took a liking to me, took me under his wing, as it were, and taught me how to pack mules and use a bullwhip. He was a personal friend of Bill Cody's, knew him from way back. He's the one who recommended me for this job, as a matter of fact. I have a lot to thank him for."

Martin scribbled for the next few minutes, covering pages with writing that looked like chicken scratches as far as Nick could see. Finally he straightened and regarded the notebook with a satisfied air. "See what you think of this." He leafed back through the pages and began to read:

> "The son of a buffalo-hunter-turned-cattle-rancher and a dark-eyed beauty from the Shoshone Indian Nation, Nicholas Rutherford—or Wyoming Nick, as he likes to be called—cut his teeth on the braided handle of a bullwhip. By the age of six, he could flick a fly off a mule's ear at twenty paces. His expertise in riding the bucking bronco he learned from his Shoshone relatives."

He looked up and grinned at Nick. "What do you think so far? Pretty good stuff, huh?"

Nick's jaw hung open. "Are you sure your name isn't Ned

Buntline? 'Wyoming Nick. . .Shoshone beauty. . .' Where did you come up with that stuff? That's about as far from the truth as it gets."

Martin held up his finger. "But it sells papers. And when papers sell, your name gets out there. And when your name gets out there, people will come in droves to buy tickets. I guarantee it." He waggled the notebook in the air. "Cody will love this."

Nick reached for the book and pulled it out of Martin's hand. Skimming through it, he removed the pages that read like the beginning of one of Buntline's dime novels.

"You have the truth right here in your notes. Try working with that."

Martin sputtered, "But you have to give the public what it wants, and the public—"

"Will come to see me. . .or not. . .for what I can do and who I really am. Not some trumped-up fairy tale." Nick tucked the notebook back into the astonished reporter's shirt pocket.

"You seem like a good sort. But if you print something like that, I might be tempted to see just how close I can come to flicking a fly off your ear."

"But. . .but. . ." Martin made a disgusted face. "I'm just trying to help you out."

"And I appreciate that. I'll take all the help you can give me. . .as long as it's based on the truth. *Firmly* based," he added as he walked out of the tent.

Cody was living up to his word. Already, the promotional wheels were turning. It would be only a matter of time before interviews like this would become a regular part of his life. He could get used to seeing his name in print—if he could manage to keep the reporters and their stories on track.

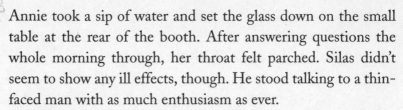

Annie took a sip of water and set the glass down on the small table at the rear of the booth. After answering questions the whole morning through, her throat felt parched. Silas didn't seem to show any ill effects, though. He stood talking to a thin-faced man with as much enthusiasm as ever.

Hearing a commotion, she looked up to see a group of people descending on the booth. Annie grimaced when she recognized the blond woman in the center.

She glanced back at Silas, still talking and blithely unaware of the retinue's approach. Annie assumed a polite expression and stepped forward. "Welcome back, Your Highness. We're glad you came to visit us again." Despite her aversion to the princess, she couldn't help but feel a quiver of excitement. *What a shame Will's parents couldn't be here to see this!*

The Infanta slowed long enough to give Annie a condescending look, then swept past her toward Silas.

"Ah, Senor Crockett. You can see I have returned as I promised. Would you favor me with another look at your marvelous carriage?"

Startled by the interruption, Silas wheeled around, a crease forming between his eyebrows. His face smoothed into a wide smile when he recognized his visitor. "Your Highness, what a pleasant surprise." He turned to the man he had been talking to. "If you would excuse me, sir, Mrs. Trenton will be able to answer any further questions you may have." He waved his hand in Annie's general direction, then bowed and escorted the Infanta over to the carriage.

The abandoned inquirer stared at the obviously important personage a moment, shot a skeptical look at Annie, and walked away.

Annie watched the byplay with gritted teeth, resisting the urge to kick the carriage wheel nearest her. *Am I not a person? Do I not look like I possess a brain?* She broke off her internal diatribe when she noticed Senor Díaz at her elbow.

"*Buenos días,* Senora Trenton." He made a quick bow. "Please do not take the attitude of the Infanta as an insult. It might interest you to know that she much admires the advances women have made in your country."

Annie sniffed, unwilling to let her ruffled feathers be smoothed so easily. "She has a peculiar way of showing it."

Díaz's white teeth shone in a sympathetic smile. "I quite understand your distress. You must understand that, in spite of her admiration, it is difficult for her to overcome years of training and adjust her own attitudes so quickly. In our country, you see, she is used to dealing with men when discussing matters of business."

"Díaz!" The Infanta's voice was sharp, imperious. "Come here. I want you to take note of this. Mr. Crockett is going to explain how the gears allow the carriage to move at different speeds."

Díaz cast an apologetic look at Annie and hurried over. Not to be left behind, Annie followed.

The Infanta fixed Díaz with a disapproving look. "You are not attending me by standing over there chatting. I expect you to anticipate my wishes."

Díaz spread his hands wide and bowed in a manner Annie found obsequious. *She won't change that attitude anytime soon if*

139

he keeps fawning over her like that.

"But of course, Your Highness. Has not my family served yours for generations?"

Silas rubbed his hands. "As I was saying, we have four gears in the gearbox in ascending ratio."

The Infanta stared at him blankly.

"Perhaps it would be easier if I showed you," Silas said. "Look here." He moved to the side of the carriage.

"Díaz, observe Mr. Crockett closely."

Annie pinched her lips together to hide the smile she felt tugging at her cheeks. The order might have been given in an imperious tone, but it was obvious the Infanta had no inkling what Silas was talking about. Apparently even members of royalty had their limitations.

Silas bent over next to the wheel. Díaz dropped to one knee beside him. Silas leaned farther forward, and his notebook slipped out of his breast pocket and landed on the ground.

He scooped it up and held it out. "Annie, would you hold this for me, please? I don't want to lose my train of thought."

Annie started to set the slim book on the table at the rear of the booth, then tucked it inside her reticule instead. It wouldn't do to take a chance on it being misplaced. Silas would be beside himself if he couldn't find it when he wanted it. Leaving the Infanta to Silas, she retreated to the edge of the booth.

"Well, hello." The voice came from behind her. "I didn't expect to find you here."

Annie turned to find herself nose-to-coat-button with a man in the uniform of the Columbian Guards. She looked up and smiled when she recognized Stephen Bridger.

"Good morning. Or is it already afternoon?"

140

Bridger chuckled. "Still morning but not for long. It's hard to keep track when you're indoors all the time, isn't it? I've been hearing about this marvelous machine and decided I had to come see it for myself. Are you connected with all this?" His gaze lit on the placard, and his face cleared. "Ah, the Crockett-*Trenton* Horseless Carriage."

Annie smiled. "My late husband was Mr. Crockett's partner."

"So you must be well versed in everything having to do with the carriage. That's wonderful! You can tell me all about it."

Annie's irritation at being ignored vanished. "I'd be glad to." She pointed to one of the posters. "The combustion engine is similar to the engine in a locomotive. You can see here how the pistons drive the main gears. There's more information on the posters on the other side."

Bridger nodded and walked behind the display to read the rest.

Annie darted a quick glance over toward the Infanta and her retinue. Díaz, on both knees now, peered under the carriage. Silas was no doubt explaining the benefits of the chain drive to him.

A familiar figure caught her attention. *Nick!* Joy welled up within her, and her heart did a funny little dance.

He strode into the booth and gave her a smile that warmed her through and through. "Would you like to go to lunch with me? I thought we might try the Marine Café."

Stephen Bridger stepped out from behind the row of posters, and Nick's expression dimmed.

"Rutherford!" Bridger extended his hand and shook Nick's with every evidence of pleasure. "I thought I recognized your voice. It's good to see you again."

"Nice to see you, too." Nick's gaze flitted from Annie to

Bridger and back again. "What about it, Annie? Are you ready for lunch?"

She hesitated and looked over at the carriage, where Silas showed no sign of ending his lecture anytime soon. "I'm sorry. I can't right now." She gestured helplessly toward the listening group. "It looks like Silas is going to be monopolized for a while. I need to be here in case someone else has a question." She held her breath and waited for his response. Surely he would offer to wait until Silas was free.

Nick nodded, somewhat curtly. "I can see you're busy. I'll let you get back to it then. Maybe I'll see you later."

Annie watched his retreating back with a sinking sensation.

Beside her, Stephen Bridger turned his attention back to the posters. "How long does it take to learn to operate one of these?"

"Young man?" A little dumpling of a woman pulled on Bridger's sleeve. "Young man! I'm looking for the exhibits from France. Someone told me how to get there; but I've tried and tried to find them, and it's no good. I'm afraid I'm hopeless with directions." She twisted her hands together. "Could you help me, please?"

"I'll be glad to, ma'am." He looked back at Annie and smiled. "I'll try to stop by again. I'd like to hear more about this vehicle."

The Infanta and her entourage swept out of the booth a moment later. Díaz alone took note of Annie's existence and gave her a courteous nod as he passed by.

Silas walked over, brushing the knees of his trousers. "That was a most enjoyable conversation." He tugged the sleeves of his jacket into place. "The Infanta seems to have a real interest in the carriage. She asked a lot of questions, all of them sensible. A thoroughly delightful woman, don't you think?"

Annie reached over to straighten his tie and forbore to answer.

Melodious chimes sounded from the clock in the central tower. Silas blinked. "Noon already? Why don't you go get some lunch, Annie? Don't worry about me. I'm far too excited to think about eating a thing."

Annie cast a longing look in the direction Nick had taken. There would be no way of catching up with him now. He'd probably be halfway back to the encampment. She nodded briskly. "Good idea. I think I'll do that."

"Take your time," Silas called.

Annie smiled wanly. "I may do that."

CHAPTER 14

Annie took a bite of frankfurter sausage and leaned back against the wooden bench, enjoying the blessed quiet. No crowds clamoring for attention, no questions to answer. Only peace and quiet.

She nodded to a pleasant-looking couple who strolled by on the path in front of her. The woman smiled and dipped her head in response. Her companion tipped his bowler in a cheerful salute. Annie smiled back. Both of them seemed to experience the same relief she did at finding a place to escape.

She sighed and felt her taut muscles start to relax. Nick was right. The Wooded Island exuded a sense of calm, a welcome respite from the incessant hubbub that went on in the rest of the fairgrounds.

What a good thing she had remembered his suggestion, even if he wasn't there to share lunch with her. Even the observation deck with its spectacular view didn't convey the same air of serenity. She bit into the sausage again, enjoying its sharp, tangy flavor.

Across the lagoon, the dazzling white buildings of the Court of Honor glittered in the early afternoon sunlight, their apparent size doubled by their reflections in the water. On the walkways connecting the buildings, hordes of people rushed to and fro as though they feared they might miss something if they slowed for an instant. But here. . . Annie closed her eyes and listened. Instead of a cacophony of voices, she could pick out the songs of robins and blackbirds, the rustling of the mulberry leaves overhead, her own steady breathing.

The heady perfume from the rose garden that adorned the south end of the island mingled with the deeper scents of trees and earth. As long as she kept her eyes closed, she could almost pretend she was on a picnic in the Indiana countryside.

Annie let a long breath escape her lungs, allowing her tension to slip out with it and float away on the breeze. Opening her eyes, she pulled her handkerchief from her left sleeve and used it to dab at her forehead, cheeks, and neck. She might have evaded the crush of the crowd, but there was no escape from the humidity. The day was distinctly muggy, even with the ever-present breeze.

A group of women walked by, fanning themselves. "Where do you want to go next?" one asked.

"At the moment, nowhere," another answered. "I need some time to catch my breath. There's only so much a person can take in all at once."

Annie watched them idly, enjoying the chance to be nothing more than an observer for once, without the need to smile and answer questions.

She popped the last bite of sausage in her mouth, licked a stray crumb from her fingers, and wadded the wrapper into

145

a ball. The afternoon stretched out before her. She could get up and leave now, head back to the Manufactures Building. Something in her resisted. She needed this time alone. But even more than time to herself. . .

She opened her reticule and pulled out Will's Bible. More than anything right now, she needed to spend time with God's Word. She held the small volume on her lap, drawing comfort from its familiar feel.

She remembered Will's delight on receiving it one Christmas, his pleasure in being able to tuck it in his pocket and carry it with him wherever he went. Since that first day, he had never been without it.

Now Annie was the one grateful for its compact size. It fit quite well in the recesses of her reticule, meaning she always had access to the most personal link that remained between her and Will. While the carriage was his brainchild, it never held the same value for him as this book he prized above all others.

She ran her fingers over the smooth cowhide, treasuring the memories it brought, wincing when she traced the deep scars made when it skidded along the macadam road on that dreadful day in Indianapolis. She shuddered. That was one memory she didn't want to dwell on.

She let the Bible fall open of its own accord. A carefully inked line marked a verse near the bottom of the right-hand page: Hebrews 13:5, one of Will's favorites.

Annie remembered him pulling the Bible from his pocket to read to her in the evenings as they sat in their cozy living room. Her favorite nights were those when the countryside lay in the throes of winter. They would sit close together before the hearth, where she could watch the glow from the fireplace turn Will's hair the color of burnished gold. Her world seemed complete on nights like that, with the day's work behind them and nothing but bright hopes for the morrow and all the other days ahead.

She focused on the verse, her memory supplying the sound of Will's mellow voice reading the words: "And be content with such things as ye have: for he hath said, I will never leave thee, nor forsake thee."

"But *you* left me, Will." The words sprang from her lips before she could stop them.

Gripped by the ache in her heart, she looked out across the placid lagoon toward the Woman's Building. Instead of the shining edifice, she saw only the image of a man with laughing blue eyes and hair the color of a wheat field.

The breeze shifted direction, ruffling the delicate pages. Annie smoothed them tenderly, pressing them flat under her fingertips. Pictures from the past sprang so readily into her mind's eye. What would she see if she could envision what Will was experiencing right now, this very moment?

He was in heaven, of course. Of that she had no doubt. In the very presence of the Lord, forever happy, forever rejoicing. He could enjoy the multitude of blessings God had prepared for him. But she was still here. . .waiting.

Annie swiped a tear away with the back of her hand. She had asked the Lord a thousand times why her own life didn't end when Will's did. In a very real sense, it *had* ended. But where Will could enjoy the delights of heaven, she was left here and must somehow find a reason to keep going.

"I will never leave thee, nor forsake thee." Her beloved husband was gone, but the Lord had never promised her Will's continued presence, only His own.

A twig snapped behind her. "Is this seat taken?"

Annie started and looked up into a pair of dark brown eyes. "Nick!" Surprise sent sparks shooting through her, mingled with a lightness she hadn't felt in a long time.

She scooted over to make room for him on the bench. "What are you doing here? Looking for a quiet spot to plan a new trick for your act?"

His smile sent goose bumps up her arms. "I felt bad about leaving so abruptly. I went back to see when you thought you might be free for lunch, but you had already gone. Uncle Silas thought you might be over at the Woman's Building or looking at the electrical exhibits. After I checked those and didn't find you, I decided I'd take a chance and try this as a last resort."

Annie couldn't stop the foolish grin that spread across her face. He came back. He was looking for her. And to cover all that ground, he'd spent quite a bit of time doing it. Speaking of which. . . "Isn't it almost time for you to get ready for your afternoon show?"

"I wasted a lot of time following Uncle Silas's leads, but we still have an hour or so to talk or to take a walk if you'd rather."

"A walk," Annie said decisively. She suddenly felt energized and knew she couldn't sit still a moment longer.

"I hope I didn't disturb you."

"Not at all." She followed his gaze to the Bible on her lap. "I was just finishing up when you came." She tucked the Bible back inside her reticule.

Nick rose and held out his hand to help her to her feet. The electric tingle she felt when their fingers touched made her want to soar, to wheel like the gulls overhead. Instead, she settled for walking demurely at Nick's side down the pathway.

148

"So that's where you get it," Nick said.

Annie stared at him. "It?"

"Your strength, that peace you have. I want you to know how much I admire the way you've been able to go on taking care of Uncle Silas and moving ahead with putting this exhibit together after all you've been through."

Only the crunch of their footsteps on the gravel marred the silence while Annie tried to formulate an answer. "Maybe it's easier for women." She laughed at his startled expression.

"We're already trained by society to be dependent," she explained. "Men are expected to handle their problems on their own without asking for help. But that's exactly what has to be done, you see. " Recognition of the truth flowed through Annie even as she spoke. "You have to call on the Lord for help at the beginning of the problem instead of thinking of Him as a last resort."

Nick gave her rueful smile. "You make it sound simple. But it must work. I can see what it's done for you."

Annie pressed her lips together. Tempting as it was to hold herself up as a model of Christian virtue, she couldn't be less than honest with him. "I try. But I feel like a dismal failure more often than not."

"That isn't the way I see it. You seem to know exactly who you are and where you're going. You have a sense of purpose that makes mine pale in comparison."

She shook her head and stared down at the pathway. "Most days, I have to remind myself to keep putting one foot in front of the other."

Nick tucked her hand into the crook of his arm. "Like now?"

Annie studied his face while their steps moved them ahead in unison. "Like now."

Nick lifted his head as though listening to the wind that rustled the mulberry leaves above them. "I used to go to church when I was a boy. And there were plenty of times out there on the range when I thought I'd be meeting God face-to-face any minute. I try to treat people fairly and do what I know is right. But I don't have what you have—that sense that God is giving you peace and the strength you need. I used to talk to God a lot, but now it feels like He's a million miles away. I guess He got tired of not hearing from me and went off and left me behind."

"He's still there, waiting," Annie said gently. "He isn't the one who moved away."

Nick seemed to be pondering her words. "Maybe you're right," he said at last.

Annie watched him out of the corner of her eye. What a difference between him and the other men who had shown interest in her—both before and after Will.

Up ahead, a figure stepped out from one of the winding paths that crisscrossed the island. As quickly as he appeared, he stepped back into the shadows of the tree-lined alley, but not before Annie got a glimpse of a narrow face under a slouch hat.

She stopped abruptly, eyes wide, feeling her heart race like a trip-hammer.

Nick halted and turned to face her. "What's the matter?"

"That man."

Nick swung around, putting himself between her and the source of her concern, then turned back to her. "What man?"

Annie felt the blood drain from her face. A buzz started in her ears, and her arm trembled when she pointed at the spot where the thin man had disappeared. "He went behind those trees. He's been following me."

Nick wrapped his hands around her icy fingers. "What makes you think he's following you?"

Without thinking about it, Annie threaded her fingers between his, grateful for their warmth. "I saw him outside Mrs. Purvis's and again on the Midway the day we saw the Infanta."

"You did?" Nick raised an eyebrow. "You didn't mention it to me then."

Annie felt a tremor along her spine. "Thousands of people come to the fairgrounds every day. I told myself it must be a coincidence. I didn't want to upset you or make myself look like a dithering ninny. The way I am right now," she added with a shaky laugh.

"But then I saw him when I went to visit Will's parents and again just now. He stepped back into the trees as soon as he realized I had noticed him. He's following me; I know it."

Nick stared at her for a long moment, as if uncertain how to respond. "It's possible," he finally said.

She could tell from his hesitation and the way he didn't quite meet her eyes that he couldn't accept the idea as a real possibility. Not here, not on the grounds of the White City where Columbian Guards patrolled the grounds and every detail had been planned to create a place of peace and beauty.

She felt an emptiness, a sense of letdown. If Nick didn't believe her. . .

"No one will bother you while you're with me," he added, as if trying to make amends for his show of doubt.

Annie tried to smile. "You're probably right." That much they agreed on at least. Who in their right mind would willingly go up against such a pillar of strength?

"Whoever it was, he's surely gone by now. We don't have

to let it ruin the rest of our time together." So saying, he placed Annie's hand back in the crook of his elbow, and they continued their walk.

When they came even with the spot where the man had vanished, Annie felt her steps lag. What if he lay in wait back there in the shadows, biding his time for the chance to leap out and. . .do what?

Nick veered to the far side of the walkway and pointed to a gondola just pulling into the boat landing on the shore.

Annie nodded, appreciating his effort to draw her attention away from the unpleasant incident but unable to stop the flow of questions that rushed through her head.

Who is that man, and why is he following me?

Did the Trentons send him to keep watch on me? But why would they? I only came here to try to heal the breach that grieved Will so. I can't possibly pose a threat to them!

Once they passed the point where the watcher had stood, Annie felt herself begin to relax. After fifteen months of having to be strong, needing to stay on top of things and push to make sure the carriage would be ready to bring to Chicago, it was comforting beyond words to have someone looking out for her for a change.

Nick Rutherford might dress like a rugged frontiersman, but she couldn't deny his gentlemanly qualities. Though different from Will in many ways, he had that same air of steadiness, the same confidence that inspired respect and trust. She felt safe when she was around him.

The way I used to feel with Will. A warm glow radiated through her. It had been a long time since she had been able to lean on someone who took her concerns seriously. *Even if he isn't quite convinced there's someone dogging my steps.*

Remembering the watcher, Annie cast a glance back over her shoulder to be sure he hadn't reappeared. The walkway stretched out behind them, empty save for a band of young boys in knickers, tossing sticks into the water.

She turned her attention back to the winding path before them, happy not to feel any pressure to make conversation. Nick seemed as content as she to stroll along in silence.

Annie felt the strength of his arm through the buckskin. She let her gaze travel up the leather jacket to the muscular shoulders it encased. What would it be like to rest her head on that strong shoulder, only inches away? She allowed her head to tilt a fraction in his direction.

A fraction too far. The brim of her hat brushed Nick's arm. She heard his breath catch. He looked down, his hand tightening on hers, and she stumbled to a stop, feeling like the worst sort of fool.

What have I done? This wasn't Will. Not her beloved husband but someone she'd known only a brief time. What must he think of her, appearing to throw herself at him that way?

From the heat that flooded her cheeks, she had no doubt that mortification stained them crimson. Her mind scrambled for some way out of this quicksand of emotions. She fastened her gaze ahead, at the column-front building that anchored the north end of the Court of Honor. "I'd like to visit the Palace of Fine Arts one day," she said brightly.

Nick looked at her strangely. "Yes, I'm sure you would enjoy it."

"I've looked at a lot of paintings before but none from the great masters represented here." She knew she was babbling but couldn't stem the tide of words that poured out of her like a flood.

What am I doing, Lord? Now he'll think I'm an idiot in addition to a flirt.

She wanted to snatch her hand out of the crook of his elbow. She wanted to leave it there and press his arm even tighter. Shame filled her when she remembered her desire to lay her head against his shoulder. At the same time, she wished with all her heart that she had done so.

Only a few clumps of sumac bushes separated them from the point where the bridge joined the north tip of the island. Annie's traitorous imagination wondered what would happen if Nick pulled her aside into the shelter of those leafy branches and folded her in his arms.

What are you thinking of, Annie Trenton? These were the feelings she had for Will, her husband, the only man she had ever loved.

Until now.

Her breath caught in her throat. Where did that errant thought come from? She had pledged her life to Will. His time on earth had been cut short, but he'd left unfinished business. She had to attend to it. It was her purpose in life, her reason to go on.

The touch of Nick's fingers warmed the back of her hand, and her pulse beat double time. *Stop it!* She couldn't—wouldn't—let herself feel this way. She was not husband hunting. Hadn't she said as much to Mrs. Purvis?

Mrs. Purvis. . . Annie could see the sprightly face in her mind's eye, the springy curls, the knowing smile. *I've seen the way he looks at you. . . .*

The heat that surged through Annie wasn't all due to the day's warmth. *Is she right?*

154

I've seen the way he looks at you. Did he have feelings for her? A warm glow flickered in her heart and spread throughout her limbs. What if he did feel something for her, something more than friendship or courtesy to a friend of his uncle's. . .what then?

More to the point, suppose she returned those feelings? The possibility that sharp-eyed Mrs. Purvis had recognized the situation before Annie was aware of it herself filled her with chagrin.

Their steps turned in unison toward the bridge, as though they had decided the route together. In a few minutes, they would be back at the booth, back to Silas and the carriage and answering the same questions over and over again. Back to normalcy as she had come to know it here in Chicago.

Part of her welcomed the chance to move back into a routine she knew. Another part of her dreaded the moment she would say good-bye to Nick.

But it would give her time to think things through, to sort out the tumult of emotions that wheeled through her mind like a flock of keening gulls. She should be glad for the respite, for the opportunity to get herself in hand again. But she wasn't.

Willow branches brushed against her sleeve when they stepped off the bridge. Nick turned south toward the Manufactures Building, then hesitated. "Would you like to go over to the Palace of Fine Arts right now?" Hope tinged his voice, but Annie saw the hesitation in his eyes. Was he experiencing the same conflicting feelings that beset her?

She longed to be with him, but she was afraid to go. She needed to think!

"Another time, perhaps." Her lips quivered. "I've been away long enough for now."

Nick nodded. Was that relief or regret she saw in his eyes?

She followed his lead as they turned their steps toward the building's north entrance, knowing that something had changed between them, something she couldn't explain. Or was afraid to.

Tonight in her room, she would take her wayward feelings out and examine them. For now, she could only think about getting back to the booth. Back to business, where conflicting emotions didn't tug at her heart with every other breath.

"What's going on over there?" Nick pointed to the entrance of the Manufactures Building.

Annie followed his gesture and saw a crowd clotting the doorway. She frowned. Instead of the usual traffic of people moving in and out of the broad archway, this was a knot that grew as more people congregated, like bits of iron filings being drawn toward a magnet. "Maybe someone is putting on some sort of demonstration."

They drew nearer to find the crowd so thick it blocked the way to the entrance. The knot of onlookers stared at whatever lay at its center like a flock of sheep with their noses pointed toward some curiosity. Annie craned her neck, looking for a way through and finding none. "This is ridiculous. They would never allow someone to block the door like that."

Nick tapped the shoulder of the man in front of them. "What's going on?"

The man barely gave them a glance. "I don't know. Maybe they're giving something away."

"Seems like a funny place to do it," Nick muttered. He looked around and shook his head. "Maybe we ought to try a different door."

Annie nodded absently, her attention still focused on the

commotion but appreciating the protective note in his voice. "Maybe so." She stood on tiptoe, trying to see over the backs and shoulders in front of her. Plenty of unusual things occurred on the fairgrounds every day—the exposition itself was an unusual event. What could be happening here to draw so much attention? She felt Nick's insistent tug on her arm and let him start to lead her away.

Off to the side, the crowd shifted as someone near its center pushed his way through, calling out, "Come on, folks. Stand back and give the man some air."

Like sheep responding to the bark of a sheepdog, the onlookers backed away. Annie hesitated, then pulled on Nick's hand. "Wait a minute, it's breaking up. Maybe we can get in here after all."

Slowly people filtered away, ready to get back to the serious business of viewing the fair. Fragments of speech drifted back to Annie and Nick:

"Is he going to be all right?"

"Looks like it. The poor fellow must have tripped and hit his head somehow, knocked himself senseless."

"No, they've called for the guards. He says he was attacked."

The words sent a chill through Annie. The sense of safety she had felt at the fair dissipated like the morning mist over Lake Michigan.

"Come on," Nick urged. "Let's go to the other door. I want to get you away from this."

"No, I want to find out what happened." If danger did exist, she needed to be aware of it and know how to protect herself and Silas.

Nick firmed his lips into a tight line. "Let the guards do the work." He nodded to the approaching group of uniformed men. "It's their job, after all." His features softened. "You can't take care of everybody, you know."

A small group of Columbian Guards hurried up. Annie's mood lifted when she recognized Stephen Bridger among them. Surely he would tell her what was going on.

The thinning crowd parted to let the guards pass. Annie saw two of them helping a shaken-looking man up off the pavement.

"Let's go," Nick urged. "We ought to be able to get through this door now."

Annie followed a few steps, then planted her feet, dragging him to a halt. "Nick, look."

"There's nothing we can do. It's best if we move along and help clear the area."

Annie shook her head and swung back around. She stared, unbelieving. "It's your uncle. It's Silas."

She elbowed her way through the last remaining stragglers. Sure enough, Silas stood between the two guards, looking older than his years. His smoky gray hair stood on end, and his glasses hung askew. Streaks of dirt splayed across his rumpled jacket and trousers. He held his right hand to his head.

"I didn't get a good look," Annie heard him tell one of the guards. He set his glasses back on his nose with hands that shook.

A furrow appeared between the guard's eyebrows. "But you must have seen—"

Annie reached Silas at last and caught him by the arm. "Are you all right?" Relief at his ability to stand on his own two feet warred with concern at his fragile appearance.

Nick ran up beside them. "What happened, Uncle?"

The crease between the guard's eyebrows deepened. "See here, I'm trying to conduct an investigation. I can't have you—"

"It's all right." Stephen Bridger joined the group. "They're with him."

Silas looked at Nick and Annie like a lost sailor spotting a beacon lighting his way home. "Yes, I'm all right." He gripped Annie's hands reassuringly, but she felt the tremor in his fingers.

The first guard cleared his throat. "We need you to tell us what happened, sir, so we can get this sorted out."

Annie moved next to Nick and shifted her weight from one foot to the other while the guard continued his questioning.

"But I didn't see them, I tell you. My glasses were knocked off the very first thing. I couldn't see anything clearly after that."

The guard let out a breath that ruffled his flowing mustache. "Are you sure you didn't just fall down and bang your head? Maybe someone tried to help you up. You were disoriented, and you thought they were attacking you."

"That isn't the case at all," Silas sputtered.

"Indeed it isn't." A well-dressed man stepped forward. "I saw the whole thing. When this poor fellow stepped out of the building, two thugs set upon him and knocked him to the ground. I was some distance away; it was all over before I could do anything to stop it."

The guard gave him a long look, taking in his meticulously tailored clothing. He nodded briefly. "Thank you, sir. If you'll wait over there, we'd like to speak with you in a moment." He turned back to Silas. "Is anything missing? Did they take your wallet?"

Silas rummaged in his pockets and drew out his wallet. "Nothing seems to be missing." His shoulders slumped. "It appears to be quite the mystery, doesn't it?"

"Hard to make any sense of it," the guard agreed. His gaze narrowed. "Do you have any enemies?"

Annie raked him with a scathing glance. "Certainly not!"

Nick crossed his arms and directed a cool gaze at the guard. "My uncle is one of the most inoffensive people you'll ever meet. I can't imagine anyone wanting to do him any harm."

The guard opened his mouth as if to argue, then took a second look at Nick and appeared to think better of it. He turned back to Silas. "You say you have an exhibit here. Could the attack be connected to it in any way?"

Silas ran his hand through his hair, leaving his hair standing on end like a porcupine's quills. "I can't imagine that being the case."

"Nor can I," Annie put in. "We have nothing of value for them to take other than the carriage itself. If they wanted to rob an exhibitor who might be carrying something of great value, why not set their sights on someone from the Tiffany exhibit or Kimberley Mining? I can think of a dozen more likely targets, but we would hardly qualify."

The guard chewed on the end of his mustache. "What about a business rival?"

Silas drew himself up. "Sir, the Crockett-Trenton Horseless Carriage has no rival."

"That doesn't give us much to go on then." The guard waved his men over to where the well-dressed man waited. "Let's see what we can learn from this witness."

Stephen Bridger lingered behind after the others moved off. "We'll do what we can to catch them, Mr. Crockett. You can count on that."

His words sounded confident enough, but Annie spotted a

shadow of worry in his eyes that made her throat constrict.

"If you don't mind my saying so," Bridger went on, "it might be best if you returned to your lodgings and got some rest. You've had a nasty shock."

Nick took a step toward Silas. "We'll take care of my uncle. You just make sure you do your part in catching the thugs who did this."

Bridger stiffened slightly. "We'll certainly do our best." He nodded to Annie and Silas, then joined the other guards.

What was that all about? Annie looked from him to Nick and back again. Never mind, it didn't matter. She had more important things to think about.

She straightened Silas's jacket lapels. "We need to get you back to the boardinghouse."

"Oh, no," he protested. "I feel perfectly fine." He fingered a spot behind his right ear and winced.

"Let me see that." Annie brushed the wisps of hair aside with gentle fingers and gasped when she saw a purplish lump rising. She appealed to Nick. "Tell him he has to lie down."

"Bridger's right." Nick grated out the words, looking like he had just bitten into a lemon.

Silas set his chin in a stubborn look. "I need to be here with the carriage."

"No arguments, Uncle." Nick jutted out his own chin. "That lump is going to be the size of a hen's egg before you know it."

Silas touched the spot on his head again and appeared to waver. "At least let me check the booth before I leave. I want to make sure those rogues didn't do any damage there."

A quick check assured them all was in order, which made the whole thing even more mystifying to Annie. There had to be a reason Silas had been singled out like that. But what?

"Come on." Nick nudged Silas's arm. "It's time for the two of you to be going."

"Not both of us," Silas protested. "I'll make my way home on my own. Annie can stay here and watch the booth."

"Not on your life." Nick's clipped statement echoed Annie's thoughts. She had a sudden vision of Silas turned loose on his own with a woozy head on top of it all.

She took a last look around the booth to make sure all was in order, then took a firm grip on Silas's elbow. "Come along. I'm taking you home."

And maybe that's exactly what we ought to do, Annie thought as they rode back to the boardinghouse in the hansom cab Nick had hailed for them. *Go home—back to Indiana.* Life there might be a bit on the boring side, but things like this never happened.

CHAPTER 15

High-pitched shrieks echoed throughout the arena:

"Ride 'im, cowboy!"

"Don't let him get away from you, Jacob!"

"Faster, Mister, faster!"

Nick nudged Ranger with his heels, pushing him out of his steady lope, and let him run the length of the arena before pulling him to a sliding stop before his cheering audience of five.

He tugged on the reins. Ranger reared up on his hind legs and struck a pose. The little boy tucked safely between Nick and the saddle horn squealed and clutched the horn for all he was worth, even though Nick never loosened his firm hold around the boy's waist.

The slender man in charge of the group reached up and helped the boy slide down. "That was quite a ride, Jacob." He tousled the boy's hair.

The youngster beamed up at him, revealing a gap-toothed

grin. "Thanks, Pastor Howell." He scampered over to join his comrades.

Howell looked up at Nick, still astride Ranger. "I really appreciate you giving up your time this way. These boys don't get a chance to do anything like this as a rule."

Nick eyed the boys' tattered clothes. He could believe it. He swung down from the saddle, wondering what it would be like to grow up in the confines of a city, surrounded by tall buildings and clouds of coal smoke instead of open fields and clean country air.

Thank goodness for ministers like Seth Howell, who looked at the children of Chicago's lower classes and saw their potential as young men of good character instead of hoodlums in the making.

A scuffle broke out among the boys, drawing his attention back to the group. He looped Ranger's reins over his arms and strode over to them, waiting until they settled down before he spoke.

"You've all had a chance to ride, right?" All four boys nodded, their eyes shining. "So do you have any questions?"

The words tumbled out all at once:

"Are there really Indians at this show?"

"Can I try your hat on?"

"Is it okay if I feed Ranger a carrot?"

"Can I shoot your gun?"

Nick blinked at the last question coming from a skinny, red-haired boy with a feisty grin. He pointed to them in the same order they had asked their questions. "Yes, yes, yes, and no."

He took his hat off and perched it on the head of the second boy. "In a minute, you'll get a chance to meet some of the other performers, including the Indians. Maybe even Standing Bear."

The kids goggled at him.

Nick dug some lumps of sugar out of his vest pocket to supplement the limp carrot one of the boys pulled out from under his shirt. Three of them thrust their hands out eagerly, then hurried over to Ranger.

Nick looked at the wiry redhead, kicking at the dirt over near the benches. He walked over to the scowling boy and pulled his Colt revolver from his holster. Thumbing open the loading gate, he half-cocked the hammer, then pulled the cylinder pin and rolled the cylinder into his left palm.

With his right hand, he lowered the hammer and closed the loading gate, then handed the pistol to the boy. "I can't let you fire it, but you can look at it. Go ahead and aim it as long as you don't point at anybody. You can't hurt anything since it isn't loaded."

The kid took the gun in both hands, blinking at its weight. He gazed at the spot where the cylinder had been. "That's why you took all the bullets out, right? So it'll be safe?"

Nick nodded. No point in telling him the cylinder held nothing but blanks ready for the afternoon show. A blank could kill a person at close range as easily as a bullet.

The boy thumbed back the hammer, then raised his arm and gazed down the barrel at an imaginary opponent. "Look at that robber," he shouted. "I got 'im in my sights!" He pulled the trigger, and the firing pin snapped harmlessly against the frame.

His grin spread from ear to ear. "Look, fellas! I just gunned down Butch Cassidy!"

Nick closed his hand around the pistol and offered the boy a lump of sugar in return. Maybe that hadn't been such a good idea after all. He stepped back and watched the youngsters swarm around Ranger.

Seth Howell walked over to him, looking almost as excited as the boys. "They're great kids, aren't they?"

Nick eyed the redhead. "They look quite the handful. Are these your troublemakers?"

Howell chuckled. "Actually they're the winners of my scripture memory contest." His smile deepened when Nick's jaw dropped. "When I contacted Colonel Cody to see if we could tour the grounds, I never expected this kind of generosity. Not everyone sees the value of kids like these. He even gave us tickets for the evening performance. This will be a day these boys will never forget."

As if on cue, Cody's errand boy, Floyd strode into the horseshoe-shaped arena and clapped his hands to get the boys' attention. "Okay, fellows, ready to go see some more?"

The boys cheered and bounded over to him. Seth Howell waved at Nick and started to follow.

Floyd held up his hand. "Don't bother. I grew up with a houseful of little brothers. I know how to take care of them. And if they don't behave. . ." He gave the pastor and Nick a broad wink. "I'll turn them over to Standing Bear. Don't worry about a thing. I'll bring them back here when we're finished." He led the way like a Pied Piper, wearing a smile as big as the boys'.

Nick gathered up Ranger's reins. "You really have a way with them. A lot more patience than my pastor ever showed when I was growing up."

"That hasn't always been the case, but I've grown to love the little scamps." Howell hooked his thumbs in his front pockets and looked at Nick thoughtfully. "One thing I've learned to recognize in working with these boys is when they have something bothering them. If you don't mind my saying so, you look like a man who has a lot on his mind."

Nick adjusted the stallion's bridle to buy himself some time to think. His mind darted back to the Reverend Tomlinson. The man probably hadn't really been as big as a giant, but it sure seemed that way to Nick when he was the age of these boys. With barely any effort, he could recall the way the pastor's voice boomed through the sanctuary like a cannon and the sound of his meaty fist pounding on the pulpit, giving the impression he was boiling mad with everyone in the congregation. . .especially Nick.

But Seth Howell didn't seem to be cast from the same mold. Nick had seen the way he operated with those kids. Anyone who had his brand of patience—especially with that little red-haired guy—just might be a man worth talking to.

Nick dropped Ranger's reins and let the horse stand in place. He pulled off his gloves and waved Howell over to a seat on the bleachers. "I do have a problem. The greatest opportunity of my career just dropped right into my lap." He went on to outline Cody's offer and their plans for his future.

Howell raised his eyebrows. "That doesn't sound like much of a problem. What's really eating at you?"

Nick rested his forearms on his knees and tried to find the right words. "This is something I've hoped for ever since I joined the show. I've worked hard for it, and here it is. It's like a dream come true."

"But?" Howell prompted.

"But it seems like something else dropped into my life at the same time. My uncle showed up out of the blue. I hadn't seen him for years."

"Has he been causing trouble?"

Nick chuckled. "Not in the way you mean. He's something of a odd duck, this uncle of mine. As much as he's a whiz at mechanics, he almost needs a keeper. He gets himself into some of the most awful messes you can imagine."

Seth Howell grinned. "He sounds like quite a character. Does he have—I think you called it—a keeper? Someone to look after him, I mean?"

Nick let out a long sigh. "That's the problem. He's here at the fair, showing one of his inventions—the only one he's ever come up with that actually worked, I might add. I can keep an eye on him while he's here—or try to. But when he goes home again. . ."

"There's no one to watch out for him there? No other family close by?"

Nick shook his head. "No one nearby. No family, that is," he amended. "But he has a partner. The widow of his partner, really. She came along to Chicago with him."

"Ah!" The pastor nodded. "You're hoping the Lord sees fit to bring the two of them together?"

"No!" Nick shot bolt upright. He saw Howell's startled reaction and lowered his voice. "Sorry, I didn't make myself clear. His partner was a much younger man. So his widow. . ."

"Is far younger, too. Far too young for your uncle, I take it." Howell's eyes lit up. "But not too young for you, is that it?" He leaned forward, propping his elbows on his knees. "Go on. This is getting interesting."

"That's it." Nick was surprised at how much lighter he felt, just having shared his secret with someone else. "I think. . .no, I know. . .I'm developing feelings for her."

"And that's bad? I don't see the problem."

Nick slapped his gloves against his thigh. "The problem is, I can't have both things at once. The show will be here for the duration of the fair, but we're moving to New York next spring.

We'll stay there for six months, and then who knows? Maybe Baltimore, maybe Europe again." He shook his head. "That isn't the kind of life I'd want for a family. Not for my family.

"That's assuming she'd marry me," he added with a hoarse laugh. "And even if she did, even if she was willing to traipse all over the world with me, where would that leave Uncle Silas? She's the only person in the world besides me who really cares for him."

Seth Howell laced his fingers and tapped his thumbs together. "You do have a dilemma then."

"I'd say so." Nick stared down at his boots, then looked up at Howell hopefully. "Do you have any advice?"

Howell pursed his lips. "I can't say I have any answers. But I know who does." He smiled at Nick. "And I think you do, too."

Nick studied Howell, then nodded slowly. "I guess I do. The Lord and I haven't exactly been on speaking terms of late. Maybe I ought to do something about that."

"No 'maybe' about it." Howell stood and clapped Nick on the shoulder. "Take your cares to Him, and He'll let you know what you ought to do."

Nick rose and gripped Howell's hand. "Thanks for listening. I know what to do now. Or where to start, anyway."

Shrill cries erupted outside, and Howell's boys came racing into the arena. They skidded to a halt at the foot of the bleachers, stirring up almost as much dust as Ranger.

"You'll never believe it, Preacher. Floyd took us around the whole place!"

"We got to climb up in the Deadwood Stagecoach!"

"We got to talk to Standing Bear himself!"

The redhead puffed out his chest. "He even let me hold his scalping knife."

Floyd trailed in behind them, looking less enthusiastic than when he left. "Yeah, but he didn't say you could try it out." He smoothed his hand over his hair. "They're all yours, Pastor Howell. I think they had a good time."

"It sounds like it." Seth Howell clapped his hands. "All right, boys, we're heading over to the exposition for the afternoon. What would you like to see there?"

"The Ferris wheel!" four voices chorused.

"I'm afraid it isn't finished yet. I'm sure you've heard about a lot of other things, though. What else sounds good to you?"

"Can we try some of them Cracker Jacks?"

"And ride on the Ice Railway?"

"And look at the big gold statue of that lady?"

"And see Little Egypt?" Nick didn't even have to guess which one came up with that idea.

Howell pointed to the boys in turn. "Yes, yes, yes. . .and no."

Nick scrubbed his hand across his face to hide his grin. "You're sure these are the winners of your scripture memory contest?"

Howell shook with laughter. "You work with what you have. Come on, boys." He walked out of the arena with the boys trailing behind him like adoring puppies.

"I don't know. Maybe I should wait until another time." Annie fidgeted with her reticule and cast a worried glance at Silas waiting patiently in the entry hall.

"Not go?" Mrs. Purvis's face twisted into a mask of consternation. "When your in-laws' carriage is already on the way? Of

170

course you're going." She nudged Annie toward the door.

Silas nodded. "Absolutely. Don't worry about the exhibit. I'll take care of everything."

Annie edged closer to Mrs. Purvis and lowered her voice to a whisper. "I'm not sure he can find his way to the fairgrounds on his own. He tends to woolgather so."

"Not to worry." Mrs. Purvis pulled her hat from its hook on the walnut hall tree and gave Annie a conspiratorial wink. "I have it all under control. I'll be glad to walk along with him and make sure he gets there."

Oh dear. Annie caught Silas's startled expression when he caught sight of the landlady donning the feather-trimmed creation. "I don't want to put you out."

"Quite right." Silas's head bobbed in agreement. "Don't go to any trouble on my account."

"No trouble at all." Mrs. Purvis favored them with her sunniest smile. "I'm all caught up on my housework, and I don't need to worry about starting dinner for hours yet. I'm perfectly free to take some time off. It just may do me a world of good." She cast a coquettish look at Silas.

"But. . ."

"Too late to change your mind now," Mrs. Purvis caroled. "Look, the driver is just pulling up."

Annie boarded the carriage and tried to put her concerns for Silas out of her mind. He couldn't get lost with Ethelinda Purvis to guide him, she reassured herself. As far as protecting his bachelor status. . .well, Silas already had years of practice at that.

She settled back against the soft leather seat, thinking how different it was to ride through Chicago at street level. No constant clack of train wheels or jarring to a stop at every station.

Only the steady *clop* of the horses' hooves and an occasional soft splash when they stepped through puddles left from a nighttime shower.

Her thoughts turned to Will's family and the mysterious letter she had received the previous evening, a politely worded request to call on them at their home this morning. Their carriage, they assured her, would be sent for her convenience. Sure enough, it showed up right on time. She hoped that boded well for the rest of the visit.

Why did they want to see her again? She scarcely dared to hope their trip to the fair had reopened their hearts to Will after all this time. But what other reason could there be? She remembered Graham's excitement at the sight of the carriage and his mother's intense interest. She recalled the look on Graham's face when she mentioned the probability of lining up investors. Excitement rippled through her. *Please, Lord, let it be a beginning.*

The driver handed her down in front of the stately brown-stone. Blevins's greeting was not effusive, but it was substantially warmer than on their previous meeting. He showed her into the drawing room.

She waited only a few moments before Mrs. Trenton swept into the room, followed by her husband and son. Will's mother stretched out her hands. "Annie, how nice it is to see you."

Mr. Trenton held back, but his eyes shone with good humor. "Yes, thank you for coming on such short notice."

Graham leaned against an étagère in the corner of the room and gave her a welcoming smile.

Annie's heart sang. They were treating her as someone well and truly accepted. . .almost as a member of the family. True, no apology had been offered for their earlier behavior or for the years of silence prior to that. But she sensed that apologies weren't part of the Trenton makeup. This reversal of behavior might well be as close to an admission of guilt as she would ever get. She smiled, deciding to accept the overture as such.

Blevins carried in a tray laden with a silver tea service. Mrs. Trenton guided Annie over to a serpentine-backed sofa covered in ivory damask and seated herself on an adjacent chair. She lifted the teapot, and Annie watched the golden liquid trickle into bone china teacups patterned with roses and greenery.

"It's Darjeeling. I hope that's all right."

"That will be fine." Annie accepted the delicate china cup and took a sip. The glow of happiness at winning over Will's family warming her more than the steaming beverage.

Mr. Trenton waved away the offer of tea and took a seat across from Annie. "My wife and son told me about their visit to the fair. They came back full of stories about this carriage of Will's." He leaned back and tented his fingers across the front of his vest. "Impressive. Most impressive."

Graham left his post in the corner and stood at his mother's elbow. "We told him this would be the conveyance of the future. Any wise investor would snap up an opportunity like this before it got away from him."

Annie's heart pounded so wildly she had to set the teacup down lest it slip from her fingers. Did this mean they were going to offer financial backing, as well?

Graham glanced at his father, who nodded. Graham placed his hand on his mother's shoulder, and his face took on an earnest expression. "Our family has been in business for many years. We understand how hard it can be to bring a new product into the marketplace."

173

Mrs. Trenton looked up at him with an approving smile and patted his arm. Annie inclined her head demurely, but inside, she shouted with exultation. *It's true—they're going to offer to help!* Joy surged through her. It was all coming together. Right now, this very moment. *Oh, Will, if you could only be here to see this!*

Tears of happiness formed on her lower lids. She blinked rapidly, not wanting to miss a single detail of this moment when all she had yearned for was about to come true.

Mr. Trenton leaned forward and took up the thread. "That is why we asked you to come. We know it must be a great burden for a young woman such as yourself to try to deal with all these matters on your own."

Annie nodded, trying to contain her elation.

"We'd like to help."

She braced herself. *Here it comes. Stay calm.* She pressed the palms of her hands together.

Mr. Trenton nodded to his son.

Graham stepped over to the rosewood side cabinet and pulled out a sheaf of papers. Holding them loosely in his hand, he turned back to Annie. "We've taken the liberty of having these documents drawn up. You're free to look them over, of course." He handed them to Annie.

She couldn't seem to get her eyes to focus on the writing. *They've already talked to their lawyer. The carriage is going to be a success.* How much were they going to offer? She didn't want to be boorish enough to ask straight out, but it would be important to know the exact figure so she and Silas would know how far it would take them. Maybe the amount was specified in the papers she held.

She almost missed Graham's next words. "What did you say?"

Mr. Trenton took over, his voice as smooth as velvet. "All you have to do is sign these papers, and you'll be free of this encumbrance. We'll take care of everything from now on."

Something in his tone alerted her. "Just a minute." She held up her hand, cutting off further speech. "Do you mean. . ."

She scanned the papers rapidly, then looked up in disbelief, her rising hopes sinking like one of the shipwrecks that littered the bottom of Lake Michigan. "Signing this would mean I've turned Will's interest in the carriage over to you."

Will's father crossed his legs and clasped his hands loosely in his lap. "That's right. It releases you from any further obligation. Success or failure, we'll be the ones to bear the responsibility." He nodded gravely as though accepting the weighty burden already.

Annie blinked and tried to put her jumbled thoughts into words. "Let me see if I understand you clearly. You're offering to take over Will's—my—interest in the carriage, not invest in it? Where does that leave me?"

Mr. Trenton gave her a paternal smile. "Free to return home and resume your life with no more worries about trying to manage business affairs that are beyond your scope. We'll be taking all the financial risks." He signaled to Graham, who produced a pen and inkwell and set them on the table in front of Annie.

He slid the sheets from her numb fingers. "We just need your signature here." He pointed to the bottom of the first page, then flipped to the end of the document. "And here."

Annie stared at the papers, then set them on the table. "I have no intention of signing that."

Mr. Trenton tapped his fingertips together. "I don't think you understand the difficulties you face. Neither you nor your partner have the business experience or connections to hope to succeed in an undertaking of this magnitude."

Annie felt her temper rising and made an effort to rein it in. She looked her father-in-law squarely in the face. "And what you don't understand is that I know Will's plans for the carriage better than anyone, and I intend to see this through, difficult or not."

Mrs. Trenton sniffed. "An inexperienced girl like you? Preposterous!"

Her husband's features sharpened, and his eyes narrowed to slits. "You refuse then?"

"I most certainly do. The carriage is going to be a great success. Will knew that; I know it. How can you possibly expect me to sign away any hope of future income from what we worked on for so long? That's nothing more than stealing."

Mrs. Trenton's lips twisted. "You don't care about my son at all. You're only after the money you think you'll make from this."

Will's father's face darkened like a thundercloud. "Isn't that just what I've said all along?"

Mrs. Trenton wept into her handkerchief. "It isn't enough you deprive us of our son. Now you want to keep everything of his for yourself."

Annie stared at the sobbing woman. "Deprive you of him? Will made the choice to leave home and pursue his own ideas long before he ever met me."

Mrs. Trenton looked up, her eyes wild with grief. "But he never would have stayed away, if it hadn't been for you."

Annie shook her head, seeking a way to deny the outrageous statement. "I had nothing to do with his decision to stay in Indiana. I would have followed him to the ends of the earth."

176

Her voice caught in her throat. "I loved Will. I only wanted what was best for him."

"Do you consider what happened to him the best thing?" Mrs. Trenton's voice rose to a shrill pitch. Her bosom heaved, and her eyes glittered. She lifted her arm and pointed her finger straight at Annie. "If he hadn't married you, my son would still be alive today. Have you ever thought of that?"

Annie rose from her chair and took a step backward.

Graham knelt by his mother and patted her arm. Mrs. Trenton pushed him away and staggered to her feet. "You call us thieves, but you're the one who stole my son."

Annie recoiled as if from a physical blow. She stretched out her hands. "Please. This isn't what Will would have wanted."

Mrs. Trenton advanced, her fingers curving into claws. "How dare you tell me what my son would have wanted. Get out of my house. Get out!"

Annie stumbled backward and threw an imploring look at Mr. Trenton. He drew himself up to his full height and looked down at her, stony-faced. "I think you had better leave."

CHAPTER 16

Nick strode through the back lot, crossing an area of the encampment seldom seen by spectators. He waved to a couple of stable hands who called out a greeting, then slipped through a narrow gap between two mountainous stacks of hay.

Alone, he hunkered down in the open space beyond. Only a few yards away, the constant activity necessary to keep the huge show going went on unabated.

Nick broke off a stem of grass protruding from the haystack and twirled it in his fingers. Now that he had the solitude he sought, he found himself at a loss for what to do next. How did he go about reestablishing a relationship he had all but walked away from?

He broke the stem in half and tossed it away. Seth Howell had known exactly the right prescription for what ailed him. Now all he had to do was figure out how to go about it. He guessed Howell's insight came from being a minister, being in tune to people's needs.

No, he corrected the thought as soon as it entered his mind. Annie would have known, too. She probably wouldn't have had to think twice about it. It would have seemed the most natural thing in the world to her. But how to start?

Maybe the best thing would be to plunge right in and see what happened. He looked up at the hazy sky and cleared his throat. "It's been a long time, Lord. Too long. . ."

To his surprise, once he started talking, the floodgates seemed to open and the words flowed forth. Nick poured out his concerns, his doubts, his need for forgiveness. By the time he finished, he felt like he had finally found his way back home.

God had listened to him; Nick knew it beyond a shadow of a doubt. No thunderbolts shook the heavens. He heard no mighty voice from on high. Yet he had an assurance that the Lord had heard him and would show him the right path to take, one step at a time.

He squeezed back through the haystacks and walked alongside one of the pens that held the show's horses. Amazing how much lighter he felt after sharing all his concerns with the Almighty. Seth Howell had been right; it felt good to get those things out in the open and dealt with. And it was a relief to lay his worries about Uncle Silas in the Lord's hands. His uncle wasn't getting any younger, after all, and yesterday's attack could have been much more serious. He still didn't know what to do on that score, but he was convinced he could trust the Lord to come up with something.

And then there was his animosity toward the guard Bridger. Nick flinched at the memory of the curt way he spoke to the man the day before. *Better watch that,* he warned himself. The actions of the past were now forgiven, but he would need to keep an eye on his attitude from here on, even if the guard did seem to turn up every time Nick was around Annie.

Annie. Nick felt as if sunlight had broken through the clouds as he remembered her smile of welcome when he came near and the feel of her hand resting trustingly on his arm. And what of her reaction when she thought she'd seen someone watching her on the Wooded Island?

Nick leaned on the top fence rail and rubbed the nose of an inquisitive bay mare who came to socialize. That look on Annie's face had been one of out-and-out fear. But was it fear of something real? That was the question.

Why would a total stranger follow Annie Trenton? She was lovely enough to attract attention anywhere she went, but it didn't make sense for a stranger to take such pointed notice of her. She'd been adamant about it, though, insisting she had seen the same man again and again. But Nick wondered.

He had traveled on two continents, been in some of the biggest cities in the world. After a while, it became easy to start categorizing people by types, rather than seeing them as individuals. He knew from experience how much people could start to resemble each other after a while. How many times had he seen someone in Europe who reminded him of his grade school teacher?

The mare nosed at his vest pocket. "Sorry," Nick told her. "I'm afraid I don't have any sugar for you." He patted her on the neck, then turned and walked on, lost in his musings.

Annie, on the other hand, had spent her life in Indiana. Not exactly a backwater, but hardly a crossroads of humanity either. He thought back to her description of the man—thin, with a narrow face, and wearing a slouch hat. How many men in Chicago would that fit? Dozens, probably. Maybe hundreds. And

180

a good many of them would likely show up on the fairgrounds at some time or other. It would be easy for her to confuse several different men with similar features. That had to be the answer.

Nick pulled off his jacket and slung it over his shoulder. Had Will Trenton realized what a lucky man he was? Women like Annie came along only once in a lifetime. Maybe not that often. He remembered how she looked when he came upon her, sitting on the bench and reading Will's Bible, holding it with such familiarity it seemed like an extension of herself. And in a way, it was. There was far more to Annie Trenton than mere outward beauty.

John James Frost checked his pocket watch for the third time in as many minutes. He snapped it shut with a decisive click and paced the narrow room, made even narrower by the presence of three other men, all watching him closely.

Burns stepped back out of his way. "They should be here any minute."

"They should be here now," Frost ground out. Late again. But why should he be surprised? The Cubans were always late.

Miller shrugged. "Maybe they're not coming."

Frost slammed his fist into his palm. "What's the matter with them? Do they think they can pull this off without our help?"

The dark-haired man in the corner stirred. "Calm yourself, my friend. They need us, but we do not need them. If necessary, everything can be set in motion without their help."

"True." Frost swung around to face him head on, hating the way the man always placed himself in the shadows. Did he do so deliberately to see without being seen? Frost wouldn't put it past him. "But a plan is only as strong as its weakest link, as you well know, Senor Díaz."

The Spaniard eyed him coolly, unruffled by his goading. "Are we sure the Cubans are our weakest link?"

"And what's that supposed to mean?"

Díaz stepped forward into the scant light afforded by the room's single window. "I refer to one small item that has gone astray." He paused long enough to let his meaning sink in. "Have you recovered your missing property?"

Frost felt his features harden into a stiff mask. "No. Not yet."

Díaz lifted one elegant eyebrow. "Then I suggest that you, and not the Cubans, may prove to be our greatest liability."

Frost scooped the inkwell off the desk and flung it against the wall. "Whose idea was this to begin with? There wouldn't be a plan without me."

"But you yourself have insisted from the first that no detail be overlooked." Díaz's voice flowed like syrup. "And so the question remains. . . . Where is it?"

It would take only an instant to spring across the narrow space between them and close his hands around the man's throat, cutting off his insolent words forever. Frost flexed his fingers and forced himself to relax. He could deal with Díaz later if he chose to. Once he no longer needed him.

Burns shrugged, unmoved by the underlying current of emotions. "I still say the girl or the old man must have it."

Frost nodded slowly, bringing his anger back under control. "They have to know where it is, at least. They obviously haven't done anything with it, or we wouldn't be standing here today." But did they plan to do something? That was the question that haunted him.

182

Miller wagged his head. "The old man doesn't have it. We went through all his pockets when we roughed him up yesterday. And we know it isn't in their rooms."

Silence settled like the dust motes that hung in the air. The four men looked at each other. Díaz tapped his fingernails on the desk, a clicking sound that gated on Frost's nerves. "Then it seems obvious." Díaz spread his hands wide. "Senora Trenton must have it."

"So what if she does?" Burns shrugged. "She's just a woman. What's she going to do?"

Miller gave a harsh laugh. "You didn't have her dogging your heels. And she knew me, too. Recognized me right off. That is one smart lady. Look at the way she figured out where we were meeting the other day."

Díaz spoke again. "She is a very perceptive woman. I have seen that myself. She could pose a significant threat to our mission." He paused long enough for his words to sink in, then added, "If she is allowed to do so."

Burns's lips curled into a crafty grin. "There's one sure way to make certain she won't talk."

"No." Frost slashed through the air with his hand. "That's one thing I won't consider. There are other options." If he didn't assert himself now and reestablish the fact that he was in command, the entire campaign could unravel before his eyes. He turned on his heel and pointed at Miller. "Thanks to you, we've already drawn the guards' attention. If she turns up dead, they might come asking questions."

He pulled out his pocket watch again. "Apparently, the Cubans have decided not to come." He nodded to Burns and Miller. "Go find them. Tell them we have made our arrangements.

If they want to be a part of them, they need to get in touch with me. Now." The two left without argument.

Facing Díaz, he went on, "Our plan will go forward, with or without them. You take care of your end, and I'll see to the rest. You can be sure of it."

He watched the door close behind Díaz, then leaned his hands on the desk and bowed his head. No one appreciated the burden of command except for those who bore it. What was he going to do about the Cubans? They were turning out to be completely unreliable. Sometimes he got the feeling they were beginning to distrust him. Did they have some foolish notion of going off on their own, trying to start a rebellion without his help?

He made a noise deep in his throat. He couldn't let that happen. The plan was his. He would be the one to bring it to fruition, a gesture so staggering it would bring two great powers to blows and result in independence for the island nation. And assure him of enough wealth to last him all his days.

But if they tried to steal a march on him. . .

The thought plagued him like a boil. Could he count on them to do as they had agreed? Not for the first time, he regretted the necessity of bringing them into the venture. What were they, anyway, but a group of ragtag renegades? Men of their stripe could easily blunder. All it would take was a word in the wrong place and. . .

"No!" The shout reverberated in the tiny room. He would not let that happen. Failure was not an option.

"Are you sure this is what Will would have wanted?" Martha Trenton stared out the tall, narrow window.

184

Richard looked at his wife, then at the tranquil room with its masculine appointments. His study. His domain. Everything within view spoke of his authority and power. He tolerated no frills, nothing to distract him from the job at hand. He glanced back at Martha, and his lips tightened. The business world was no place for sentimentality.

"It doesn't matter. He wasn't thinking clearly; that much is obvious. He didn't know himself what he wanted." Richard ran his fingers along the edge of his vest lapel. "Will made the choice to turn away from us. He has to bear the consequences."

"But Will won't be the one who has to live with them, will he? He isn't here for you to punish anymore." His wife looked at him, her eyes deep pools of sadness.

"No, it will be that snippy upstart who'll have to pay the piper." The corners of his mouth drew down when he remembered how she stood up to him, the arrogant way she rebuffed his offer. "What was she thinking of, refusing to concede she is incapable of handling business affairs of that magnitude? Preposterous!" He punctuated the statement with a blow of his fist on the desk blotter.

"Did Will truly love her, do you think?"

Richard glared at his wife. "What difference does that make? He may have been besotted by her, but she obviously has no more business sense than any other woman. She's out of her mind if she doesn't recognize the fact that our family has the ability, the *right* to handle Will's affairs."

Martha stared at him a long moment as if seeing him for the first time. "Sometimes I wonder if you aren't more concerned with business than with losing your son." She left the room without a backward glance.

Richard clasped his hands behind his back and paced the floor. Physical activity had always proven a good means of letting off steam. So Martha believed him to be a cold fish who never thought about their son.

A foolish notion, that. A day never passed that he didn't think of Will. He lifted the silver-framed photo from his desk and stroked the glass. His lips twisted. *What were you thinking of, Son, to leave us like that? To go off with that. . .that. . .*

That what? The words he had used for the past few years to describe his son's wife no longer seemed appropriate now that he had seen her in the flesh and heard her voice.

Listening to the woman talk about Will, it was almost as though he could hear his son's voice again, see the bright smile that used to bring a glow to his heart and fill his soul with paternal pride. If he closed his eyes right now, he felt sure he would see Will as he used to be, with the wind ruffling his fair hair and excitement lighting his eyes.

He pressed his eyelids shut to test his theory but saw nothing except a dim grayness. A swell of emotion tightened his throat until he could barely draw breath. What wouldn't he give to see his son again, talk to him one more time? Maybe this time he could convince him his destiny lay here in Chicago instead of chasing an engineering degree in the hinterlands of Purdue.

Or perhaps Will would do the convincing this time.

His eyes sprang open, and he felt a trace of moisture along his lower lids. If he had it all to do over again, would it be so bad to let Will go, knowing he was only a day's journey distant? A few hours away, instead of an eternity out of reach?

If only he could see him, touch him, talk to him again. . .

And if he could. . . Even the possibility made his heart ache.

What would Will say? If he had the chance to speak to his father one more time, what would his message be?

Take care of Annie.

The words came unbidden as clearly as if Will were in the room, speaking directly to him. Tears stung his eyes, and he stretched out his hand as if he could reach across the great divide and touch his son once more.

Take care of Annie. Could he do that? Perform this one last act of love for his son? Excitement seized him. Perhaps he could arrange to showcase the horseless carriage somehow, maybe put it on permanent exhibit here in Chicago after the exposition ended in October.

His enthusiasm mounted. With enough exposure and financial backing, the carriage's commercial success would be assured. There would be income enough to satisfy them all, Annie included.

"Sir." Blevins stood in the doorway, a silver tray in his hands. "A message has just arrived."

Richard took the square envelope Blevins proffered and broke the seal. He scanned the missive quickly. An invitation to a reception Bertha Palmer planned to give for the visiting Spanish princess. *Perfect.*

According to Graham and Martha, the Spaniards were interested in the carriage, as well. He could use this opportunity to spread the word about Will's grand invention right away, make the horseless carriage known to the most influential men in the city. . .and beyond the borders of the country, given the international nature of this gathering.

He might even speak to the princess herself and make sure she knew him as the father of the great inventor William Trenton.

As the father of a dreamer who threw away his heritage as the scion of one of Chicago's finest families.

He stretched out his hand again, but this time to bolster himself against the door frame. What was he thinking? He had been about to admit—no, *embrace*—the fact that his son spent his short lifetime as little more than a grease-stained laborer.

He shook his head like a swimmer emerging from a deep pool. That woman must have cast a spell over him to twist his thinking so. He looked at the invitation dangling from his fingers and shuddered at the thought of what an admission like that would mean.

He would never be able to hold his head up in Chicago society again.

Richard dropped into his leather desk chair and stared at the wall. By all accounts, this invention of Will's had the potential to capture the attention of the nation, perhaps the world. The profits could be staggering. And those profits by rights should belong to Will's family. His parents, his brother.

He rested his hand on the desktop and drummed his fingers on the satiny wood. There ought to be a way for them to lay claim to the carriage. And he thought he knew what that was.

CHAPTER 17

S ilas, I'm going out for a bit." Annie gathered up her hat and reticule and started to walk away from the booth.

"Again?" Silas's tone wasn't quite aggrieved, but his brow crinkled.

"I'm sorry. I know I haven't been much help today. I just can't seem to concentrate." What would this make—her fifth foray outside the building in the course of the last few hours? Her sixth? But if she stayed within its confines one moment longer, she might lose control and tell him every detail of her disastrous visit to the Trentons. That was something she simply could not do. Not for anything did she want Silas's heart to be broken by the things they said. . .or by their attempt to gain control of her share of the carriage. "Would you like me to bring you a lemonade when I come back?"

Silas's features smoothed back into their usual cheerful lines. "That would be nice." His gaze fastened on a point over Annie's right shoulder, and his face took on a hunted expression.

"What is she doing here again?"

Annie turned. At the far end of the aisle, she could see a merry-faced figure coming their way. Gray curls bobbed with every step. "Mrs. Purvis?"

Silas tugged at his collar. "I told her on our walk over here this morning that we probably wouldn't be home for dinner. I need to stay to meet with Ned and Herman Winslow. They've shown some significant interest in investing. Do you think she forgot and came looking for us?"

"The Winslows!" Annie clapped her hand to her forehead. "I forgot all about them." She set her hat and reticule under the table. "I'll stay here and help."

"No, that's all right. I'll be fine talking to them." He turned to Annie. "I do perfectly well, you know, when I'm discussing mechanics."

He refocused his attention on Ethelinda Purvis's approach. "I must say the woman surprised me. I expected her to go off and have a look around once we arrived. Instead, she stayed right by my elbow all morning. She showed an amazing interest in the carriage, practically hung on my every word. Not what I would have expected at all."

He glanced back at Annie and made shooing motions with his hand. "Go on. I'll be all right. You do look like you could use a breath of fresh air."

Annie wavered, then scooped up her hat and reticule and bolted for the exit, feeling only marginally guilty for abandoning Silas to Mrs. Purvis for the second time in one day.

He really would be fine, she assured herself. If he hadn't succumbed to Mrs. Purvis's overtures by now, he had already shown a decided level of immunity. And he would do a far better job of explaining the intricacies of the carriage to the Winslows than she could in her present state of mind.

She cleared the doorway and took a grateful breath of outside air. Crossing Government Plaza as quickly as she could, she wove her way through couples and family groups who seemed content to see the sights at a strolling pace.

She broke through at last to a clear spot on the plaza and forged ahead with all the speed she could muster. Expending energy had helped calm her roiling spirit during similar outings throughout the day, but the relief never seemed to last long. The ugly memories kept rising to the surface.

How could I have been so wrong? No wonder Will had to get away from his family. They're simply unspeakable!

When she reached the north inlet, she stopped to catch her breath and decide what to do next. Where to go this time? Earlier attempts to walk off the aftereffects of the morning's painful encounter had taken her to the Agriculture Building, where she gave due attention to the mammoth cheese from Canada and a fifteen-hundred-pound, chocolate Venus de Milo, and past the Viking ship anchored by the north pier.

She gazed around, still breathing hard from her exertion. The Woman's Building, she decided. Perhaps meandering through a series of exhibits devoted to the accomplishments of women would help bolster her flagging spirits.

Instead of balm for her spirit, she found yet another irritant inside. Two women pressed close behind Annie, peering over her shoulder at a display of tapa cloth from Polynesia. "Isn't it exciting?" one chirped. "Royalty, here in Chicago!"

Annie stiffened. Surely they couldn't be talking about. . .

"And from Spain, no less," the second woman said, confirming

Annie's fears. "Imagine, a ruler of the land of sun-drenched beaches and orange groves, the home of Cervantes and Velázquez. And she's right here among us."

Annie moved on, unfortunately at the same pace as the talkative ladies.

"Did you hear about her visit to the Libbey Glass exhibit? My dear, she ordered a *dress* from them. Made of spun glass, can you imagine?"

A long *ahh* emanated from her companion's lips.

Annie ducked around the pair and headed into the rotunda. She paused between two rows of cases containing specimens of needlework and ivory painting and congratulated herself on making good her escape.

But only for a moment. Near the central fountain, three women stood in animated conversation.

"The Infanta Eulalia? Why, everyone is talking about her, simply everyone!"

Everyone in the Woman's Building at least, Annie thought peevishly.

Why her? Why the ill-tempered, imperious, obnoxious Infanta? Plenty of other important personages spent time at the fairgrounds. Yet everywhere she turned, she heard people talking about the charming Infanta Eulalia.

Or maybe not so charming. With her ears attuned to any mention of Spanish royalty, Annie picked up on another conversation just ahead.

"Yes, she snubbed Bertha Palmer, of all people." The speaker's harsh whisper carried far beyond her two eager listeners in the cavernous building. "Simply snubbed her—the queen of Chicago society! It seems Mrs. Palmer invited the Infanta to a reception at her home. The Infanta is staying at the Palmer House, of course. Only the best hotel accommodations in Chicago for the likes of her. And when the princess looked at the name on the invitation and realized it was from the wife of the man who owned the hotel. . ." She broke off, convulsed with laughter.

"Do go on," urged one of the other women.

"Why, then she drew herself up and asked, 'Am I to have dinner with the wife of my innkeeper?' "

"You don't mean it?"

"I most certainly do." The woman tapped her fan against her hand. "And you can imagine Mrs. Palmer's reaction to that!" The three women tittered behind their hands.

Annie felt moderately ashamed of the satisfaction that flooded her at this revelation. But only moderately. What was the fascination people had with royalty? They were only people, after all. Surrounded by pomp and ceremony, they did inspire a certain degree of awe, but seen up close, their flaws were all too evident.

Or maybe that was true of everyone, a part of being human. She put that thought away. She didn't have the patience to deal with philosophical matters right now.

She rounded a corner and came face-to-face with the twittering ladies she'd encountered when she first entered the building. Annie tensed, waiting for the inevitable. Sure enough, it came.

"And you'll never believe what else I heard about the princess."

Annie didn't wait to find out. Her hopes of finding pleasant distraction in the Woman's Building had been dashed the moment the Infanta's name was mentioned. Her eyes darted back and forth like a fox at bay. Maybe what she needed was not distraction, but a place where there were no distractions. And she knew just where to find one.

Evening light filtered through the trees on the Wooded Island, growing fainter by the minute. Annie gripped Will's Bible in both hands, drawing reassurance from its very presence.

Noise from the main grounds receded into the distance. Annie let the relative quiet of the island seep into her soul. Where to begin reading? She flipped through the familiar pages to the Psalms: "I will bless the Lord at all times: his praise shall continually be in my mouth."

According to the note at the beginning of the psalm, David's life had been in danger when he wrote those words, but he continued to praise God even in those circumstances. Her eyes moved farther down the page: "I sought the Lord, and he heard me, and delivered me from all my fears."

Annie held the pages of tiny print close and studied the words in the twilight's glow. She could understand deliverance from some of her fears. But all of them? From worries about the Trentons' planned takeover and the fear of losing everything she, Will, and Silas had worked so hard for?

She read the verse again. "I sought the Lord, and he heard me." Had she sought the Lord's guidance or pushed her way ahead? She squirmed on the wooden bench and skipped to a later part of the psalm, seeking words of comfort instead of conviction.

"Keep thy tongue from evil, and thy lips from speaking guile. Depart from evil, and do good; seek peace, and pursue it."

Seek peace. Hadn't she made every effort to do just that? She'd done everything she could think of to fulfill Will's wish and make peace with his family, but all she had succeeded in doing was to stir up a hornet's nest.

A pair of purple martins swooped low, making an evening meal of some tiny insect. Annie watched them, her thoughts tumbling like the soaring birds. What more could she do? Her main goal in coming to Chicago was to see Will's carriage receive the recognition it was due.

Judging from the steady stream of viewers and inquirers, she had been successful in that, at least. But that success created a whole new set of problems. Her anger rose again at the memory of being driven from her in-laws' house like some mercenary interloper.

Annie squeezed the Bible's cover until her fingers ached. *I just wanted to bring about a reconciliation, Lord. But those people are utterly contemptible! I still can't believe the way they were ready to practically throw me to the wolves!* Her earlier peace faded away like the rays of the sinking sun.

She set the Bible on top of her reticule and paced the area around the bench, needing to give her frustration some means of release. *They were planning to steal it from me, just take it outright.*

A hopeful duck waddled up on the bank, as if expecting her to scatter a largesse of crumbs. *In their eyes, I don't have any rights,* Annie fumed. *They don't even see me as a person!* She stomped her foot, sending the duck scuttling back into the lagoon.

Annie caught her breath and glanced around, hoping no one but the duck had witnessed her outburst of temper. She pressed her fingers to her temples. She saw herself as a rational person, able to make sense of reasonable situations. But the Trentons' actions were far from rational. She had been willing to put the past behind her and extend the olive branch, and what had they done? Snatched it from her hand and slashed her across the face with it.

What had Will's mother said? "If he hadn't married you, my son would still be alive." Annie closed her eyes and could see again the pain etched on the older woman's face as she spat out the words. It was obvious they were all still grieving, just as she was. But that didn't excuse their venom or their appalling behavior. She scuffed at the dirt and sent a pebble skittering across the pathway.

Her sense of outrage surfaced again. Abominable, that's what it was! *How can they blame me for Will's death?*

So much for her naive assumption that they had seen the error of their ways and decided to welcome her into the family at last. At this point, she didn't care whether they ever came around to accepting her or not.

She snatched up the Bible and smoothed her palm across the cover. "Did they really think I would be foolish enough to sign those papers?" Her words floated out on the evening breeze. If they did, they had another think coming! She wasn't about to do anything that would rob her of control of the carriage.

How could they expect her to give it up without protest? She had worked by Will's side on the project, encouraging him and Silas every step of the way. More than just a combination of wood and steel, it had become an integral part of their lives together. Losing it would be like losing Will all over again.

How could her sweet, loving Will have sprung from such a family? She pressed the Bible to her chest and continued her circuit around the bench. Maybe the reason wasn't so difficult to fathom after all. His loving nature was due to his relationship with his heavenly Father, not his earthly one. Without the love of God in his heart, Will might have turned out exactly like the rest of them.

Annie turned this new idea over in her mind and nodded. That was what the other Trentons lacked—the presence of God in their lives. The thought stopped her dead in her tracks.

Will understood that. That was the reason he wanted so much to make peace with his family, to tell them of their need for Christ. But he didn't get the chance. Annie felt the familiar ache in her throat. So that left it up to her. And what had she done with her opportunity? Alienated them, fractured their already tenuous relationship probably beyond all hope of repair. Maybe even driven them away from the Lord altogether.

A cold feeling settled over her. What if maintaining control of the carriage drove the Trentons away from Christ? Would anything she gained in Will's name be worth that?

She sank back onto the bench and closed her eyes for a long moment. When she opened them again, she realized how long the shadows had grown.

She felt a tickle of apprehension. What was she doing here alone with darkness only a few minutes away? In her haste to find a private spot, she had forgotten about this being the last place she'd seen the man in the slouch hat. She darted a fearful glance from side to side, then scooped up the Bible and stowed it back inside her reticule. She needed to leave. Leave *now*.

Footsteps crunched on the gravel behind her, and a low voice said, "So there you are."

Annie leaped to her feet and whirled around.

"I didn't mean to startle you." Nick walked forward, already regretting his choice not to announce his presence earlier. A

197

closer look at Annie's pallid features made him want to kick himself. This was more than just a brief moment of alarm; he was looking into a face filled with fear.

Without hesitating, he reached out and drew her into his arms. She trembled like a willow leaf in his embrace. "No need to panic," he said soothingly. "It's only me." To his delight, she didn't pull away but stayed within the circle of his arms.

He felt tempted to hold her tighter but didn't want to take advantage of her panic. He tilted her chin up so he could look into her face. "What's got you so keyed up? Uncle Silas said you've been as jumpy as a cat on hot bricks all day." He saw the flicker of surprise in her eyes.

"He told you that?"

Nick chuckled. "I know. It isn't like him to be so perceptive. I figured it must be something pretty important to make you edgy enough that he would notice." She stirred, and he loosened his hold, thrilling when she stayed close to him.

Annie lowered her gaze. Her lashes fluttered against her cheeks. "I thought you might be that man, the one I saw the last time we were here."

"I see." That explained her fright when he came up on her like that. But it wouldn't have made her jumpy all day.

Annie blinked rapidly, then looked up at him. A tiny frown puckered her brow. "It's getting late. Shouldn't you be getting ready for the show?"

"It's all right." He raised his hand and wiped a tear from her cheek. "My part doesn't come until later. I decided to skip the grand entry tonight. It was more important to see you."

Annie's eyes widened, and he could see the sparkle of unshed tears. "You were looking for me?"

"Mm-hm." Her vulnerability made him want to sweep her into the protection of his arms again. "I've been in and out of Manufactures half a dozen times, but it seems like I've missed you all day." *And in more ways than one.* "When Uncle Silas finally mentioned you being upset, I figured you'd be looking for a place to get away and collect your thoughts."

"What did you want to see me about?"

"Well, for one thing, after talking to my uncle, I couldn't begin to concentrate on the show until I'd seen you and determined that you were all right." *And I'm still not convinced of that.* "And I wanted to tell you something else. I met a preacher this morning."

He outlined his visit with Seth Howell, ending by telling her of his time spent in prayer.

"I feel like I'm back on the right track for the first time in quite a while. Though I didn't hear any great revelation or a voice from on high, I know God is a part of my life again, and I plan to keep it that way."

A sweet smile curved Annie's lips. "I'm glad." She pressed his fingers in hers, then glanced around, her nervousness apparent again. "I suppose I ought to get back to the booth."

Nick cupped her shoulders in his hands. "Stay awhile. Please."

"I really should go. Silas is going to talk to some men who are interested in investing in the carriage. I know he'll do a fine job, but I need to be there in case anyone else comes. I never should have deserted him like this."

"He was doing fine the last time I stopped by. He was talking to a couple of men."

Annie's face lit up. "It must have been the Winslows. I'm glad it seemed to be going well. A pair of stout, bearded men about Silas's age?"

"No." Nick tried to picture them in his mind. "One was younger, slender, with wavy blond hair. The other man was older, rather thin-faced." He broke off when Annie gave a low cry and swayed. He tightened his grip on her shoulders, afraid she might faint. "What is it? Do you know them?"

Even in the waning light, he could see her lips stiffen. She pulled back and turned away from him. "They're the Trentons. . .my in-laws." She spun back to face him, a mute appeal in her eyes. "I don't know whether to go straight back there and try to protect Silas or run as far as I can in the opposite direction. I'd just as soon never see them again." She moved away and wrapped her arms around herself. "The first visit didn't go well, and this morning was even worse." Her voice faded until he had to strain to hear the last few words.

Nick took a step toward her, ready to shelter her in his arms against whatever it was that threatened her. *Whoa, there. You'll scare her off if you move too fast.* He forced his arms back down to his sides and held his ground. "What happened this morning?"

He could see the shudder that rippled through her. She tightened her grip around her waist. "They invited me to their house. I was foolish enough to go there with the hope that they were ready to make amends for the past."

It didn't take much effort to know that hadn't been the case. They'd hurt her—he could see it in the taut lines of her body. "What happened?"

Annie wrapped the strings of her reticule around her fingers and twisted them tight. "They said they wanted to help, that they'd had papers drawn up to that effect." She looked at him, her eyes pools of misery. "What they really wanted was to take everything away from me, to keep all of Will's part in the carriage for themselves."

"What? That's outrageous!"

"And then his mother accused me of taking Will away from them. . . ." She choked on a sob. "Of causing his death."

Compassion overcame restraint. Nick was beside her in an instant. Without a word, he drew her into his embrace. For the second time that evening, she came willingly. Even as his heart went out to her in her distress, he exulted in the heady sensation of holding the woman he. . .

Loved? *Yes.* He admitted it to himself. He wanted to crush her to him, but she felt so delicate, nestled there in his arms. Her slender frame was far too fragile to carry the load she bore.

A sob shook Annie's shoulders. She pulled a handkerchief from her sleeve and dabbed at her nose, then looked up, shame-faced. "I'm sorry. I'm afraid I'm an awful baby."

"Not at all." His voice came out in a husky rasp. "I want you to know I'm willing to do anything I can to help. I don't want anything to hurt you like this, ever again."

Annie glanced down, then tilted her face up again. Gratitude shone in her eyes. Nick felt his breath come faster. Her lips were close, so close to his. Lips made for laughter, not sorrow. He cupped her cheek with one hand. Her eyes flared wide, and he heard her breath catch.

He raised his other hand to cradle her face and felt her quiver. An electric charge seemed to shoot up his arm. Her eyes searched his face, as if seeking his intent. Sensing her hesitation, he started to draw back.

No. He'd felt that same tingle of electricity run between them the last time they walked on this island, and he'd held back then.

201

He wasn't going to make the same mistake this time. He lowered his face to hers and saw her eyelids flutter closed.

Her lips were warm and tender, just the way he'd imagined them. He felt Annie's fingers twine themselves in the fringe at the front of his jacket. Did she pull him closer, or did he imagine it?

A dull roar filled his ears. The sound of angels shouting their approval? He pulled back and opened his eyes, seeing a reflection of his own sense of wonder in Annie's sea blue gaze. He heard the roar again. This time he recognized it for what it was—crowds of fairgoers cheering the moment when the lights of the fairgrounds went on, turning dusk to dawn in the space of an instant.

Hundreds—no, thousands—of tiny bulbs outlined the buildings of the Court of Honor. Overhead, mighty searchlights pierced the night sky, strobing through the heavens. To the south, the great fountains of the Grand Basin sent colored streams of water 150 feet in the air. The entire fairgrounds was awash in brightness and wonder. But not as wondrous as the glow in Annie's eyes.

Nick traced the contour of her cheek with his finger. "I've wanted to do that since the first time I saw you."

Annie gave him a radiant smile that threatened to undo him completely. "But you didn't know me then."

Nick stared into her eyes with a hunger that shook him. "My heart did."

Annie made no reply but simply rested her head against his jacket and stared out at the reflections shimmering in the lagoon. "The lights look like a fairyland," she said.

Nick dropped a gentle kiss on the top of her head. There

was enchantment in the air, all right, but it had nothing to do with Mr. Edison's incandescent filaments.

After a long, sweet moment, Annie stirred and heaved a sigh. "I really ought to get back. It's getting late, and Silas may want to go home soon. And you—" She tugged on a string of the buckskin fringe and gave him a wistful smile. "You shouldn't miss your performance. What would Colonel Cody say?"

Nick nodded. The enchantment couldn't last forever. "I'll walk you to the building before I head back." He took her hand in his and held it in the crook of his arm. Once again, they strolled the island in silence, but he felt as though their hearts were still talking.

Near the bridge, Annie spoke again. "Thank you for letting me pour out all my woes. It was good of you to listen to me." A frown marred her forehead. "I just hope my in-laws haven't caused Silas any problems."

Nick puffed out his chest. "If they make any more trouble for you, just let me know. I'll take Standing Bear and some of his men over there, and we'll have a talk with them."

Once again, Annie's shoulders shook, but this time with laughter—a musical sound he found irresistible. And Nick didn't want to resist. At the near end of the bridge, a cluster of willow trees formed a pocket of deep shadow. Veering to the right, he steered Annie into the inky darkness and pulled her into his arms again.

Their second kiss was every bit as satisfying as the first. And there was no doubt about it this time—Annie's arms crept up around his neck with a willingness that sent his heart soaring.

CHAPTER 18

The gatekeeper barely glanced at the exhibitors' passes Annie showed him before waving her through the turnstile. Silas followed in her wake, getting his coat caught in the metal arm in the process.

Annie helped him untangle himself. "How did your conversation with the Winslows go? Did they seem interested? We didn't get a chance to talk about it last night."

Or maybe they had. Given the daze she'd walked in ever since Nick's kisses, they might have discussed the Winslows at length, for all she knew. This morning she felt as absentminded as Silas.

Silas drew his eyebrows together. "It wasn't what I hoped for at all. They'd been over to the Electricity Building earlier. That fellow at the American Battery Company display had already convinced them that Morrison's electric horseless carriage is going to outdo any gas-powered conveyance." His shoulders slumped. "At least they showed the courtesy of stopping by to tell me they

204

were going to put their money into his carriage and not ours."

"Oh." One less potential investor to pin their hopes on. Annie digested the information, then looked out at the glittering White City. Adopting a casual tone, she said, "Nick told me about some men he saw at the booth last night. From his description, they almost sounded like Will's father and brother." She gave a brittle laugh. "But of course, it couldn't have been them, could it?"

Silas brightened. "Did you talk to Nick? He came by looking for you, but I forgot to mention it. I'm glad he found you."

"Was it the Trentons?"

"Why, yes. Indeed it was. That was the other thing I meant to tell you last night. I can't imagine how it slipped my mind."

Annie felt the skin tighten across her shoulders. "What did they want? Did they ask for me?"

"Not at all. Their whole attention was focused on the carriage. Will's father seemed particularly interested. He kept asking about Will's part in the process and how our partnership came about."

He straightened his shoulders. "You would have been proud of me, Annie. I told him at least a dozen times how Will came up with the idea to begin with and how this will make his mark in history. Maybe they are going to come around and give Will his rightful due as one of the great inventors of our time."

Annie tried to decide what to make of this latest visit. Had the Trentons changed their minds? Twenty-four hours before, she would have been elated at this news. Today, she wasn't sure how she felt.

A stray breeze from the lake threatened to tug her straw skimmer loose, and she clapped it tight against her head. By lunchtime, the wind would change course and be blowing back out toward the water. She readjusted her hatpin, thinking as she did so that the Trentons' attitude seemed to shift more often than the lakeside breeze—and with far less predictability.

She pondered the Trentons' appearance at the fair while she and Silas crossed the broad plaza. Had they realized the depth of their treachery? Suffered remorse after driving her from their home? She tugged at Silas's elbow, pulling him to a stop to let a rolling chair pass by.

At least Will's father had come to see the carriage for himself. She could take comfort in that. And in the questions he asked Silas, she could read the reality of his grief, however harsh and unfeeling he might appear on the surface. With a supreme effort, she put her musings aside. She had more pressing matters facing her at the moment.

Silas fumbled in his inside coat pocket. "Morrison says his carriage will run for thirteen hours before the batteries need to be recharged. The Winslows seemed to feel that was an advantage over ours." He patted his other coat pockets and then his vest with a bemused expression. "I need to come up with a way to let the public know that all you have to do to keep the Crockett-Trenton carriage running indefinitely is to refill the gas tank when it's empty. Far simpler to do that than find a place to recharge a bank of batteries."

He stopped to rummage through the pockets of his pants. Coming up empty-handed, he scratched his head. "I can't find my notebook, Annie. I need to jot down some of these ideas while they're still fresh in my mind. Do you have any idea where I could have left it this time?"

Annie pulled the notebook from her reticule and handed

it to him. "You asked me to hold it when the Infanta stopped by, remember? I should have thought to give it back to you before now."

They passed a view of the Wooded Island that usually tempted her to slow her steps and linger. Today, she walked by without a second glance. She hated to do anything to cast a shadow on Silas's day, but it was time to fill him in on what was happening with the Trentons. After what she had been through the day before, she simply couldn't bring herself to trust them. There was no telling what they might be up to next.

"I'm glad to know Will's family showed such interest," she began, "but there may be more to it than meets the eye." Without going into great detail, she outlined their attempt to wrest Will's interest in the carriage from her.

Silas gasped and came to a full stop just outside the entrance of the Manufactures Building. "You didn't sign those papers, did you?"

"Of course not." She forced a laugh. "Do you think I'd be cruel enough to throw you into partnership with them? Besides, they weren't there for Will when you two were developing the carriage. Why should they be allowed to step in and take over just when it looks like it's going to be a success? That would be a betrayal of Will and everything he worked for. I couldn't hurt him like that."

Silas's features twisted into a look of dismay. "Hurt him? But, Annie. . .Will is gone."

A hammer blow to her chest couldn't have stunned Annie more. She fought to push words past the tears that clogged her throat. "Don't you think I realize that? Every morning when I wake up and don't see his head on the pillow next to mine?

Every time I put two place settings on the table by mistake?"

Her chin trembled, and she knotted her hands into fists. "Don't you understand that I live with that knowledge every moment of every single day?"

Even through her tears, she could see the stricken look on Silas's face. She ought to apologize for her harsh tone, take back the angry words, but she couldn't. She didn't have any strength left to comfort someone else.

Ignoring the hand he stretched out to her, she whirled and dashed away.

Annie ran, shoving through the crowd, heedless of the startled glances and sharp protests as she pushed her way along. *I have to get away.* With her breath tearing in and out of her lungs, she ran until her legs felt like limp noodles. Still, she pressed on.

Up ahead. The bridge across the north inlet. She could lose herself in the crowds on the other side. Gasping, she ran toward it.

A sharp pain shot through her ribs. Annie clutched at her side, jolting to a stop at the near end of the bridge. She clung to the railing, doubled over and fighting for air.

A piping voice spoke up, "Mama, is that lady all right?" The mother hurried her child past. Annie couldn't blame her. She must look like a madwoman with her flyaway hair and tear-streaked face.

Edging nearer the willow and mulberry trees that grew in a cluster near the end of the bridge, she saw an open space between their trunks. She slid into it, grateful to find a little space to call her own. What was Silas thinking of? How could he, or anyone, imagine that Will didn't fill her thoughts day and night? He was—would always be—a part of her life. They had joined together, become one flesh. A bond like that didn't just go away.

The stitch in her side eased. Staying within the shelter of the trees, she planted her elbows on the bridge's railing and drove her fingers through her hair. *What am I going to do?* Regardless of what Silas might think, the thought of betraying Will by turning control of the carriage over to his parents was tearing her apart.

And what about those kisses she had shared with Nick the night before? Memories of the feelings they stirred—feelings she assumed had died with Will—flooded her mind and brought a flush of shame to her cheeks. Wasn't that betrayal of an even worse kind? She couldn't feel like that about another man. Not only fifteen months after losing Will.

She covered her face with her hands. *What kind of woman am I, Lord?*

"Excuse me, are you all right?"

The voice at her elbow made her jump. She glanced up to see Stephen Bridger standing beside her, face creased with concern. She looked away long enough to blot her tears and compose herself.

"I thought you looked upset," he went on. "I just wanted to make sure there hadn't been any other unpleasant incidents."

Not unless you count my in-laws trying to rob me blind, not to mention my own wayward behavior. She turned back to face him, trying to manufacture a cheerful smile. "No, I was just taking a break from the booth. It was good of you to stop and check, though."

His pleasant smile warmed her. "I'll be making my rounds then. If you do have any further problems, you know who to call." He touched the brim of his hat and walked off.

Annie's mood lightened at his show of kindness. And what was she to think about that? Was she developing some hitherto unsuspected susceptibility to developing tender feelings toward any man who showed her the least bit of compassion?

And if that turned out to be the case, what should she make of her feelings for Nick?

Annie leaned against the bridge railing, watching the crowd pass by—the small groups, the families, and the couples. Especially the couples. She and Will used to walk like that—arm in arm, heads bent toward one another, enjoying the warmth of the moment, the sureness of their love.

Memories sprang into her mind as sharp and clear as if she had seen him only yesterday. It took no effort at all to imagine him standing beside her now. The golden couple with the golden future. *What happened, Will?*

She looked up at the trees above her and blinked back the tears that filmed her eyes. A breeze swayed the limbs, and a mulberry dropped from its branch. Annie watched it fall into the clear lagoon and saw the ripples spread outward. The surface smoothed over again, and she saw her reflection in the water—a lone woman with no one beside her. Tears stung her eyes, and her vision blurred again.

Who was she, that woman in the reflection who came to the fair with a plan firmly in mind and full of the determination needed to see it through? She had come this far, but what lay in store for her future?

It could never be the one she and Will had planned

together. No matter how many accolades the carriage might garner, an award sitting on her mantel at home wouldn't bring Will back to her.

Pain shot through Annie's chest. She had tried her best, worked so hard. No one could say otherwise. But when it came down to it, Silas was right. Nothing she could do would ever make any difference to Will. All the preparations for the fair, the resolve to see Will's genius recognized hadn't been for him at all. Every one of her dogged efforts benefitted only one person: herself.

She felt a chill in spite of the sun shining high overhead. And if that was the case, whom did she have left to do anything for now? She looked into the future and saw a life without purpose, a terrifying thought.

Annie rubbed her hands along the railing, brushing a cluster of fallen willow leaves off the ledge and sending them down to the water below. They floated there, aimless and drifting.

Just like me.

The realization stunned her. "What's to become of me?" she whispered. The frenzied activity of the past fifteen months had helped to keep her pain at bay. But now. . .what would fill the rest of her days?

Leaning against the railing, she studied the passersby from a fresh perspective, seeing smiles and laughter, excitement and purpose. Life swelled around her, keen and fresh.

Her heaviness began to lighten as though she had been under water for a long time and now rose to the surface, ready to take in a gulp of life-giving air. The world hadn't stopped turning when Will died. She had spent fifteen months in a dungeon of her own making.

It was time to start living again. She could no longer do anything for Will, but love still bloomed in her heart, demanding someone to share it with.

Someone like Nick?

Memories rushed through her, bringing the warmth back into her veins: the way Nick's arms enveloped her, making any threat of danger seem far away. The look in his eyes that sent all other thoughts to the farthest corners of her mind. And the crescendo of joy that sang in her heart when his lips bore down on hers.

She pressed her fingertips against her lips, reliving the wonder of that moment. In Nick's arms, thoughts of the carriage, the Trentons—even Will—had been pushed out of her mind altogether.

Annie broke off the tip of a willow twig and traced his name on the bridge railing. What would a future with Nick Rutherford be like? He had no reservations about voicing his desire to stay with the Wild West Show. How would she deal with traveling constantly from one place to another and never having a real home?

She crumbled the willow twig between her fingers. Foolishness to even be thinking this way! Nick had kissed her; he hadn't proposed. Maybe that was the furthest thing from his mind.

Three little boys raced across the bridge. Ignoring their parents' shouts to wait, they plunged headlong into the leafy nook that sheltered Annie and stared up at her when they found the place was already occupied.

"Whatcha doing here?" the smallest one asked.

Annie couldn't bring herself to speak. *What am I doing here? Grieving for one man, longing for another, wondering who I really am.*

She had to move, to get out of there. Too many people were around, too many memories, too many questions for which she had no answers. She had to leave, find a place to regain her equilibrium.

The booth? No, she couldn't face going back to that crowded building right now. Ignoring the twinge of guilt she felt at abandoning Silas, she turned and started walking north.

"Good day, Uncle." Nick stepped into the booth. "Where's Annie? I thought I might take her to lunch." He held out a small packet. "I brought you one of those hamburger sandwiches, since I knew you probably wouldn't want to leave the booth."

Silas's eyes gleamed as he held the steaming wrapper under his nose and took a whiff. "I've become quite partial to these. Thank you. That was very thoughtful."

Nick shrugged off the praise. Providing lunch for his uncle had been the best way he could think of to assure some time alone with Annie. They could grab a bite to eat at one of the cafés, then take a leisurely stroll out to the Midway and see what progress Ferris's men were making on the great wheel, maybe even go for a ride on the Ice Railway. Anything would do so long as they were together.

And somewhere out there. . . Surely on these vast grounds there would be some secluded nook where he could steal another kiss, even in broad daylight.

Absorbed in his plans, he almost missed what his uncle was saying. "What was that?"

"I said I don't know where she is. She ran off soon after we arrived on the grounds."

Nick felt like someone had hit him with a sledgehammer. "Ran off? Why would she do that?"

"I'm afraid I upset her with a comment I made about Will." His uncle sighed. "They loved each other very much, you know."

Nick flinched. He knew. Every time she spoke the man's name, her whole face lit up. But last night on the island. . .

He relived the memory of her lips clinging to his, her arms urging him closer. She seemed to have forgotten Will for that moment at least. "Do you think she'll ever be ready to love someone else?"

Uncle Silas gave a rueful laugh. "I'd much rather you asked me about gears or chain drives. I'm afraid I don't understand the first thing about women."

"Does any man?" Nick raked his fingers through his hair and gazed down the length of Columbia Avenue. "How long has it been since she left?"

"It was just after we arrived. I really didn't take note of the time. She didn't even come inside the building."

"That long?" It must have been hours by now. He thought of Annie wandering the grounds all that time, alone and unhappy. "I'm going to look for her."

Silas shook his head. "But I don't have the least notion where she may have gone."

"I think I may have an idea. If I don't find her, I'll check back with you later." Nick strode off with a sense of purpose. Twice before, Annie had gone off for a respite from the crowds. Both times he had found her on the Wooded Island.

His spirits rose again. And the last time he found her there, things had turned out exceptionally well.

214

CHAPTER 19

Annie's steps dragged as she passed another building. What was this one? She glanced up at the plaque mounted above the second-floor balcony, proclaiming it had been erected by the great state of Idaho. She stumbled to a stop and tried to get her bearings, shielding her eyes from the sun's relentless glare.

Where on earth was she? In a corner of the grounds she had never seen before, that much was certain. Her stomach rumbled, and she grimaced when she noted the position of the sun, already past its zenith. She must have been wandering for hours.

Annie swayed and pressed her hands against her temples. It was high time she got back to the booth and started acting like a responsible adult again. If she felt lightheaded from hunger, Silas must surely be in even worse shape. He'd barely picked at his breakfast. Probably fretting about the electric carriage he'd heard about the night before, if only she had bothered to listen. But she had been too consumed by her own turmoil to pay any attention to his.

215

What had she been thinking of, running away like that? Behaving like this, she was of no use to Silas or anyone else. She should have known she couldn't outrun her problems. Her worries came right along with her—the Trentons and their threats, her feelings for Nick—the thoughts forming and reforming in her mind like images seen in a kaleidoscope.

And now, she didn't even know where she was. She heaved a sigh that seemed to come from the depths of her being. There was nothing else for it; she had to keep walking. She'd gotten here somehow, and she would have to find her way back.

Hunger tore at her again. If she'd been thinking straight, she could have stopped at that outdoor café she had noticed some time back. She glanced back over her shoulder, her mouth watering at the thought of a chicken sandwich and a carbonated soda. Where had she seen it?

"Mama?" The quavering cry hung suspended in the air.

Annie swung around, responding to the note of desperation in that one brief word.

"Mama–a–a!" There it came again from a lone figure huddled by a hydrangea bush.

Annie rushed over and knelt beside the little girl. "What's the matter, sweetheart? Are you lost?"

The child swiped a hand across her tearstained cheeks. "Do you know where my mama is?"

Annie hugged the little girl to her chest and stroked her matted curls. "I'm sorry, I don't. But maybe I can help you find her."

The toddler sniffled and looked up at Annie. "How?"

Good question. How could she help a lost child when she didn't even know where she was herself?

"Oh, the poor dear. Is she yours?" A pleasant-faced matron

bent over Annie. "I heard her crying. I'm so glad she's found you."

"But I'm not—she isn't—" Annie fumbled to a stop. "She isn't mine. She can't find her mother, and I don't know where to start looking for her."

"I can help with that." The woman lifted the child in capable arms and gave Annie a reassuring smile. "I'll take her over to the Children's Building. They'll know what to do, and she'll be well cared for until her mother is found." She reached into her reticule and produced a lemon drop. "Here you are. You can suck on that while Mrs. Connors takes you to some people who can help you find your mama."

She set off at a brisk clip. The little girl popped the lemon drop in her mouth and nestled her head on the woman's shoulder with an air of trust that tugged at Annie's heart.

Now she was back to her original problem: how to find Silas or food or both. She struck her forehead with the heel of her hand. Why hadn't she asked Mrs. Connors for directions before she left?

She turned back toward the place where she remembered seeing the café, then stopped. No, she would follow the direction Mrs. Connors took. If that led toward the Children's Building, it would lead toward the lagoon and the buildings that made up the Court of Honor. She had to get back to Silas.

"Hello-o!"

Silas blew a speck of dust off the carriage seat and looked up. He thought he recognized that merry trill, but it didn't belong here at the fairgrounds. He scanned the people milling along the passage and spotted a feathered hat perched atop springy iron gray curls.

Ethelinda Purvis waved cheerily with one hand. The other clutched the handle of a large basket. "How are you on this lovely day, Mr. Crockett?" She sailed past two men examining the posters and walked right into the booth as though she belonged there. She hefted the hamper and set it on the little table with a thump.

Silas shook his head as if trying to clear away the remnants of a bad dream. What was she doing here? He liked things done in an orderly fashion. A place for everything, and everything in its place. . .at least when he could remember where the proper places were. Mrs. Purvis's place was at the boardinghouse, not here. The booth belonged to him and Annie.

Annie. She was always there when he needed her. He turned his head from side to side, half expecting her to show up and rescue him now.

"I brought some food for you. And Annie, of course." Mrs. Purvis pulled off her hat and set it next to what he now recognized as a picnic hamper. *A picnic? Here in the Manufactures Building?* That made even less sense than their landlady's unannounced appearance.

Silas shut his eyes. Sometimes when he had been working too hard, he tended to imagine things. This must be a mirage, the product of an overtired mind. He waited for a slow count of five, then reopened them.

Mrs. Purvis, now comfortably seated in one of the straight-backed chairs, beamed up at him. "And I must confess I brought enough for myself, as well." Her eyes twinkled while she pulled out plates, forks, and knives. "I've enjoyed our evening meals so much. We seem almost like a family, don't you think?"

She loaded two plates with pieces of golden brown fried chicken and fragrant rolls. Silas's mouth watered. He'd finished the hamburger Nick gave him a good twenty minutes before. Surely it was too soon to think of eating again. But that chicken looked luscious, and he already had a high opinion of Mrs. Purvis's bread-making skills. It wouldn't hurt to take a bite, at least. Or maybe two. He'd hate to hurt her feelings after she went to the trouble of bringing the meal all the way to the fairgrounds.

"There's always so much to see here," Mrs. Purvis said, spooning a dollop of jam onto the rim of Silas's plate.

He stared at the glistening mound. That couldn't be gooseberry jam, could it? Why, he hadn't eaten that since he was a boy. He dipped a corner of his roll into it and brought it to his lips.

Aah. Gooseberry indeed. His eyes hadn't deceived him. "Wonderful. Absolutely delicious."

A delicate wave of pink tinted Mrs. Purvis's cheeks. "How kind of you to say so. Here, have some more." She ladled more jam onto his plate with abandon. "I remembered you mentioning the other night that you've hardly had a chance to see any of the fair, what with tending to the booth all the time."

She hitched her chair a few inches closer to his. "I thought perhaps Annie could stay here after we finish our meal and let you look around a bit. I'd be happy to show you around."

Silas choked on his roll and gasped for air. "Annie isn't here. I don't know when she'll be back." With any luck, she would stay away until Mrs. Purvis grew tired of waiting and decided to leave. The thought cheered him.

"Oh." Disappointment washed over the landlady's features.

Silas took another bite of the tender chicken, grateful for the first time for Annie's prolonged absence. Food, extra attention, offers to act as his guide around the fair—he could see where this was headed. He hadn't stayed a bachelor all these years without learning to recognize the signs.

Mrs. Purvis was a nice enough woman and a marvelous cook. He wouldn't want to hurt her feelings, but he had to remain vigilant. And inaccessible.

Marital bliss wouldn't be bliss for him at all. Not even with gooseberry jam thrown in.

Annie's resentment flared as she trudged past yet another unfamiliar building. Silas was old enough to be her father! Couldn't he take care of himself once in a while? Her breath caught on a sob. She was tired, so tired, of always having to be the responsible one.

Remorse smote her. *I'm sorry, Lord. That sounds so petty after everything Silas has done for me. I'm just so tired!*

She marched along, planting one weary foot ahead of the other. The other fairgoers blurred into a meaningless pattern of colors; their conversations dwindled to a dull buzz. Nothing could attract her attention now except her own exhaustion. Not the crowds, not the beautiful setting, not even the magnificent buildings.

A man bumped hard against her, then hurried off, murmuring an apology. Jolted out of her stupor, Annie glanced up and took stock of her surroundings. Nothing looked familiar. Panic fluttered in her stomach.

There has to be a landmark you can spot. Look for it! She spun around, waiting for something to strike a familiar chord. It was no use. Hemmed in by buildings representing various states and countries, she couldn't even see the vast green roof of the Manufactures Building.

She was lost. There was no denying it. Panic moved from a flutter to a pounding throb. She wanted to plop down right there in the walkway and howl like that lost little girl.

Suppose she did. Would someone hurry over to comfort her? Hand her a lemon drop and lead her to a place of safety? They'd be more likely to put her in a home for the mentally unbalanced, she thought with a humorless laugh. And wouldn't the Trentons love that?

She bit her lip and fought back the tears. What she would give right now to see a familiar face! No sooner had she formed the thought than she saw one she recognized. Her elation turned to despair when the realization sank in.

It was the man in the slouch hat. He had found her again.

Annie ducked behind a nearby wall. Her fingers scraped against its rough stucco surface. Had he seen her yet? Her thoughts flew to Nick and the safety she felt in his arms the night before. How she would love to be wrapped in his embrace right now and have this nightmare go away. Tears squeezed past her eyelids. Nick wasn't here; her pursuer was. She had to get away.

As stealthily as she could, she leaned past the edge of the wall and peered around the corner. He stood in the same spot as before. Annie stepped back quickly and tried to marshal her thoughts. Maybe he hadn't seen her. Maybe Nick was right—he was no more than an innocent visitor out to see the fair. Happenstance had put them in the same spot at the same time.

But in her heart, she knew it wasn't so. Mere chance could not have caused their paths to cross so many times. No, this was something personal, though she didn't have the slightest idea what it could be. What did he want with her? It seemed ridiculous for him to be pursuing her in broad daylight if he had some evil plan in mind. What could he do in the middle of the day with dozens of other people milling past?

She didn't intend to stay around and find out. But how could she leave? The only means of escape lay along the street where he stood. She couldn't even duck inside one of the buildings without him seeing her. *Think!* There had to be a way.

With infinite care, she looked past the corner again. He hadn't moved far, only to a spot a few yards away. But now he was pivoting, turning in a slow circle as though looking for someone.

Looking for her. Maybe she could call for help. But what could she say? Nick hadn't believed her story about the man following her; why should a stranger? She had to move—now. A group of people swept toward her, all seeming to talk at once in a language Annie didn't understand. She recognized her chance and seized it. The moment they drew even with her, she slipped into their midst, elbowing her way to the center of the group.

The angular woman next to her turned astonished eyes on Annie. *"Was tun Sie?"* she demanded in a tone that made it clear she wanted to know what Annie thought she was doing.

"I'm so sorry," Annie babbled. "It's that man back there. He's following me and. . .and you don't have the least idea what I'm saying."

She risked a glance over her shoulder, just in time to see her pursuer complete his revolution. As he came to a stop, his eyes focused directly on her. For an instant, their gazes locked. Annie saw the flash of recognition on his face, and he started toward her.

"No!" she cried. Shoving her way past the startled foreigners, she bolted and fled down a narrow alleyway. A cart piled high with supplies blocked her passage.

Not now! Annie threw a glance over her shoulder. He was turning toward the alleyway, and although he was still some distance away, he was advancing steadily. Once again, their gazes met, and this time, he smiled.

Terror flooded her, giving her the impetus to force her way through the narrow gap between the cart and the wall. As she cleared the front of the cart, she barreled into one of the men pulling it and knocked him into his partner. The impact swerved the cart sideways, plugging the passageway as effectively as a cork in a bottle. Annie ran on, heedless of the men's angry shouts.

She had done it! Whatever the man's purpose in following her, she had thwarted it. Annie nearly sobbed with relief. She looked over her shoulder again, just to be sure, but she saw no sign of her pursuer. She slowed her headlong dash to a more sedate walk.

The alleyway opened onto a broad avenue. Ahead of her, a lofty dome rose into the sky. Annie's heart skipped a beat. Even from the back side, she recognized the Illinois Building. And beyond that should be. . .

Yes! Relief surged through her at the sight of the north tip of the lagoon. Beyond that lay the Manufactures Building, which meant Silas, the booth, and safety.

Annie forged ahead, her confidence rising now that she was nearing familiar territory. Back near the center of things, the crowds thickened. She threaded her way straight into the congestion, ignoring the glares when she shouldered her way into the center of the mass. Normally she would have gone out of her way to avoid a crush like this; today, being surrounded meant security.

The swarm of people seemed to press in on her. A stocky woman jostled her, and she nearly lost her footing. Maybe the center wasn't the best place to be after all.

She moved to the outside edge of the crowd and immediately breathed more freely. From here, she could see the north end of the Manufactures Building past the U.S. Government Building. Nearer to hand lay the lagoon, and on its bank stood a tall figure in a buckskin jacket.

Annie's heart leaped when Nick glanced her way, letting his gaze skim over the crowd. She waved her arm over her head, hoping to attract his attention.

She saw the smile break out on his face, and he hurried toward her. Annie held her reticule close to her side and looked for an opening, ready to dart through the first opening in the crowd between them. There—as soon as those two women were past. She slowed her steps, watching for her chance.

A hard shove caught her squarely in the middle of her back. Annie stumbled and tried to regain her balance. Her feet tangled in the hem of her skirt, and she fell, landing facedown on the pavement.

CHAPTER 20

Nick frowned and scanned the crowd again. Where was Annie? She'd been there one instant, then simply disappeared the next. Maybe someone had moved in front of her and screened her from his view. He climbed up on a nearby bench to get a better look.

Still no Annie, but from here, he could see a disturbance in the crowd, an eddy pooling around something that disrupted the flow of traffic. Someone cried out, the words incoherent at this distance, and more people turned back to gather around the obstruction. Nick jumped down off the bench and hurried in that direction, a sick feeling gnawing at his gut.

A man slipped out of the press of people. His quick, furtive movements caught Nick's attention. He saw the fellow slide something under his coat, then stride briskly in the direction of the Grand Basin. Something about him made Nick take a second look. Had he seen the man before? What seemed familiar? Was it his build, his walk, the way he wore his slouch hat tipped down over one eye?

A slouch hat. Annie's fears on the island came back to him in a rush. He took two steps in pursuit of the other man, then wheeled about and ran toward the crowd and whatever lay hidden at its center.

A cold sweat broke out on his face when he saw the still figure on the ground. "Annie!" He sprang to her side and turned her over, cradling her in his arms. "Can you hear me? Are you all right?"

"Must've been the heat," a man said. "She just keeled over, right beside me."

"No." Annie blinked her eyes and gazed up at Nick with a puzzled expression. "Someone pushed me."

"Pushed you? But who—" He broke off, remembering the man in the slouch hat. Dark feelings rose in a tumult. He should have grabbed him when he had the chance.

Annie stirred, and Nick helped her sit up. She explored her forehead with her fingertips. "I must have caught myself with my hands. I don't seem to have a bump anywhere."

No, but her palms were scored by their contact with the unforgiving pavement. If he ever got hold of that fellow, he'd wring his neck. "Let me help you up," he said, assisting her to her feet. He steadied her when she swayed and held her until she recovered her balance.

"I'm all right, I think." She cradled her forehead in her palm for a moment, then looked up at him. "Why would someone want to knock me down?" She caught her breath and looked to and fro on the pavement. "My reticule! Where is it?"

The picture of a furtive man stuffing an object under his coat sprang unbidden to Nick's mind. He went through the motions of helping her look for it, but he was certain the man had accosted Annie for the specific purpose of stealing her purse.

"Let me through!" A burly man forced his way to where Nick and Annie stood. "I'm sorry, ma'am. I tried to catch him."

"Catch who?" Annie's forehead puckered.

"The fellow who snatched your bag. I thought I could get him, but he lost me in the crowds by the train station." He pulled out a bandanna and mopped his face. "They'll never find him now."

"Ah, Rutherford." Nick turned to find his boss standing behind him. "Every time I see you over here, I find you in the company of this lovely lady." He swept off his white hat and bowed to Annie. "Bill Cody at your service, ma'am. I am delighted to make your acquaintance at last."

Annie gave him a wobbly smile and extended her hand. "I'm Annie Trenton. I'm pleased to meet you, though I'm afraid I don't look my best at the moment."

Cody's brows drew together, taking in her disheveled appearance. "What's this? Has there been an accident?"

"Nothing accidental about it." Nick put his arm around Annie's shoulder and drew her close. "Some thief just knocked her down and made off with her purse."

Cody's eyes bulged. "That's an outrage! To think that some bounder would do such a thing to any woman, let alone as fair a flower as this. . . ."

Nick saw the hint of a smile play over Annie's lips at the compliment.

"I can't make up for what has happened." Cody pulled two passes to the show from his vest pocket and presented them to Annie with a flourish. "You and your partner—Nick's uncle, I

227

believe?—will be my guests at tonight's show. You'll be seated in my own private box, reserved for special dignitaries."

Annie stared at the tickets. "Thank you, but I couldn't think of doing it tonight. Not after what's just happened."

Nick took the passes from Cody and pressed them into her hand. "You ought to go. It might be just the thing to take your mind off this."

"It's settled then. I'll look forward to seeing you this evening." Cody turned to Nick. "Take good care of her. If you need to skip the afternoon performance, I'll understand." He placed his hat on his head and gave them both a wink. "I'll see you later."

Annie made a move as if to put the tickets away, then her face fell. "I forgot. I don't have my purse anymore."

Her tragic expression made him long to get his hands on the fellow who had done this. "Were you carrying a lot of money?"

"No." Tears welled in Annie's eyes. "Just a couple of dollars. But Will's Bible. . . It's gone. Oh, Nick!" She buried her face in his chest.

He cradled her in his arms for a moment, then said, "Let's get you back to the booth, and then I'll take you and Uncle Silas home."

Annie swiped at her cheeks with her fingers. "Please don't tell him what happened. It will only distress him." She gave him a look of such pleading, he couldn't find it in his heart to deny her.

"All right, but I want you to promise me something. I don't want you going off on your own anymore. Stay with someone you know you can trust: me, Uncle Silas. . .even Bridger. But no more running off by yourself—not until the thief has been caught. Promise?"

She nodded her head solemnly. "I promise."

Keeping one arm wrapped around her, he led her back toward the Manufactures Building, berating himself with every step. If only he'd listened to Annie's fears about the man in the slouch hat, this ugly incident might never have happened.

He couldn't undo what had already occurred, but he knew one thing for certain: He would never fail to take Annie seriously again.

John James Frost hurried along the south end of Machinery Hall and ducked into a warren of mechanics' sheds. With a quick look around to be sure no one was watching, he pushed open the door of the little building he had come to look on as his temporary headquarters. Burns slid in through the door behind him and let it click shut.

Frost blinked, waiting for his eyes to adjust to the gloomy interior. Miller stood near the window. Leon Ames sat on a corner of the battered desk, his slouch hat tipped down over one eye. Frost looked from one to the other. "Burns said you wanted to see me. What's happened?"

Miller jerked his head toward the man on the desk. "Ames has something to show you."

Frost turned to the skinny man. "What are you doing here? No one is supposed to suspect a connection between us. And you're supposed to be out watching that woman."

Ames grinned, revealing a full set of large, yellow teeth. "I did more than watch her today." He reached under his coat and drew out a reticule. Holding it by the strings, he dangled it in front of Frost. "You said you'd like to know what she was carrying around with her. Here it is."

Frost's eyes bulged. "How did you get that?"

Ames's chuckle grated on Frost's ears. "It was like taking candy from a baby. She didn't even know she'd lost it until I was long gone."

Frost felt a tremor of excitement. Maybe all was not lost after all. "Give it to me." He snatched the bag from Ames's grasp. Yanking at the drawstrings, he ripped the purse open and shook its contents out onto the desk. It only took a moment to rummage through the small pile of items. A thin, cold thread of fear snaked its way up his spine. He raised his head slowly. "It isn't here."

The grin slid off Ames's face. He stood and backed away. "It has to be. I got everything she had." He jabbed his finger at the small mound on the desk. "Right there, that little leather book. Isn't that what you were looking for?"

Frost gripped the small volume and held it up. "This? Hardly." He flipped it open and felt the blood rush to his face. "You idiot! This is a Bible." He flung the book away from him and turned on his inept henchman. "Do you realize what you've done? You've called attention to yourself. You let her know she's being watched. Now she'll be on her guard. And worst of all. . ." His voice rose to a shout in spite of his efforts to control it. "You may have pushed me into a position of doing something I don't want to do." He swept his arm across the desk, sending the contents of the reticule flying.

Miller stepped away from the window. "Calm down, Boss. The thing to do now is figure out what to do next. Maybe they don't even have it."

Frost riveted him with an icy stare. "They *have* to have it.

230

The satchel was fastened securely. She told me herself she went through it trying to identify the owner. There's no other place it could be."

Miller shook his head. "We've looked everywhere. It isn't in their rooms, and the old man didn't have it on him. If the woman wasn't carrying it—" He spread his arms wide. "Where else is there?"

Burns shrugged. "I don't know, but the boss is right. They have to have it, and that puts us in a bad spot. The old guy doesn't notice much anyway, but you said yourself that woman is plenty smart. And she's the type who'd try to interfere if she figures things out."

Ames shuffled his feet. "Maybe she won't. Figure it out, I mean."

Burns sneered his derision. "Yeah, but why take that chance. If she opens her mouth—"

"Enough!" Frost brought his hands down on the desk. "Let me think." The Trenton woman might hold the key to his ruin. He knew all too well what would happen if she talked to the authorities. He spoke slowly, putting his thoughts into words. "She hasn't said anything yet, or everything would have come crashing down around us by now. All right then. We can assume that she doesn't know—"

"Yet," Burns stated flatly. He pulled a knife from his pocket and opened the blade. "Think it through. There's too much at stake, and time's getting short. We may not be able to stop her from getting wise to the plan, but we can make sure she doesn't tell anyone."

Frost whipped his head around. "Meaning what?"

Burns shrugged again and started cleaning his fingernails

with the tip of the blade. "It's hard to talk from the bottom of Lake Michigan."

Frost pounded his fist into his palm. "No! I don't hold with killing women."

Ames laughed. "What're you talking about? Look what we've got planned for tomorrow."

"A different situation entirely," Frost said. "The other matter is the means to an end. It's political, not personal. Killing Mrs. Trenton would be nothing short of murder."

Burns folded his knife and slid it back into his pocket. "It's too big a risk. We can't have her out walking around, ready to spoil everything at the last minute."

Frost advanced on the man, backing him into the farthest corner. "Then keep her from walking around. Put her someplace where she can't talk. Get her out of the way; that will be fine." He leaned forward until his face was only inches away from the other man's. "But don't kill her."

"Are you sure you've given this due consideration?" Wendell McAllister, attorney-at-law, looked up from his notes and rested his elbows on his massive mahogany desk. "It might not be in your best interests if it became public knowledge you're taking your former daughter-in-law to court."

Richard Trenton's gaze sharpened. "That's hardly the point. I simply want to rectify a situation that should never have been allowed to occur in the first place."

"That may be the way you see it, but it's hardly the light in which other people will view it—a wealthy businessman taking the bread from the mouth of a young widow, so to speak."

Richard eyed him steadily. "I am counting on you to make sure this matter stays out of the public eye. I pay you a substantial amount of money; I expect you to be worth it."

McAllister cleared his throat. "If that's the way you want it, Mr. Trenton, that's the way it will be."

"Good. We understand each other." Richard crossed his legs. "I've worked hard to build my family's reputation and to secure our position, both financially and socially. By all rights, both my sons should have joined the family business." The pain rose up in him as it always did at the thought of Will's defection. He pushed himself out of his chair and walked to the window that overlooked the bustling activity of State Street.

"If Will felt he had to do something different, he only needed to tell me so. He could have opened a branch office in some other city—New York, perhaps—if he didn't feel he could stay in Chicago." His lips stiffened so he could hardly get the words out. "He certainly didn't have to dirty his hands in some dingy workshop."

He turned his back on the view of the city. "At the same time, his invention has the potential to become a household word. Since it bears our family name, I intend to see that it is marketed in such a way that our reputation is upheld. And the only way to do that is to have complete control of the project from this point on."

McAllister eyed him closely. "And complete control of the profits it will bring?"

Richard permitted himself a small smile. "Of course."

The lawyer shuffled through the papers in front of him. "According to what I see here, your son had a partner, someone who would have a reasonable expectation of profits, too." He raised his bushy gray eyebrows. "Surely you don't expect him just to walk away from it all."

Richard gave a short bark of laughter. "But the invention was my son's idea. Even his so-called partner admitted it freely." His lips curled at the memory. The man had emphasized that fact over and over again during their brief conversation, little dreaming he was providing the ammunition for his own downfall. "As the originator, the majority of the rights for the carriage should go to my son. Once I have control of that, I can deal with Mr. Crockett."

"But your son's widow. . ."

Richard waved away the objection as if swatting at a pesky fly. "She isn't a Trenton."

The lawyer sputtered. "Not by blood, certainly, but by marriage."

"It was not a marriage that was sanctioned by the family. She is to be cut out of this completely. Can't you get that through your head?"

McAllister's chair squeaked when he leaned back in it. He shook his head. "I am obliged to tell you that if this goes to court, I think you'll find you don't have a leg to stand on. A judge or jury would find her position much stronger than yours."

Ah, they were finally getting around to the main issue. "It doesn't have to go to court. All that's necessary is the threat of doing so. Neither she nor Crockett have the means to pursue this through legal channels, but she is quite aware that I do. It would hardly be worth her while to be drawn into a legal battle she can't finance."

"In other words, you plan to use intimidation."

Richard fixed him with a wordless stare.

"I see." The lawyer sighed and picked up his pen. "You're determined to go through with this?"

"I wouldn't be talking to you if I weren't, would I? Here are your instructions." He leaned forward, tapping the desk with his fingers for emphasis. "I want you to draft a letter in the strongest terms possible. Tell her if she doesn't sign the papers, we are prepared to take her to court. We will ask the court to freeze the assets of the company and stop any further business transactions until the matter is settled. Make sure she understands that we intend to prevail and will spare no expense in doing so." He leaned back and ran his fingers along the lapels of his vest. "That should take care of it nicely."

McAllister nodded. "I understand. I'll get right on it."

Richard Trenton rose to leave. "See that you do. I want her to have that letter today, if possible. Tomorrow at the latest."

CHAPTER 21

Lights glittered everywhere, illuminating the horseshoe-shaped arena. In the near distance, horses stamped and whinnied. Broad sheets of canvas hung over the tiered rows of benches to protect the spectators from the elements, but the arena itself lay open to the night sky.

Annie looked about her, marveling at the sheer numbers of people who swarmed the vast stadium. Thousands of people populated the exposition grounds at any given time, but there, they were always on the move and spread out over the six hundred-plus acres. Here, all were gathered together in one place, a great, teeming throng.

Annie watched as more people filed in, taking their places and chattering eagerly with those in the neighboring seats. She hugged herself and let the contagious air of anticipation wash over her. To think she had almost decided not to come, to stay home at Mrs. Purvis's instead and spend the night moping in her room!

Beside her, Silas stared at the spectacle with the excitement of a child on Christmas morning. "I've always envied my nephew's opportunity to experience life on the wild frontier. Tonight we're going to get a real taste of it!"

Annie smiled, glad she had changed her mind for Silas's sake, as well as her own. She needed something like this, something that would drive the ugliness of the afternoon's attack out of her thoughts.

A few feet away, two couples slid onto benches on the other side of a wooden partition, eyeing Annie and Silas with ill-concealed curiosity. Annie sat a little straighter in her padded chair, keenly aware of the attention they were attracting just by being seated in Colonel Cody's private box.

With her interest in Annie and Silas apparently exhausted, one of the ladies leaned toward the woman beside her. "Did you hear? That high-and-mighty Spanish princess left town today. It was in the evening paper."

Her neighbor clucked her tongue. "Good riddance, says I. Imagine making such a fuss over someone who's just flesh and blood, same as you and me."

The first woman tittered. "Isn't that the truth? I guess Chicago will just have to get used to doing without royalty."

"Oh, I don't know." The other woman nodded her head in the direction of Colonel Cody's box. "Who do you suppose they are? Must be someone pretty highfalutin to rate that kind of special treatment." She shot an envious glance toward Annie, then turned back to her friend.

Annie sat stunned. Highfalutin? She and Silas? Ludicrous as it was, the assumption stung. How could they assume such a thing about her? *They don't even know me.* The thought struck her. . .*any more than I know the Infanta.*

What was it the second woman had said in her disdain for the princess? *Ah yes, "flesh and blood, just like you and me."* The truth of the statement struck home. Had the Infanta Eulalia felt the same way when people talked about her, when they made unfounded presumptions and whispered behind their hands? *Just like I did.*

What would it be like to have to endure that for a lifetime? She'd been uncomfortable enough with that kind of attention after only a few minutes. Having a royal bloodline wouldn't serve as a shield against the wounds suffered from barbed comments flung her way.

Lord, forgive me. Another thought caught her up short. When it came down to it, the Infanta truly was just flesh and blood, a woman not so different from Annie herself. She would have to stand before God one day just like every other mortal who ever lived. A claim to earthly royalty wouldn't sway judgment on that day. The only thing that would matter was whether or not she was a child of the heavenly King.

While Annie wrestled with these sobering thoughts, a man stepped out and bellowed in a stentorian voice, "Ladies and gentlemen, please take your seats. The show is about to begin!"

Before his words faded away, hoofbeats thundered through the arena as hundreds of riders burst through the open end of the stadium and filled the open ground. Annie sat spellbound as cowboys and Indians, gauchos and Cossacks, and horsemen carrying flags of nations from around the world galloped in an enormous circle, forming a mighty pinwheel of man and beast.

When the last of them had taken his position, a lone rider bearing the American flag galloped in, followed by Colonel Cody himself, resplendent in buckskin, thigh-high boots, and fringed gauntlets, astride a white stallion.

The audience cheered and rose to their feet as one at his entry. The colonel made a stately circuit of the arena, bowing graciously to one and all. When he drew even with the box, he paused long enough to tip his hat to Annie and Silas, drawing even more inquisitive stares their way.

Annie felt a flush creep up her neck. She smiled and nodded back to him, but her eyes kept roving over the sea of horsemen, seeking one particular face.

And there he was. Halfway across the arena, she spotted him. The warmth in her cheeks deepened when she realized he was gazing straight at her. Nick sent a smile in her direction, a smile meant just for her. The roar of the crowd receded into the distance. Somehow in the midst of that mass of humanity, Annie felt as if only the two of them existed.

Colonel Cody's voice cut into her reverie as he took a position in front of the assembly and shouted at the top of his voice, "Ladies and gentlemen, permit me to introduce you to the Rough Riders of the World!" The audience responded with deafening applause. Colonel Cody swept his hand in a grand gesture, and the riders wheeled and exited.

Annie's gaze never left Nick. She watched him ride along in a smooth, fluid motion that seemed to make him one with his mount. He raised his hand to her when he reached the opening at the end of the arena, and then he was gone. Annie caught her breath and sat back in her chair, wondering if the rest of the show could possibly live up to the excitement of that moment.

For the next hour, she sat enthralled while Annie Oakley shot glass balls tossed into the air and otherwise proved her claim to be the greatest woman sharpshooter in the world. She watched in awe while cowboys rode bucking broncos and roped steers. She cheered wildly during the horseback races, then held her breath at a living representation of an Indian attack on a settler's cabin.

By the time intermission arrived, she felt exhausted by the sheer glory of it all. Silas tottered to his feet, mopping his forehead with his handkerchief. "I don't believe I've had that much excitement all at one time in my life. I wonder if the second half can be as thrilling as the first."

Annie smiled. Of course it could: Nick would be in it. She had already found and marked the page in the program that described his upcoming act.

Silas took a deep breath. "I feel the need to move about. Would you care to join me?"

"What a good idea." Annie didn't need a second invitation. Padded chairs or no, she welcomed the opportunity to walk around. It looked like nearly everyone else had the same idea. She descended the steps from the box behind Silas, and they joined the crowd in walking the length of the arena.

At the farthest end, Annie spied a little alcove near the grandstand stairs where the crush wasn't so dense. She slipped into it gratefully and leaned against a part of the scaffolding.

Silas followed. He bounced on his toes, as eager as a boy. "I tell you, when that warrior grabbed the settler's hair and raised his knife, it took my breath away."

Annie nodded, half her attention focused on a conversation taking place just behind her.

"I thought you would enjoy the show. I'm glad you think it lives up to its reputation."

Annie narrowed her eyes. Where had she heard that voice

before? She leaned her head back and listened intently.

"A good way to soften me up before you try to loosen my purse strings, eh?" A hearty chuckle followed.

Annie waited for the man she had heard first to speak again.

"It's always nice when you can mix business with pleasure. But since you brought it up, let me point out that our sugarcane production is increasing all the time. And we expect some big opportunities to open up in the near future that will mean major growth for the company."

Annie closed her eyes. She recognized the voice, but from where?

"That's all very promising," the second speaker said. "But I've heard things are a bit dicey between Cuba and Spain. What's to keep it all from blowing up in your face?"

The first man lowered his voice so much that Annie had to strain to hear it. "Put your fears aside on that score. I have it on good authority that the situation in Cuba will be stabilizing very soon. I'm only offering this opportunity to a few select investors. You're one of the first I've contacted. . . ." The voices faded as if the men were moving away.

Annie shook her head. She almost had it. Her mind conjured up the image of a dapper man with dark eyes. Her eyelids snapped open. *Frost!* Could it be him?

She leaned around the scaffolding to see. Yes, there he was. He stood talking to a well-dressed man in a pin-striped suit. At that moment, he lifted his head and looked directly into her eyes. Annie flinched at his cold expression and turned away, eager to put some distance between the odious man and herself.

She plucked at Silas's sleeve. "Let's get back to our seats. The second half should be starting soon."

241

Annie's attention remained riveted on the next few acts, as the thrill of the buffalo hunt and the Cossacks' feats of daring took the distaste of seeing Frost from her mind.

The last of the Russian riders charged out of the arena. A crew of workers moved in swiftly, setting up standards that held Japanese lanterns at intervals around the perimeter. Their work done, they darted out again. A hush fell over the audience. Annie clasped her hands tightly in her lap. This was the moment she had been waiting for.

Heralded by the blast of a trumpet fanfare, Nick galloped into the arena, a coiled bullwhip in one hand. With a flick of his wrist, the coil snaked out in a graceful arc, and a resounding *crack* shattered the silence.

Around the stadium he rode, and with each crack of the whip, a lantern dropped to the ground, neatly clipped from its hanger. He completed his circuit with nary a miss, then turned his mount to face the center of the arena where a hoop hung suspended well above the ground. A worker ran out with a torch in his hand and used it to set the top half of the hoop aflame.

With only a moment's pause to recoil the bullwhip and hang it over his saddle horn, Nick sent his horse on a headlong dash straight toward the flaming ring. Annie leaped to her feet and pressed her hands over her mouth, unable to tear her gaze away as he pulled himself up to a standing position in the saddle.

The rushing steed drew nearer to the ring of fire, and Annie thought her heart would beat right out of her chest. What was he going to do? Even from this distance, she could see Nick poise himself in the saddle. Not a sound could be heard other than the pounding hooves.

The instant the horse passed under the lower edge of the hoop, Nick leaped into the air, vaulting through the center of the fiery circle to land back safely in the saddle on the other side.

He slid quickly to a sitting position and brought the horse to a sliding stop not ten feet in front of Cody's box. Doffing his hat in acknowledgment of the thunderous roar from the crowd, he gave Annie a slow wink that set the blood throbbing in her veins.

He was gone again before she could catch her breath, let alone respond to his salute.

The rest of the show—the thwarted robbery of the Deadwood Stagecoach, the attack on the immigrant train, and the Grand Salute—passed with Annie paying no more than fleeting attention to the spectacle. Her thoughts were consumed with Nick and his amazing ride.

She basked in a flush of pride and wonder. If she felt this way, what must Nick experience at every performance? No wonder he wanted to continue with the show.

The reminder brought a rush of emptiness. Nick belonged here. This was his life. . .and how could she ever fit into that?

She and Silas remained in their seats after the other patrons filed out. Workers came out to clear up the area and glanced at them curiously but didn't bother them. Obviously, being a guest of Colonel Cody's carried its privileges.

Silas, still bouncing with excitement, turned to talk to a couple of men who lingered near the edge of the box. Annie waved away his invitation for her to join them, glad for the chance to sit quietly and try to sort her thoughts.

It seemed but a moment before Nick reappeared at the edge of the stadium and beckoned to her. Assuring herself Silas was still occupied with his new acquaintances, she hurried over to where Nick waited. He drew her back into a corner under the grandstand where they had a modicum of privacy and clasped her hands in his strong grip.

"How did you like the show?"

She tightened her fingers around his. "Oh, it was wonderful! But you nearly scared me to death. My heart was up in my throat when I saw you jump through that fiery ring." Her heart seemed to be up to some other tricks of its own this evening. Just his nearness was enough to make it race.

"I'm glad. I've been working hard on that one." He fell silent. Stepping back, he pulled her farther into the shadows and brushed her cheek with the backs of his fingers. "I can't tell you what it meant for me to see you out there, watching." His voice took on a husky timbre. "It seems like that's all I've had on my mind the whole day—wanting to see you again."

"I'm here now."

Nick nodded. "So you are." He cupped his hands behind her head and lowered his mouth to hers.

All her doubts and fears melted away. This was right. They belonged together. Somehow they would find a way to make it work. She pressed her cheek against his chest and felt the beat of his heart through his buckskin jacket.

Nick sighed. "This is no good."

Annie jerked her head back. "What do you mean?"

He waved his arm toward the arena where workers moved to shut things down for the night. "There's a crowd, always a crowd. We need some time away, just the two of us."

244

He ran his hands up and down her arms, sending a shiver of delight coursing through her. "What would you say to meeting me tomorrow. . . ." He dropped a kiss on her forehead. "At the clock tower. . ." She closed her eyes and felt his next kiss graze her left ear. "About ten thirty?"

His lips swept across her cheek and pressed against her mouth once more. "Do you think you could manage that?"

Annie nodded, unable to speak. She rested her forehead against his chest and clutched the front of his jacket. Her knees felt as though they had turned to putty.

Nick wrapped his arms around her and pulled her tight against him. "We can walk down the beach and find a quiet spot where we can be alone." He trailed his fingers along her cheek. "We have some things we need to talk about."

Annie couldn't find her voice, so she answered him with a kiss.

"Nick! Hey, Rutherford, wait up!" Lost in a happy daze of plans for the morrow, it took a moment for Nick to register the words. He pivoted on his heel and saw two men hurrying toward him.

He squinted, trying to make the figures out. They drew nearer, finally entering the bright circle cast by one of the gas lanterns that offered light to the encampment.

"Tom Harper, is that you?" He grinned, recognizing a pal from his ranching days in Wyoming. "What are you doing here?"

Harper slapped him on the back and took a moment to catch his breath. "I rode in on the train with a shipment of cattle. Decided I might as well stop over for a couple of days to see the fair and the show. You've made quite a name for yourself back home, you know. It'll be something to tell folks I got to see you in action."

He gestured to his companion. "Meet Fletcher King. He helped me bring those cows, and I talked him into coming to the show tonight." He elbowed the older man. "It didn't take too much persuading, especially when I told him I knew one of the stars. Right, Fletch?"

Nick studied King, whose seamed face spoke of years of toil and hardship, and extended his hand. "Glad to meet you, sir. I hope you enjoyed the performance."

King shifted the wad of tobacco in his cheek and spat on the ground. Avoiding Nick's eyes, he stared off into the distance. "You got some of it down, all right," he finally said. "There were stagecoach robberies and Indian raids aplenty in those days."

He hooked his thumbs in his belt and turned to face Nick directly. "But I was there, son. I was part of it." His voice roughened. "Out there, people died. When men went down, they didn't get back up again when all the shooting was over. And for those of us lucky enough to be alive at the end. . ."

He gave Nick a piercing gaze that seemed to penetrate his soul. "Well, there wasn't any grand music playing. No crowds standing and cheering either. We just waited for the dust to settle so we could bury our dead, knowing some of our best friends were gone and we'd never see 'em again. Not until Judgment Day at least." He scrubbed at his mouth with the back of his hand. "Sure not in time for the next show."

Silence stretched out after he finished. Finally Nick found his voice. "You're right," he said slowly. "I've seen some of that myself. Our intent is to give people a picture of what life was like

246

on the frontier. We never meant to make light of what happened there."

King patted him on the shoulder with a gnarled hand. "Don't take it too hard. You seem like a good sort, and I'm sure you meant well. I didn't mean to stomp on your toes before I barely made your acquaintance." He scraped his palm along his stubbly cheek. "That's just the opinion of a tired old man who's lived a lot of years and seen too much."

Tom Harper edged to one side. "I guess we better be going. I just wanted to say hello. It was sure good to see you again."

Nick clasped his friend's hand in a firm grip. "I'm glad you stopped by." Turning to King, he added, "It was good to meet you, sir. And I want to thank you for saying what you did. You've given me a lot to think about."

John James Frost strode down the dimly lit street, feeling like he might explode at any moment. *That woman!* Had she been listening to him? Watching him? The prospect made his stomach roil.

He left the streetlights behind and turned the corner toward his lodging house. The near darkness gave him a renewed sense of security. No one could watch him here.

His breath hissed between his teeth. What was she up to, always in the wrong place at the wrong time? And just when all his carefully laid plans were ready to be set in motion. His chest tightened. It almost seemed as though fate was playing a cruel joke on him. His foot struck an empty bottle, sending it clinking off into the darkness.

But fate had ordained this plan. He felt it, had known it from the first. His breathing eased again. Yes, it was foreordained. He would go ahead as he intended. Wasn't his a righteous cause? Wasn't it considered good, even noble, to end oppression?

And if he himself derived a benefit, as well, who could say anything against it? It would only be his just reward. A liberator deserved his due.

A shadowy figure darted across his path. Frost sucked in his breath, then let it out slowly. A cat, only a cat. Surely not an omen.

He forced himself to remain calm. Once Cuba had been set free from Spain's tyranny and his personal fortune had been assured, he would never again have to lower himself to stay in such squalid surroundings in order to remain out of the limelight. The world would be his and all the luxury it had to offer. The only drawback in his grand scheme was the people he had to work with.

A flicker of doubt smote him. Would he be able to depend on the men he had recruited? Miller, Ames, and Burns were little more than common thugs, and the Cubans' loyalty had always been open to question. What about Díaz? Was the man as trustworthy as he made himself appear?

It didn't matter. Let them all abandon him if they chose. The only loss would be to themselves. He would see it through. He would be at the appointed place himself, ready to take the whole matter into his own hands if need be.

He didn't need any of them anymore, not at this point. Things had gone too far for that.

CHAPTER 22

Annie picked up her blue-and-white-striped shirtwaist and held it against her royal blue gored skirt, studying the effect in her mirror. She jumped when a sharp tap rattled the door.

"I'm ready to go," Silas called. "I'll meet you downstairs."

Already? Annie stared at the mound of skirts and dresses piled on her bed. Where had the time gone? She needed to quit dithering and get moving. She still hadn't decided what to wear. She clapped her hands to her head. Or done her hair!

She pulled on the skirt and shirtwaist and ran down the stairs, narrowly avoiding a collision with Mrs. Purvis in the doorway to the entry hall. Silas blinked when he saw Annie's hair hanging loose.

"I'm sorry," Annie panted. "It's going to take me a bit longer, I'm afraid. Do you mind waiting?"

Silas fiddled with his watch fob. "But we really do need to get down there. I wanted to be at the booth as soon as people start arriving." He chuckled. "Things are looking more promising by the day, but you can't catch a fish if you don't go to the lake."

Annie touched her hair again. She couldn't go looking like this, not for her special meeting with Nick.

Through the front window, she spied a hansom cab coming down Blackstone Avenue. The sight galvanized her into action. Towing Silas behind her, she yanked the door open and waved at the driver to stop.

She pulled Silas out onto the porch and down the steps. "Would you mind going on ahead? I'll meet you there as soon as I'm able."

Silas pulled back and held up his index finger. "Nick said we shouldn't be separated. He was most emphatic about it."

Annie tugged on his sleeve, inching him closer to the sidewalk. "I'll have the driver come back and pick me up. That should be every bit as safe as being with you or Nick or one of the guards."

Still, Silas dallied. The driver tapped the handle of his whip against the side of the cab. "Do you want a ride, or don't you?"

Mrs. Purvis trotted down the front steps with her feather-laden hat in her hands and inserted herself between them. "I couldn't help but overhear. If you'd like to save some money, I'd be happy to walk with Mr. Crockett again this morning."

Annie smiled, then noticed Silas flailing his arms at her behind the landlady's back. "Thank you, but I think we can afford to splurge this once." She dragged Silas to the curb and pushed him into the cab.

He leaned toward her and cast a furtive glance at Mrs. Purvis. "Bless you, Annie. Do you realize what that woman is up to?"

Annie patted his arm and closed the door firmly. She gave

the driver instructions, then added, "And could you come back for me, please? In. . .thirty minutes?"

He saluted with his whip and started the horse off at a smart clip. Silas waved out of the open window.

"Remember," Annie called. "Look for the green roof and head straight for that. Once you get inside the building, you'll be fine."

She gave Mrs. Purvis a quick hug, then rushed up the steps. Thirty minutes. . . Could she be ready by then?

Twenty-eight minutes and three changes of clothes later, Annie barreled down the stairs wearing the royal blue outfit she had started out in. In the entry hall, she tucked her handkerchief into her sleeve and paused long enough to glance at the mirror in the hall tree.

Nothing had changed since she had checked her appearance in the glass in her room—cheeks flushed a rosy hue, her eyes bright and sparkling. She adjusted her hat a fraction and tilted her head to study the effect. Instead of her straw skimmer, she had decided to wear a small hat with flowers at the back of the crown. Would Nick like it?

"Good-bye!" she called toward the interior of the house, wondering if Mrs. Purvis was still mooning over missing an opportunity to spend more time with Silas. Her lips quirked upward. The poor dear. Annie hoped she found someone to spend her remaining years with someday, but Silas Crockett wouldn't make the kind of husband she was looking for.

She clattered down the steps just as the cab pulled up to

the curb. The cabbie jumped down and reached for the door handle. Annie lifted the hem of her skirt and raised her foot to the step.

"Excuse me!" A stout man hurried up, wheezing. "Are you Mrs. Trenton?"

Annie turned her head. "Yes, I am."

"Then this is for you." The man placed a long envelope bearing the imprint of W. McAllister, attorney-at-law, in her hand and tipped his hat. "Good day."

Seagulls wheeled above the lake in a cloudless field of blue. A long blast heralded the arrival of another steamship bringing visitors from downtown Chicago to the fair. John James Frost stood near the peristyle and watched the ship disgorge its passengers, sending another swarm along the half-mile trek down the pier.

He shifted his gaze to where a knot of silent men stood beside a nearby column and enjoyed a moment of quiet relief. When all was said and done, his confederates hadn't failed him. Even the Cubans had shown up.

The crowds poured past, oblivious to the group of conspirators or the world-changing events about to be set in motion, intent only upon seeing the great fair. For a moment, Frost felt a twinge of envy. What would it be like to feel the same breathless exhilaration, to concentrate solely on the enjoyment of the moment? Even the weather seemed to pronounce a blessing on the air of frivolity, having provided a clear sky, fine temperatures, and a light breeze that carried with it the fresh scent of the lake.

For an instant, the wind shifted. Frost's nostrils twitched at the momentary smell of death that wafted from the direction of the stockyards. The thought of bovine carnage brought him back to the moment.

Though not suspected by the pleasure-seeking masses, death nonetheless hung in the air. One death that would lead to more but would hopefully result in freedom for many. . .along with the culmination of his dreams of success.

Never again would he or anyone else doubt his ability to lead, not after throwing two mighty nations into turmoil. Once the assassin held the Infanta in his sights, the instant his finger tightened on the trigger. . .

A sigh of pure pleasure escaped his lips. That would be his crowning moment. Nothing must be allowed to stop it. Not even Annie Trenton.

He shook his head. What was it that kept her going despite their repeated assaults? She was a woman of considerable resource; he had to admit that. Despite her delicate appearance, she showed a strength he never would have guessed she possessed. Which led him to wonder what she might yet be capable of doing.

John James Frost, soon to be the catalyst that brought the United States and Spain to blows and delivered independence to the Cuban people, looked out across the teeming mass of people and felt his misgivings take root.

Maybe he should let them kill the woman after all.

"It works very much like a tiller on a boat." Silas leaned over to demonstrate. "You push this lever from side to side, and it changes the direction of the wheels."

"Remarkable!" His visitor stepped back and surveyed the carriage with delight. "Amazing what you scientific chaps have come up with lately. To think of the things we have to look forward to in the new century!" He wrung Silas's hand enthusiastically. "A privilege to meet you, sir. It's men like you who will revolutionize the future."

Silas felt his chest expand as the man left. *This is what I was made for.* A wonderful thing when a man knew he was in his element. In most situations, he was keenly aware of being an outsider, but here at the exposition. . .

He drew in a deep breath of air. Did it smell sweeter, cleaner here? For the first time in his life, he experienced the heady knowledge that people understood what he was doing and approved of it. Even royalty!

He watched people filter by, preening himself when many gave the carriage an admiring glance. So nice to be seen as a knowledgeable person rather than a blunderer.

"Silas!"

He looked to see who had called his name. Ah, Annie had arrived. "I'm glad you're here. You'll never guess what a man just. . ." The words died on his lips when she drew close. Her face looked as brittle as one of the plaster statues that guarded the bridges of the fairgrounds. Her lips trembled, and she looked like she was on the verge on tears. Or had she already been crying?

He grasped her hand. "What's wrong?"

Annie held out a crumpled envelope. "A man handed this to me just as I was leaving. They're going to take control!"

"What? Who?"

"Will's parents. It's all in this letter." She thrust the envelope into his hand and paced the width of the booth. Tears slid down her cheeks. "I wish I'd never contacted them. Their lawyer says they're going to take me to court."

"For Will's share of the carriage? But Annie—"

"I can't fight them, Silas. I might be able to win in time, but I don't have the money to outlast them. And it isn't just me—you don't know what they're like! They'll eat you alive if you wind up in partnership with them." She covered her face with her hands. "Will's dream was for this to bring in enough income to support all three of us. We were close, so close. But it's all gone now."

She turned on her heel and started out of the booth. "I need some time to think."

"Wait. Where are you going? Nick made it quite clear—"

Annie cut him off. "I won't go out of sight of the booth. I just can't stand still a moment longer."

"But, Annie." Silas stretched out his hand, but she was already out of reach.

CHAPTER 23

Annie stumbled away from the booth, fighting for composure. How could the Trentons do this? She couldn't let them win. She had to find some way to fight back!

Panic seized her. What would she do, what would she live on, if all hope for future income from the carriage was gone?

Chimes rang from the clock tower. Nine o'clock. Not long now until her meeting with Nick. She pressed the heels of her hands against her eyes and wiped away the tears. She'd been so happy, looking forward to being with him, letting her hopes run free when he hinted at talking about the future. But now. . .

Was she being wise in agreeing to meet him? For that matter, had she shown wisdom in anything she had done since coming to Chicago?

She reached reflexively for her reticule. If ever she needed the comfort of God's Word, she needed it now. Her hand closed on empty air. The reminder took her breath away. She didn't have Will's Bible anymore. It was gone—taken from her just as Will had been.

Annie clamped her hand against her lips and tried to stifle the sobs that shook her. She looked around wildly. She needed to be alone, but how could she be in this mob of people?

Behind her, someone cleared his throat. "Mrs. Trenton?"

Annie whirled, half expecting to find the stout man from Mrs. Purvis's ready to thrust another ominous envelope at her. Instead, she found herself face-to-face with a man in the uniform of the Columbian Guards. "What is it?"

"Mr. Crockett told me I'd find you here. Mr. Thorndyke, the administrative facilitator, would like to speak with you. Something about an irregularity with your booth." He gestured toward the exit. "If you'll come with me."

Annie shook her head. "I can't leave the building."

"This will only take a few moments. He said it was urgent."

Annie turned back to the booth. "I need to let Silas—Mr. Crockett—know."

The guard moved in front of her. "I've already spoken to him. He's aware of the situation."

Annie looked back down the broad aisle and saw Silas looking at them. He smiled and waved at her. Still, she hesitated. "Surely Mr. Crockett would be the person he'd want to talk to."

The guard chuckled. "To tell you the truth, he seems a little vague. I'm sure you'd be better suited to talk to Mr. Thorndyke."

Annie thought of Nick and of her promise to stay with him or Silas. But he'd also mentioned Stephen Bridger. How could she be safer than in the company of a Columbian Guard?

She cast one more look back at Silas. "All right. I'll go see him."

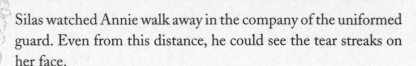

Silas watched Annie walk away in the company of the uniformed guard. Even from this distance, he could see the tear streaks on her face.

Annie, crying? He hadn't seen that since just after Will died. Oh dear. She was even more upset than he'd suspected. He stared at the thick white envelope in his hand. And all because she'd tried to make peace with Will's family.

He tapped the envelope against his palm, feeling a weight of responsibility settle over him. He had come to depend on Annie, but now she was the one who needed help. It was up to him to come up with a solution. The heavy paper crinkled in his fingers. *All right, think it through. What would Annie do in a similar situation?* She'd find a way to fix it; she always did. But this time, the job wasn't Annie's. It was his.

What to do? What to *do?* Silas clutched at his hair with both hands. He was not a man of action; he never had been. But before him lay a moment that required action and required it now. He rapped his knuckles against his forehead. If this were a faulty gear or a sticky linkage, he could find a way to take care of it. Why, oh why, did he have to be such a muddleheaded fool when it came to normal, everyday matters?

The sense of failure bowed his shoulders. His whole body sagged. Everyone was right. They always had been. He was nothing more than a worthless dreamer. He looked up, gazing around the great exhibit hall as though he had never seen it before. The place that seemed so friendly and welcoming only moments before reverted into a confusion of lights, noises, and milling crowds.

258

Maybe he could find a solution if he tried to approach this like a mechanical problem. An idea crept into his mind just beyond the fringes of conscious thought. Silas squeezed his eyes tight, trying to capture it before it flitted away. *Think. Think!*

Maybe if he related the problem to something he understood. An engine needed certain things in order to run: fuel, air, a spark. Annie was under the threat of being taken to court. What did she need in order to fight this thing, to win?

The answer struck him full force, with the clarity of one of Edison's electric bulbs. He turned the idea over in his mind, examining it from every angle. He nodded, excitement coursing through him. Yes, that would solve everything. He felt sure of it.

"Excuse me, sir." A man wearing a top hat and a frock coat spoke from the edge of the booth. "I'd like a moment of your time."

"Later, perhaps." Silas stuffed the envelope in his pocket. "I have something I must attend to immediately."

"But, sir." His visitor glanced at the placard. "You are Mr. Crockett, are you not?"

"What? Oh, yes, certainly." Silas gathered up his satchel and bowler. He started past the man but found his elbow caught in a firm grip.

"I don't believe you understand." He offered Silas a card. "My name is Hilliard. I've been looking at your vehicle, and I'd like to offer—"

Silas pulled his arm free. "You'll have to come back another time. I must take care of an important matter."

Hilliard sputtered a protest, but Silas clapped his hat on his head and went on his way, feeling like a knight ready for battle.

A sudden rush of vitality swept over him. For once in his life, he knew exactly the right thing to do.

Silas Crockett to the rescue!

Annie strode alongside the guard, hurrying to keep up with his rapid pace. What could this man Thorndyke want of her? She rubbed the tight muscles at the back of her neck. How much more could go wrong today?

They turned to cross the bridge that spanned the north canal. Annie looked over at the tall, sturdily built man. "What is this about? Can you tell me?"

He shot her a sidelong glance and shook his head. "I was told he needed to speak to you. It's an urgent matter; that's all I know." He lengthened his stride even more.

Annie fell silent and let her thoughts return to the problem with the Trentons. Will would have wanted her to receive the income from the carriage. She knew that beyond any shadow of a doubt. Throwing that away and living in poverty would only dishonor him.

But if she fought the Trentons and forced them to take her to court, would that harden their hearts and serve to turn them away from God? Nothing would be worth that.

They skirted a group of visitors who stood, entranced, at the edge of the great Columbian Fountain. What if she gave in and allowed Will's family to take over? Did it necessarily follow that they would reconcile themselves to God as a result? Annie sighed. There didn't seem to be any easy answers to this dilemma.

She turned toward the entrance to the Administration Building, but the guard touched her elbow. "Not there. He's back in the maintenance area behind Machinery Hall." At her look of astonishment, he hastened to explain, "He planned to see you in his office, but another emergency came up, one that he had to deal with right away. He regrets the inconvenience, but there are so many things to be taken care of, all at once. It's a busy time for everyone. He was sure you would understand."

"I thought you said this would only take a short time. I have another appointment scheduled, myself." If Mr. Thorndyke could sound busy, so could she. Her meeting with Nick was still almost an hour away, but she didn't want to cut things too close.

The guard only picked up his pace. When they rounded the south end of Machinery Hall, he led her into an area filled with warehouses and sheds. Annie blinked, startled by the contrast between it and the pristine Court of Honor. She hurried to keep up with her escort, glad to be in the company of one of the Columbian Guards. She never would have ventured back here on her own. He stopped before a small, nondescript building and opened the door.

Annie hesitated. "Is this it?" She stepped inside the dingy room, then turned to the guard. "Where is he? I thought you said he'd be here."

"He must have been delayed by that other matter. He'll be along directly. I'll wait outside and make sure no one bothers you." The door clicked shut behind him.

Annie stared after him, her indignation rising. Who did Mr. Thorndyke think he was, to demand her immediate presence and then make her wait? She planted her hands on her hips.

261

Administrator or not, he was going to get a piece of her mind as soon as he got there!

She let her eyes drift around the little room. Hardly something fit for a fair official, in her estimation, with only a scarred desk, a few chairs, and a set of shelves tucked back into the darkest corner. It must be a place chosen for its proximity to whatever else he was attending to. It certainly hadn't been selected for her convenience or comfort.

She started to sit on one of the chairs but held herself back. No telling how much dust would rub off on her clothes, and she had no intention of dirtying her handkerchief to wipe it off.

Annie drummed her fingers on the desk. Where was the man? She would give him another five minutes, ten at the most, then demand to be escorted back to the booth.

Nick walked east along Adams Street. The buildings at the fairgrounds might be enormous, but there was still room to catch a breath between them. Being in the midst of these tall buildings laid out in tight rows made him feel like he had entered a canyon. He rolled his shoulders under his jacket, wishing he could see the horizon. Even out West, he'd never found a canyon a comfortable place to be.

Today, though, he was willing to put up with a little discomfort. He'd already broken his usual routine by breakfasting in one of the city's downtown cafés, wanting to get an early start on his errand. Besides, it felt like a day to do something out of the ordinary. When a man faced a turning point in his life, he needed to look at things from a fresh perspective.

He had spent the night before thinking the matter through. Annie Oakley and fellow star Frank Butler were married, and staying with the show hadn't seemed to cause a problem for them. He could name other married couples in the company, as well. While it might not be the norm, there was certainly a precedent.

He stopped at the next corner to let a streetcar pass and looked up at the mighty buildings towering above him. How would Annie feel about New York? The show was booked for six months there next season. Would she be able to adapt? He had to believe she would. She seemed to take everything in stride.

Dodging a horse-drawn cart, he hurried across the street. It might take her some time to adjust, but from what he'd seen of Annie, he felt sure she would find a way to take root and blossom no matter what her surroundings. And what a rare bloom she'd be! Her beauty would grace any setting.

But would it be the best thing for Annie? Would *he* be the best thing for her? That was the question that haunted him. Maybe he was rushing things. She might not be ready to take such a big step. Maybe he needed to give her more time. Speaking of which. . .

He checked his pocket watch and relaxed. Plenty of time to finish his business downtown before he needed to start back to meet Annie. He spotted a likely looking store on the corner and turned in.

CHAPTER 24

A rms crossed, Annie paced the floor of the little building. She wasn't getting a thing accomplished in this dusty shed. What kind of business was conducted in here anyway? It looked more like a toolshed—and an ill-kept one, at that—than a setting suitable for someone of Mr. Thorndyke's stature.

She made a slow circuit of the room, passing the desk and the rickety chairs. She kept her distance from the shelves in the farthest corner. Who knew what kind of vermin might be lurking in those dim recesses? She moved back to the desk and what light the lone window afforded.

Had it been ten minutes yet? If Mr. Thorndyke wanted to talk to her this morning, he'd better hurry up. The thin north light illuminated a large paper spread across the desktop. Annie stepped around to the other side of the desk to peer at it more closely, wondering if it had anything to do with the reason the fair administrator wanted to see her.

It was a sketch of some kind. She bent over it, intrigued.

How many times had she and Will pored over some mechanical drawing, examining every detail? At least it offered a means of staving off boredom.

Annie frowned. It appeared to be a map of the grounds or a portion of it. Was that the Manufactures Building, or rather, the south end of it? Yes, there was the front of the Agriculture Building across from it. Now that she knew what to look for, she recognized the Grand Basin in between, with the peristyle marking the east end where the waters of the basin connected with those of the lake.

She leaned closer, her interest piqued in spite of her irritation with the tardy Mr. Thorndyke. Keeping her finger above the drawing and whatever dust might coat its surface, she traced the lines of the buildings, trying to determine the drawing's purpose. Was it a plan for putting in electric lines, a water system?

She frowned and tilted her head. There had to be some way to make sense of it, but she could see nothing except a few scribbles and arrows, apparently scattered at random across the center of the page.

She pulled her handkerchief from her sleeve and dabbed at her face and neck. The temperature must have risen ten degrees since she arrived. She fanned her hand in front of her face. It was getting entirely too stuffy. She needed fresh air.

Her patience reached its end. She had better things to do than wait for his "urgent" meeting, and she was thoroughly tired of this dismal little room.

Annie marched to the door and wrenched the handle, but the door refused to open. She rattled the handle again but couldn't get it to budge. She banged on the wooden slab with the flat of her hand. "Hello! The door seems to be stuck. Would you open it, please?"

"Be patient, ma'am. It won't be much longer."

Annie pounded harder against the unyielding door. "You don't understand. It's stifling in here, and I'm tired of waiting. I want you to take me back to my booth now."

"No, you don't understand." The guard's voice lost its courteous veneer. "You're not leaving until I say you do. Just sit down and behave yourself. We'll let you go eventually. . .if you keep quiet."

Nick fidgeted, tapping his fingers on the glass-topped counter. He wouldn't have thought his request would be so difficult to fill in a city of this size. He held his breath when the clerk returned from the back of the store.

"I'm afraid we're all out, sir. We do have some very nice ones available but none in the size you're looking for. Would you like to see the others?"

Nick hesitated. Three stores now, and no success. "Thanks, but I'll keep looking." He still had a little time. He knew what he wanted; he was determined to get it right.

Outside, he looked at his pocket watch and winced. If he didn't get moving pretty soon, he wouldn't make it back on time. And he didn't want to be late for his meeting with Annie.

He snapped his watch shut and shoved it back into his vest pocket. Maybe it was more important to talk than to bring her the special gift he had planned. He took two steps toward the el station on the corner. But he didn't want to go empty-handed.

One more store. There was one right across the street. If that didn't have it, he would leave, successful or not. He really ought to be on his way right now. He swung the door open and described his needs to the clerk. Like the others, this one disappeared into the recesses of the store, leaving Nick standing at the counter.

He jiggled his leg and willed the man to hurry up. Would Annie like it, or would she think he had overstepped his bounds? He tried to picture what she might be doing at that very moment. Was she looking forward to their time together as eagerly as he was? Or was she going about business as usual, helping Silas in her calm, competent way?

Nick shifted from one foot to the other. He was going to be late; he knew it. What would happen when he didn't show up at the appointed time? Would Annie be worried? Offended? Or would she even notice?

The clerk reappeared, beaming. "Here it is. I was sure we had one."

"That's great. I'll take it." He pulled the money from his pocket while the clerk wrapped his purchase; then he bolted out of the store, tucking the parcel into the front pocket of his jacket. He sprinted toward the el station like a runner out of the starting blocks, his thoughts churning as quickly as his legs.

Had he done something that would bring a glow of pleasure to Annie's eyes, or was he about to make a complete fool of himself? He raced up the steps to the station and threw himself through the door of the train just before it pulled out.

Nick flopped into a seat and drew the small parcel from his pocket. He untied the string and pulled off the brown paper wrapping. The small black volume fit neatly in his hands. He turned it over, inspecting it more closely than he'd had time to do in the store. Who'd have thought finding a pocket-sized Bible would turn into such a challenging quest?

267

He rubbed his thumb along the smooth grain. Would she like it? It wasn't an exact match, and it would never replace the stolen Bible she grieved over, but maybe it would bring her some measure of solace.

He replaced the wrapping and tucked the package deep into his pocket. Whatever her reaction, he'd know it soon. He leaned forward in his seat as if he could help push the train more quickly toward its goal.

Annie pounded on the rough door with both fists. "Let me out of here!"

The guard's voice sounded muffled as if he didn't want to be overheard. "Lady, if you know what's good for you, you'll just settle down and keep quiet."

"What are you doing, Burns, talking to yourself?"

Annie nearly wept with relief at the sound of another voice. She beat on the door with renewed vigor. "Help! Please help me! He's locked me in here, and he won't let me out."

She listened intently through the silence that followed. The second voice spoke again, "Are you out of your mind? She sounds like she's right there at the door. You just shut her in there and let her run loose? You didn't tie her up or anything?"

Annie staggered back. Surely she hadn't heard correctly. She stepped forward again and pressed her ear to the door, trying to still her breathing so as not to miss a word.

"I didn't want her getting excited and screaming or trying to make a break for it." She recognized her captor's voice. "So I just let her in and locked the door behind her. It made it nice and easy. No one but you and I are going to hear her through that heavy door."

"But the plans, you idiot! They're lying out there on the desk in plain sight."

"So? It isn't like she's going to be telling anyone about them." The ominous tone in the man's voice made Annie's knees go weak.

"Wait a minute." The newcomer's voice held a note of warning. "You know what the boss said about not hurting her."

The so-called Columbian Guard let out a string of words that made Annie suck in her breath. "I don't care what Frost says. Our necks are on the line, the same as his. You think she won't identify me if we just let her go? You know how quick she spotted you when you snatched that wallet. I'm not taking any chances. Once the other one is dead, this one is next."

Icy fingers of dread clutched at Annie's throat. She tottered away from the door and propped herself against the desk. What had she stumbled into? No, not stumbled—been thrust into by unknown hands.

Who were these men, and what plans were they talking about? She looked again at the paper spread open on the desk. It didn't make a bit more sense to her than it had before. Someone was going to die; that much was certain. But what could a map have to do with that?

She pushed herself away from the desk. She didn't have time to waste on speculation now. Something horrible was about to happen, and soon. She could try to figure it all out later. Right now, she had to get out. . .in a hurry.

What could she do? She tried to make her paralyzed brain function. Absurd to think she was being held captive right on

269

the grounds of the fair, but it had happened. The *why* of the situation didn't matter anymore, only its reality. She had to find a way to escape.

She prowled the room, taking in more details of her surroundings. The desk and chairs offered no solutions. She looked at the shelves deep in the shadowy corner and shuddered. What about the walls? She ran her hands along them. Plaster and lath. Given enough time and the right tools, she might be able to break through, but not without making enough noise to alert the guards to her efforts. And time was something she didn't have.

Annie eyed the solitary window set high in the north wall. Was there any way to reach it? She looked at the shelves again. If she could move those, drag them over to the window. . .

Her excitement rose at the possibilities. Perhaps she could climb the shelves, use them as a ladder to reach the window and freedom.

She looked at the window again. It was only about two feet square. Could she squeeze through, even if she did reach it? She would have to. There was no other choice.

Her mind made up, she strode over to the shelves. They swayed when she wiggled them back and forth. A sigh of relief escaped her lips. They weren't attached to the wall. On closer examination, her spirits rose even more. Consisting only of rough boards nailed to uprights, they didn't even have a solid back. They should be light enough for her to move.

She gripped one side in each hand and tugged. A small paint can dropped off the top shelf and thudded against the plank floor. A thump rattled the door. "Keep quiet in there. I'll tie you up if I have to."

Annie caught her breath. She would have to do this without

making any further noise. She tried to marshal her thoughts. The shelves held a collection of items that looked like they had been tossed there haphazardly. The first order of business, then, would be to unload the shelves so nothing else could fall.

Working feverishly in the dim light, she lifted the items one at a time and set them out of the way on the floor. Her hands closed around a small book. Disbelief flooded her at the sense of familiarity. *No, it couldn't be.*

She carried the book over toward the window, but even before she could hold it up to the light, her fingers had traced the well-known scars and assured her of its identity. *Will's Bible!* She clutched it to her. But what could it be doing there in that dingy shed?

She ran back over to the shelves and pawed around the spot where she had found the Bible. Did it hold any more surprises? Her fingers touched a slender volume, and she carried it back to the light.

Silas's notebook? She flipped through the pages, seeing his familiar handwriting. But hadn't she seen him scribbling in it only that morning? She turned to the last page with writing on it and recognized the notes he had made on the train the day they arrived in Chicago.

On the train. Images whirled through her mind: the train, the station, the collision with Frost, the switched satchels. Annie sucked in her breath. Could Silas have pulled the other notebook from Frost's satchel that night before he realized the mix-up and slipped it into his pocket without thinking? If that were the case. . .

Pieces of the puzzle started fitting together with lightning speed. All the strange occurrences since their arrival—their rooms being ransacked, the attacks on Silas and herself, and now hearing Frost's name again through the door. It was all connected. She felt sure of it. And now she was being held captive, and the men outside the door were planning to kill her.

Annie rushed back to the shelves and unloaded the last of their contents, desperate to keep her thoughts clear despite the agony of fear that gripped her.

She had to get out.

Richard Trenton stared at the man across his desk. "The letter was delivered?"

"Earlier this morning." McAllister held out a sheet of paper. "Here's a copy."

Richard took in the concise paragraphs at a glance and laid the paper in the center of his desk blotter. His gaze returned to McAllister's face. "How did she take it?"

"I really can't say. My man told me she was just getting ready to step into a cab when he gave it to her. I suppose she read it after she got inside."

Richard nodded slowly. *Of course.* Curiosity would have compelled her to. He picked up a brass letter opener, enjoying the cool, smooth feel of the metal. She would have had time to read it through several times by now. And more importantly, react to it.

He glanced at the letter again and allowed a small smile to touch his lips. He must have thrown fear into McAllister yesterday. The man had outdone himself. He slid his thumb along the edge of the blade. By now, she must be beside herself.

He laid the letter opener down, adjusting it so it lined up

precisely with the edge of the blotter, then looked at the glass-domed clock. Give her another hour to let it all sink in. She'd be cowering in her shoes by then, ready to do whatever it took to ward off this legal threat.

He rose and ushered McAllister toward the study door. "Good work. I'll let you know when she's signed the papers." He let Blevins see the lawyer to the front door and trotted upstairs, his sense of well-being growing with every step.

"Martha," he called, "get ready. We're going to the fair."

CHAPTER 25

Annie tipped the shelves against the wall, easing them into place gently in order to make no sound. She put one foot on the bottom shelf, testing her weight and praying it would hold. She glanced up at the window. Would it open easily, or would she be forced to break it?

If she had to shatter the glass, she would need something to protect her hand. She looked around for something she could use. A rag lay wadded up in the corner near the desk. She bent to retrieve it and uttered a soft cry. It wasn't a rag; it was her reticule. She set it on the desk and stuffed the Bible and notebook inside, then snatched up the drawing and put it in with them. Maybe someone could make sense of it in time to stop whatever was being planned.

The window slid up easily with only a minimum of noise. Annie poised herself on the narrow sill and gathered her skirts. Leaning out backwards, she reached for the edge of the roof and pulled herself up until her feet rested on the window ledge.

Holding her breath, she pushed off with her feet and dropped to the ground.

The landing took her breath away. She took a moment to recover, straightening her hat and dusting off as much as she could of the grime and cobwebs that clung to her skirt and shirtwaist.

What now? She had to find her way back to the Manufactures Building. With every passing moment, the feeling grew stronger that the notebook now in Silas's possession held the key to all the strange goings-on.

She glanced at the shed behind her. No sign yet that the guards were aware of her escape. Keeping the building between her and them, she made her way to the edge of Machinery Hall, then moved rapidly to the corner where she could follow the south canal back to the plaza.

John James Frost stood near the east end of the Grand Basin, enjoying the warmth of the morning sun on his back. He held his umbrella at his side and tapped it gently against his leg. With the beautiful weather the sky promised, he wouldn't need the umbrella for shelter from the rain. Today it would serve a much more important purpose.

Sunlight glinted off the Statue of the Republic to his left and shimmered across the waters of the Grand Basin. Frost smiled to himself. It seemed symbolic. Today would mark a shining moment in his life. The time was at hand. All his planning, all his dreams were about to be realized. He turned to the dark-haired man standing beside him. "Any trouble persuading the Infanta to come back?"

Miguel Díaz smiled, looking every bit as pleased as Frost

felt. "Not at all. I told her a man approached me just before our departure, saying he had information about an assassination plot against one of the royal family but would only give the details to her personally."

Frost threw back his head and laughed. "Very clever."

Díaz gave a slight bow. "I wanted to appeal to her sense of adventure, make it seem like a—how do you call it?—a cloak-and-dagger affair. She was more than happy to slip off the train at the next stop and return to the fairgrounds incognito. She loves playacting of that kind, you know."

Frost smirked. "Not a wise choice for a public figure. Going off alone like that could prove risky."

"I have warned her about this many times already." Díaz assumed a grave expression. "As her chief of security, I followed her back here as soon as it was learned she was missing."

"Of course." Frost pressed his lips together and tried not to laugh.

A slight smile lifted the corners of Díaz's lips. "It is a shame that when I catch up to her it will be too late to avert a tragedy."

"But just in time to express outrage over her assassination, eh?"

Díaz's eyes gleamed. "Ah, yes. I shall be quite vocal in pointing out the shame of this despicable act taking place on American soil while a member of Spain's royal family is here as an honored guest." Their gazes met and a look of understanding passed between them.

Frost rocked on his heels and looked around. From where he stood, he could see four of the Cubans stationed at various points around the basin's perimeter. Immediately after the shooting, they would pull out the sheaves of papers they held under their jackets and scatter them to the winds, pamphlets denouncing Spain's tyranny and demanding the liberation of Cuba.

And over there should be. . . He shifted his weight and craned his neck. Yes, the fifth Cuban was in place just behind one of the columns that lined the south end of the Manufactures Building. It was an ideal location, chosen after careful study and deliberation. It would conceal the shooter from the notice of passersby while leaving him in a perfect position to aim and fire when Frost gave the signal.

As soon as the shot was fired, the other Cubans would fling their pamphlets into the air, then make their exit across the plaza and out through Terminal Station, while attention was focused on the slain Infanta. The assassin would dart back into the Manufactures Building and lose himself in all the confusion. And just in case something went wrong with his escape plan. . .

Nearer to the door of the building and out of the gunman's line of sight, Leon Ames was waiting. If the Cuban muffed his opportunity and it looked like he was about to be apprehended, Ames would pull out his own gun and drop him on the spot, ensuring the man's silence while making himself look like a hero.

Frost jingled the coins in his pocket. Even Díaz didn't know about that additional bit of preparation. It was always wise to have a secondary plan in place, just in case something went wrong.

Everything was ready. The players were all in place. By now, Annie Trenton would be safely locked away. The Infanta should be on her way soon.

All they had to do was wait.

"Silas!" Annie bolted into the booth, fighting for air after her mad dash across the grounds.

Silas turned from polishing the carriage trim. A smile broke out on his face when he saw her. "Annie, my dear. I have some wonderful news."

"I need your notebook."

"Eh? What?" He pulled it from his inside coat pocket and held it out to her, a frown creasing his face.

Annie grabbed the notebook and turned it over in her hands. Not an exact duplicate but a close enough match if one didn't pay careful attention. Her fingers tightened on the leather binding as she thought about the invasion of their rooms and the way both she and Silas had been attacked. This had to be what Frost and his men had been looking for. They had done everything in their power to find it, yet it had remained just beyond their reach.

"Here." She pulled the other notebook from her reticule and thrust it at Silas.

"What's this?"

Annie riffled through the pages of the book in her hands, the one that had caused all the trouble. "It's your notebook."

"But didn't I just—"

She warded off his questions with her upraised hand. "I don't have time to explain now. I need to look at this." Only a few pages held any writing at all. She scanned the brief notations. Nothing leaped out at her.

"As I started to tell you—"

"Not now, Silas. I have to think." They wouldn't have made such efforts to retrieve the notebook if it didn't hold important information. If she could only find out what was being planned and alert the authorities in time to stop it from happening!

"But, Annie, you'll be so pleased—"

"I'm sure I will," she murmured. Her sense of urgency was mounting. Whatever the reason her captors felt she needed to be detained, surely they wouldn't have planned to lock her away days ahead of the event. No, something was going to happen very soon, and the answer had to be right in front of her.

Waving away Silas's attempts to gain her attention, she squeezed her eyes tight and tried to shut out the babel of sounds around her.

Silas tugged on her arm. It was no good. She needed privacy. But where? Did a quiet place exist in this cavernous building?

Yes, it did. Relief swept over her. She tucked the notebook in her reticule. "I'll be back."

"But, Annie, you just got here. And Nick said—"

"Don't worry. I won't leave the building. I promise."

She hurried up the nearest staircase and pushed open the door to the observation deck. Leaning back against it, she pressed the notebook against her chest and looked around.

Where to go next? Annie stared in dismay at the couples and families strolling along the promenade. Surely there was a quiet spot up here. There had to be. She hurried down the length of the building, looking in vain for a place that would suit her purpose. At the south end, she found an unoccupied bench in a secluded corner.

She pulled the drawing from the reticule and spread it open on the bench beside her, smoothing out the wrinkles from where she had hastily wadded it into her purse. Looking out at the view before her, she realized she sat directly above the area shown on the map. By all rights, everything ought to become clear right now. She waited for inspiration to strike, but it eluded her.

Shaking her head, she took out the notebook and leafed

through it again. Inspiration couldn't be relied on. An orderly, logical approach, that was what she needed. But where to start? She found the place where Silas's notes began and flipped back to the page with writing prior to that:

> *once IE disposed of, dec. of war should follow within days*
> *two days at most for Col. M to seize Havana*
> *new govt. in place by end of week*
> *assume control plantations by month's end*

Annie's brow furrowed. What war? What plantations? Feeling like she was trying to find her way through a dense fog, she turned back to the previous page:

> *meet with Cubans, assure cooperation*
> *find location*
> *D to have princess in place on the day*

She stared at the pages, tears of frustration scalding her eyes. It was no use. She had set herself an impossible task. Making sense of these obscure scrawls would be as likely as. . .

As deciphering a meeting time and place from a few scribbles found in a switched satchel. She had done it once; maybe she could do it again. Thus heartened, she looked at the notes once more, searching for some common thread.

The satchel belonged to Frost; thus, this notebook must be his, as well. She closed her eyes, trying to remember the conversation she had overheard during last night's intermission. Something about trouble between Cuba and Spain and the expectation that the situation would stabilize in the near future. She nodded.

There was one connection, but she had no idea what to make of it. What could plans for taking over Havana, Cuba, have to do with the White City?

She skimmed the notes again. "D to have princess in place." In place for what? She turned to the following page once more. "Once IE is disposed of. . ." Disposed of—could that mean dead? Perhaps this IE was the target of their plot. She went back over the two lists, her pulse quickening. Did Cuba have a princess? No, Cuba was controlled by Spain.

Spain? Annie's hand flew to her mouth. Could *IE* signify the Infanta Eulalia? With growing horror, she saw the pieces of the puzzle fall into place.

Frost was in Chicago. The Infanta Eulalia, princess of Spain, was in Chicago. Could that mean. . . ? *No.* Relief flowed through her. The Infanta had left the city the day before.

Annie tossed the notebook down on the bench and picked up the map again. There had to be something here. She looked at the drawing again, studying every detail. There was the Manufactures Building, on top of which she sat. To the south lay the Grand Basin and the Statue of the Republic.

She studied the paper intently, able to see more clearly here in the sunlight than in the gloom of the shed. There was a smudge at the bottom of the page as though someone had made a note, then tried to rub it out. She peered at it closely, able at last to make out a date—*June 15th*—and then the notation *a.m.*

June 15! Annie straightened and stared straight out across the Grand Basin. But that was today. And the morning was nearly spent. That meant whatever had been planned was scheduled to take place soon.

CHAPTER 26

Nick burst through the doorway of the Manufactures Building and rushed down the broad walkway that bisected the interior from north to south. He looked ahead, searching for Annie, straining for a glimpse of her sweet face. He'd spent more time downtown than he should have, but it was all going to be worth it when he saw the glow in her eyes as he placed the Bible in her hands.

He searched the area at the base of the clock tower but didn't see her standing there. But she didn't know which direction to expect him to come from, he reminded himself. Maybe she was standing on the other side, or—he grinned—maybe she had moved across the walkway to take another look at the Tiffany exhibit while she waited.

He made a complete circuit of the tower and stopped, baffled. He glanced up at the clock and compared it to his watch. Only a few minutes past the appointed time. Why hadn't she waited? He peered down the length of Columbia Avenue in the direction of the booth. She must have gotten caught up in something and hadn't been able to get away yet.

He took up a position from which he'd be able to see her when she started his way. On the other hand, why stand around using up more precious time? He would meet her at the booth instead, and they would go ahead as planned.

Nick checked the faces he passed as he walked along, not wanting to miss her on the way. He didn't see her in the crowd. . . or in the booth when he arrived.

Over in the corner, Silas was busy talking to a man in a checkered coat. Nick walked over to them and cleared his throat. "Do you know where Annie is?"

Silas paused in midsentence and looked around. "She was here earlier, but she went off with one of those Columbian Guards. Then she returned, all in a dither." He smiled indulgently. "She took my notebook—well, the one I thought was my notebook. It turns out she had mine with her. Curious, don't you think?"

Nick didn't even attempt to make sense of that. Trying to follow Silas's thoughts was like chasing feathers in a whirlwind. "But where is she now?"

"She went off again. And just when I had the most marvelous news. Nick, I—"

"She just left?"

"Yes." Silas's face sagged; then he brightened. "But she did say she wouldn't leave the building. We both remembered what you said." He gave Nick a reassuring smile and turned back to the man he'd been talking to.

Nick walked to the edge of the booth and looked up and down the walkway. Still no sign of Annie. She had agreed to meet him. Where was she? He felt a stirring of doubt, and his

283

face tightened. Maybe meeting each other wasn't as important to her as it was to him.

But she'd made a promise about staying close to Silas. He scanned the crowd again. What was she thinking? Staying inside the building didn't guarantee her safety.

And according to Uncle Silas, it wasn't the first time she'd disappeared that morning. What was it he said—she came back all in a dither? That wasn't like Annie. Something was wrong.

Nick clenched his jaw and set out along Columbia Avenue. If she was in the building, he would find her.

Snatching up the drawing, Annie stepped to the railing. From the rooftop, she had an unobstructed view of the area below. She held the map up, trying to pinpoint the locations marked by the initials and arrows scribbled on the page. Who or what did they indicate? She let her gaze roam over the crowd and felt her frustration mounting. How could she hope to find someone if she didn't know who she was looking for?

She began again, taking the area one section at a time. Machinery Hall. The Administration Building. She passed over the area near the Columbian Fountain, then returned to it and looked again. What was it that caught her attention?

She singled out a figure, a lone woman striding along. Something about the way she carried herself, her proud, regal bearing—Annie pressed against the railing, unable to believe her eyes. It was her, the Infanta. She'd know that walk anywhere, even from this lofty height. And she was alone.

Annie watched the princess move along with an air of purpose, skirting the fountain, then walking east along the near bank of the Grand Basin. Annie looked at the drawing again. One set of initials near the dot that marked the Statue of the Republic caught her attention: *JJF.* Her eyes widened. *John James Frost?*

She noted the position marked by the initials. Nick had once told her he could find a face in a mass of confusion if he had it fixed firmly in his mind. She summoned Frost's appearance from her memory and focused her gaze on the east end of the basin.

There he was, standing beside another man, not far from the gilded statue.

She whipped her head around and looked back at the Infanta. It was going to happen. She opened her mouth to scream a warning, then realized how futile that would be. There was no time to summon help or try to explain the situation to anyone else. The Infanta was in mortal danger, and Annie was the only one who could stop it.

She swiveled her head, looking for the quickest way down, then plunged toward the south stairway.

This is crazy. Nick fidgeted near the clock tower. After traversing half the length of the building, he realized what a fool's errand he'd set for himself. How did he imagine he'd be able to find Annie in all of this? All these walls and partitions—there were simply too many obstacles.

He raked his hand through his hair. *Annie, where are you?* According to Uncle Silas, she said she wouldn't leave the building. Some help that was. She had promised to stay within the confines of the largest building ever constructed.

He heard shrill voices overhead and looked up to see two children running along the gallery. Maybe looking at things from a higher perspective would help. He found the nearest staircase and went up one level. He moved quickly along the galleries, looking at each face he passed and scanning the throng below. He stopped when he had covered half the distance to the south end without success. *This is ridiculous. I might as well go back to the booth and wait.*

Instead, he pressed on, driven by a sense of urgency he couldn't explain. He would go as far as the end of the building and then decide what to do next. Annie needed him; he couldn't let her down.

Annie dashed down the stairs, clinging to the rail with one hand and holding up the hem of her skirt with the other. Her alarm increased with every passing second. Where would the Infanta be by now? Had Frost already set his deadly plan in motion?

She eyed the distance to the gallery level and to the ground floor beyond and let out a moan of despair. She would never make it in time. *God, help me!*

She reached the landing and started down the second set of steps. A knot of people meandering up to the galleries blocked her way.

"Excuse me. Please, I must get past." Annie squeezed between a heavyset woman and the stair rail.

The woman staggered into the man beside her. "Well, I never!"

"Watch where you're going," called her companion.

She made it through the impasse and continued her head-long rush. Fairgoers milled about on the floor below. Despair washed over her. So many people, but not one she could turn to for help. There was no time for explanations.

There was no time at all.

I give up. Nick slapped his palm against the gallery railing. *It was a fool idea anyway.* He might as well head back to the booth. And then what? He walked to the nearby staircase, weighing his options.

Voices floated up to him from a group of people a few steps below: "What's wrong with that girl?"

"She's going to knock someone down if she goes flying along like that." A ruddy-faced man wagged his head in disapproval.

Nick looked over their heads and spotted Annie farther down, nearly at the bottom of the stairs.

"Excuse me!" He threaded his way between the man and the wall, taking the steps two at a time. Why was she hurrying like that? Was she running from something. . .or someone?

"Annie!" he shouted.

Without slacking her pace, she turned her head from side to side, searching the crowd below.

"Up here!" he called.

This time, she looked up and saw him. "Nick!"

His heart leaped at the joy that lit her face. He bounded down the stairs, ready to take her in his arms.

Instead of waiting, she waved at him to come on. "Hurry!"

287

She raced down the last few steps, then sprinted toward the exit.

He caught up with her at the doorway. "Hold on a minute. What's gong on?"

She headed straight outside, never missing a step. "They're going to kill the Infanta." She swiveled her head from side to side. "Where *is* she?" She sidestepped a woman leading two children by the hand and broke into a headlong run in the direction of the Statue of the Republic.

"What? Who's going to kill her?" Nick dodged the woman and her children and hurried to Annie's side. "Annie, what's happening?"

"There's no time to explain. It's going to happen any second."

The desperate look on her face convinced him. He'd seen enough to know he could believe what Annie said, no matter how improbable it seemed. Danger was at hand, and she was rushing straight toward it.

"Tell me what's going on, and I'll take care of it. I don't want you getting—"

"There she is!" Annie pointed at a woman not twenty yards ahead of them and redoubled her speed.

CHAPTER 27

Show me what to do, Lord! Annie pounded along the pavement with Nick right beside her. In only moments, they would close the distance between them and the Infanta. How could she make the princess pay attention to what she had to say?

She took her eyes off the Infanta long enough to glance in Frost's direction. He still stood in the same spot. . .and was that Senor Díaz beside him? Annie's mind whirled. Something was wrong—those two shouldn't be together. The metallic taste of fear filled her mouth. Did she have time to cry out, to warn the Infanta?

She saw Frost smile and raise his furled umbrella in a mock salute. Just ahead of her and Nick, a man stepped out from the shadows of the colonnade. The sunlight flashed on something in his hand.

"Nick!" She waved her arm toward the man. "He has a gun!" She needed a weapon. She had none—only herself.

Annie launched herself at the Infanta Eulalia.

While they tumbled to the pavement, she heard the crack of gunfire. At the edge of her vision, she could see Nick falling to the ground.

No! Annie felt as though the shot had penetrated her own heart. *Not Nick!*

Beneath her, the Infanta struggled, shrieking like a banshee. "*¡Quítate, animal!* Get off me!" Annie slid to one side and let her get up. The Infanta rattled off angry words like machine gunfire.

Annie remained facedown on the ground, unable to make herself get up and see what she knew she would find. In her rush to save the princess, she had sacrificed the man she loved. A cacophony of shrieks and screams split the air around her. Still, she couldn't bring herself to move.

"Annie? *Annie!*" Strong hands gripped her and turned her over gently. "Are you hurt, Annie? Speak to me."

She looked up, unbelieving, into Nick's eyes, dark with dread. With a joyful sob, she let him pull her to her feet and into his arms. She inhaled the smell of leather and felt the strength of his grip holding her tight against him. The steady beating of his heart reassured her that he was still alive, still with her. Tilting her chin, she looked up at him, wanting to see that look of concern in his eyes once more.

A clawlike grip seized her arm and whirled her around. "You!" The Infanta stood beside them, her eyes flaring wide. "*¡Idiota!* What do you mean by this outrage?"

"Your Highness! Are you all right?" Senor Díaz dashed up to them with Frost at his side. "We saw the whole thing, the way this woman attacked you—"

"What's going on here?" A Columbian Guard looked at each

290

member of the group in turn. "Is anyone hurt?"

"This woman!" The Infanta pointed a trembling finger at Annie. "She attacked me, knocked me to the ground! I demand you arrest her immediately."

The guard flicked a look at Annie. "She didn't fire that shot, though, did she?" He turned back to her accuser. "What is your name, ma'am?"

The Infanta drew herself up. "I am the Infanta Eulalia, princess of Spain."

The guard looked skeptical. "I heard the princess left yesterday."

Díaz stepped in. "Begging your pardon, I can assure you of the Infanta's identity. I am Miguel Díaz, chief of security for Her Highness. I saw everything that happened." He nodded toward Annie and Nick. "This woman and her cowboy partner rushed up behind the Infanta and knocked her to the ground. I heard a shot. I thought they had killed her."

He turned to the Infanta, "You are all right. *Gracias a Dios.*"

Annie trembled from head to toe. She shook her head. "No!"

Nick put his arm around her and lowered his head like a bull ready to charge. "Wait a minute here. That's not what happened."

"Mr. Díaz is right," Frost interjected. "I was standing beside him and saw the whole thing. I demand you arrest these two at once."

The Columbian Guard looked back and forth, clearly at a loss.

"Come now." Díaz's tone was clipped. "Who are you going to believe. . .a representative of the royal family or this pair of ruffians?"

"I, for one, would take the word of these two." Stephen

Bridger shouldered his way into the circle. "Moreover, I've been talking to some of the other witnesses. We have the gunman, thanks to Mr. Rutherford." He smiled at Nick. "And I've already had some dealings with Mr. Frost." He sent the businessman a steely glare.

Annie felt her courage return. She pointed at Frost. "He's the one who planned it all. I think he and Díaz are in it together." She flinched at the look of hatred Frost gave her but stood her ground.

"Impossible!" The Infanta spat out the word. "She is trying to cover up her own misdeeds by blaming another."

Díaz's face suffused with color. "That is right; she lies. I have been a faithful servant of the royal household my entire life."

Stephen Bridger took a step closer to the two men. He leveled a sober look at Annie. "That's a serious charge. Do you have anything to back it up?"

"Yes," Frost sneered. "Where's your proof?"

Annie moved closer into the circle of Nick's arm. "It's up there." She pointed to the observation deck. "I can take you to it."

Stephen Bridger leaned over the railing of the observation deck and shouted to the men below. "I have everything we need. Take them all to the guard station, and we'll get it sorted out there."

He turned back to Nick and Annie and held up the notebook she had gotten from Silas. "With everything you've been able to tell me, this should give us what we need to make them talk. I'd appreciate it if you'll come by later and give us an official statement."

He looked at Annie, and a slow smile spread across his face. "That was an amazing thing you did out there. You probably saved us from an international incident, maybe even from a war." He tucked the notebook into his uniform pocket. "You've had quite a day from the sound of it. I'd tell you to be careful, but it looks like you're in good hands now."

Annie tilted her head to look up at Nick. "Yes," she said. "I am."

Nick waited until Bridger left, then turned to face her without letting her go. "I thought you promised me you wouldn't go off on your own anymore."

She leaned against his arm, grateful for the support. "You said you trusted Stephen Bridger. The man wore a guard's uniform. I assumed he would be safe. I never dreamed he was one of Frost's men. . .until it was too late." She shuddered.

Nick's arms tightened around her. Pulling her close, he rubbed his cheek against her hair. "If Colonel Cody hears about this, he'll wind up offering you a star role in the show."

A soft laugh escaped her lips at his attempt to lighten the mood. "I could drive the carriage around the arena," she quipped. "It might be good advertising." She felt the rumble of his laughter against her cheek.

He tucked a tendril of hair behind her ear. "Are you up to that walk now?"

Annie looked up at him. "Could we just go back to the booth? I think I need to catch my breath for a while. And I'd like to make sure Silas is all right."

They descended the stairs to the ground floor at a much slower pace than the last time. Annie felt a sense of normalcy returning. Maybe she should have taken Nick up on his offer to walk along the beach. She was fairly certain Silas would be fine. Surely all the ominous goings-on had ended now that Frost and his men were in custody.

Sure enough, Silas stood near the placard talking to a dignified, silver-haired man. Annie wanted to weep with relief at the scene's air of normality.

Silas looked up when they approached. "Here they come now." He led the other man over to them. "Nick and Annie, I'd like you to meet—"

A stern voice broke in. "Young woman, are you ready to sign those papers?"

Annie spun on her heel. Richard Trenton stood behind her with his wife beside him. The two of them stared at her coldly. Her elation at having saved the Infanta evaporated like morning dew.

Mr. Trenton advanced on her and looked down on her from his advantage in height. "You received a letter from my attorney this morning. Don't bother to deny it."

Nick held up his hand. "Just a moment. I don't know what you're up to—"

Mr. Trenton barely spared him a glance. "You, sir, are not a part of this conversation." He turned back to Annie. "It would be easier on everyone if you would put an end to the matter now. All I need is your signature, and we'll be on our way." He drew a set of papers from his inside coat pocket and held them out to Annie.

Annie felt the veins in her neck throb. Sweeping her arm out, she snatched the papers from him and crumpled them in her hand. "Go away."

His slacked-jawed astonishment fueled her courage. She stepped away from Nick and advanced on Will's father, her outrage growing stronger by the moment. "How dare you use your money and position to try to take away what Will worked so hard to achieve?"

"Annie," Silas said, "you don't have to—"

"Yes, I do." She knew she was probably making things worse for herself, but after what God had just done to protect her and Nick, she had no trouble believing He would take care of her somehow, even if all the income from the carriage was stripped away.

She threw the wad of papers on the floor. "If I were the only one concerned, I would walk away from this, but agreeing to your demands would mean leaving Silas at your mercy. I'd be letting you hurt a decent man who has been a good friend to both your son and me."

"Not to mention being my uncle." Nick moved up beside her. "If you think I'm going to stand by and let you do anything to hurt either one of them, you are sadly mistaken."

Mr. Trenton gave a snort of derision. "None of you have any idea what you're letting yourselves in for."

Silas patted the air with his hands. "If you'd all just listen for a moment—"

Her father-in-law's face was the color of a ripe tomato. "Let me explain what you can expect if you continue in your attempts to put off the inevitable—"

Annie jabbed her finger at him. "You never showed one bit of interest while Will was alive. What makes you think—"

A piercing whistle splintered the air. Silas waved his arms. "Would everyone please be quiet?"

CHAPTER 28

"Much better." Silas beamed and straightened his jacket. "I think I can put an end to this discussion. Allow me to introduce Mr. Charles Bailey." He indicated the man he had been talking to when Annie and Nick arrived. "He stopped by the other day to take a look at the carriage, and we had quite a pleasant chat. When Annie showed me the letter she had received this morning, I decided to pay him a visit."

The group's attention turned to the gray-haired man at his side. Richard Trenton snorted. "What kind of nonsense is this? I fail to see what your social life has to do with the matter at hand."

Charles Bailey smiled and cleared his throat. "I can answer that. Mr. Crockett and I did indeed have a pleasant conversation regarding this fine vehicle several days ago. What he neglected to mention is that I am an attorney."

Annie didn't miss the start Will's father gave.

Bailey continued, "During our visit, I mentioned that I've

been spending quite a bit of time over at the Clifton Coal exhibit in Mines and Mining, going over some rather intricate contracts they've asked me to draw up. That is where Mr. Crockett found me a little while ago."

"Silas went to see you?" Annie stared at him. "I don't understand."

"Who Crockett chooses to speak to is neither here nor there," her father-in-law put in. "This woman is the one I'm dealing with here—or trying to."

Charles Bailey gave him a look that made Mr. Trenton clamp his lips together. "Mr. Crockett asked me to look over the letter sent by Richard Trenton's attorney, as well as a partnership agreement signed by both Mr. Crockett and William Trenton." He gave Annie a fatherly smile. "This young lady's late husband, if I'm not mistaken."

Annie nodded, trying to work her way through the explanation. "An agreement? What agreement, Silas?"

"It's something we had drawn up at the beginning of our partnership. After Will died, I didn't see any need to burden you with the details, considering everything else you had to think about."

Mr. Trenton sniffed. "And you just happened to have this agreement with you? Here, in Chicago?"

Silas blinked. "Of course. I brought all the papers I thought might be important in case we decided to sell the rights to the carriage. I keep them in my satchel."

"Go on, Mr. Bailey," Nick urged. "What does this agreement involve?"

Bailey clasped his hands loosely in front of him. "According to the agreement, both partners had an equal share in the invention and its proceeds unless one of them should die. In that case, the surviving partner would then command a controlling interest. In other words. . ." He looked at Silas. "In any matter regarding the carriage—development, sales, marketing, anything—Mr. Crockett has the final say."

Hope fluttered, then took wing. "So even if I lose control of Will's share," Annie said, "Silas is still the one who's in charge. Is that right?"

Bailey nodded. "Precisely."

Mrs. Trenton looked up at her husband. "Does that mean we've lost, Richard?"

"Hardly." His face grew rigid. "Will originated the idea. Even if he signed that agreement, we can still contest it. And we will."

The faint hope that had stirred within Annie withered and died.

Charles Bailey turned to Mr. Trenton. "You might want to hear the rest of Mr. Crockett's announcement before you decide to do that." He gestured to Silas.

Silas looked as though he were about to burst. "After I returned with Mr. Bailey, I found another gentleman waiting for me, a Mr. Hilliard." His chest expanded. "He has looked the carriage over and wants to be a part of what we're doing. Annie, he's put up the money for us to go into production!"

Annie felt the booth spin around her. "Oh, Nick!" She reached out for him.

Nick put his arm around her and held her tight. "Where does that leave Annie in regard to this legal threat?"

Bailey positioned himself next to Annie. "It means she is on extremely solid footing." He looked directly at the Trentons.

"Sir, you must be aware you have no legal grounds for this abominable attempt to deprive Mrs. Trenton of what is rightfully hers. Not only that, but you might be interested to know that the agreement Mr. Crockett has entered into with Mr. Hilliard is an extremely lucrative one. She will have at her disposal all the financial resources she needs to fight you in court. . . and win."

The attorney turned a softer gaze on Annie. "If you wish to avail yourself of my services, I would be happy to represent you in this matter."

Mr. Trenton stiffened. "You can't hope to get away with this. My name is known all over this city. I have a reputation here, a standing in the community."

"Annie will, too, as soon as word gets out about what happened this morning," Nick told him. "Do you really want to be known as the man who tried to swindle the woman who saved the life of the princess of Spain and kept America out of a war?"

Her father-in-law's jaw dropped. "What? What are you talking about?"

Nick grinned. "You can read about it in the evening paper."

Mr. Trenton looked around the circle of faces, ending with his gaze resting on Annie. His chest heaved, and his lips drew back. "You have caused nothing but trouble for this family since the day you met my son. Come along, Martha. We're leaving." He wheeled around and stalked away.

His wife stayed where she was and looked straight at Annie.

Annie couldn't discern what lay behind her expression. Pity stirred within her. She felt compelled to reach out in some way, knowing this would probably be the last time she would ever see the woman who gave Will life.

What would Will do? She felt the weight of the reticule pulling on her wrist. She touched it, her fingers tracing the solid shape of Will's Bible. Without any sense of consciously working through the problem, she knew what she had to do.

Annie pulled the reticule open and drew out the Bible. "This was Will's." She held it out, trying to keep her hand steady. "I think he would want you to have it."

From farther along the aisle, they heard a bellow: "Martha, come away from there now!"

Mrs. Trenton stared at Annie. Their gazes locked and held. Annie felt a quiver when her mother-in-law touched the book and took it in her hand. "Thank you. I will always cherish this as a memento of my son."

Annie forced her fingers to release the last tangible reminder of Will's love and their life together. "Don't just cherish it; read it. Please. That would have meant more to Will than anything."

Mrs. Trenton drew the small volume from Annie's hand. "I will." With the air of someone holding a lifeline, she clutched the Bible to her and hurried to catch up to her husband.

Annie watched her go through tear-filmed eyes. Whether they were tears of joy or sorrow, she couldn't be sure. *I did the best I could, Will.* She was sure she only thought the words until she saw Nick's sympathetic glance.

She turned, wanting to hide her raw emotions from the others. Her reticule swung wide when she spun around, its lightness a poignant reminder of what she had done.

"Annie?" Nick stood beside her, his eyes filled with compassion. "This isn't the best time, certainly not what I would have chosen." He broke off, looking uncharacteristically hesitant, then held out a paper-wrapped parcel. "Would you accept this?

I know it will never hold the same place in your heart that Will's did, but. . ."

Annie stared at him, trying to read his thoughts. His expression remained blank. She reached out and touched the package and drew it into her hand. With trembling fingers, she pulled off the paper and saw the small Bible inside.

"Oh, my." She examined it, turning it over in her hands. It was slightly larger than Will's. A bit heavier, too. She stroked the cover with her fingertips. It felt smooth and fresh, not worn from loving use. She opened it, liking the way the crisp pages flipped beneath her fingers.

No, it wasn't Will's Bible. But that didn't change the message it contained. And Nick had gone to all the trouble of finding it just for her. Tears clogged her throat. She looked into his eyes and saw the warmth there. . .warmth and something more.

"Thank you." It was all she could manage to say. It took a bit of work to tuck the Bible inside her reticule, but by stretching the opening a bit, she could make it fit. She needed to buy a new reticule anyway after the rough treatment this one had gone through. She would look for a new one when she got home.

Home. Her shoulders lifted at the thought. Her need to stay on at the fair had ended. She had accomplished her mission as much as she was able. She had seen Will's carriage receive the acclaim it deserved. While she couldn't claim success at effecting a reconciliation with Will's family, she had done her best. Remembering the look on his mother's face when she carried the Bible away, Annie thought it possible Will's mother might become reconciled to her heavenly Father at least. And that was infinitely more important.

And Silas had managed to elude Mrs. Purvis's most blatant

hints about matrimony. Her lips quirked up at the thought.

Yes, it was time to go home. She looked up at Nick again and felt like her heart had stopped beating. It was time to go home. . .unless someone gave her a reason to stay.

CHAPTER 29

Annie watched the colors of the sunset dim as twilight crept across the grounds. She edged closer to Nick, appreciating the reassurance of his solid bulk beside her in the waiting crowd.

The knot of people moved a few feet forward, then stopped again. Nick squeezed her shoulder. "It's been a long week, hasn't it?"

Annie gave a shaky laugh. "The longest I can remember. I had no idea there would be so much involved in telling the police everything I learned about Frost and his activities, not to mention all the time Silas and I had to spend with Mr. Bailey, trying to work out all the details on this new agreement."

The tight knot of people moved ahead again, several yards this time. Nick's brow furrowed. "I still can't figure Frost. What would make a man willing to do what he did?"

Annie stared along the length of the Midway, watching the lights twinkle on. "Stephen Bridger told me more of the story after Frost was questioned. It seems his agreement with the Cubans would have given him control of a number of sugar plantations as soon as they won their independence. If his plan had worked, it would have made him a millionaire several times over."

"And plunged his own country into a war at the cost of the Infanta's life and who knows how many others?" Nick shook his head. "Amazing what greed will do to some people."

The breeze picked up. He put his arm around Annie and drew her closer. "Well, at least one good thing has happened this week. They finally finished the work on this." He looked up.

Annie tilted her head back and followed his gaze up, up, up to the top of the mammoth wheel that loomed overhead. "How high did you say this thing is?"

"It's 264 feet." Nick didn't take his eyes off the cars moving through their slow revolution. "Isn't that something?"

"You're sure it's safe?"

Her question drew his attention away from the monstrous steel circle. Nick cupped her chin in his hand and looked at her intently. "I would never, ever knowingly put you in any danger." The corners of his mouth turned up, and he tapped his finger on the tip of her nose. "You do a pretty thorough job of that on your own."

Annie laughed in spite of the tremor that rippled through her at the thought of ascending to that dizzying height.

"Have you heard any more about Díaz?" Nick asked. "He was as much a traitor as Frost, maybe even more so."

Sadness engulfed Annie. "It was greed again. That and resentment at feeling like he was being shunted aside. His family has served the royalty of Spain for generations. Time after time, they were promised advancement and gifts of land, but those promises were never kept. Frost guaranteed him a position in the new Cuban government as a reward for delivering the princess, and he saw a chance to finally have his day in the sun."

She leaned against Nick's arm. "He seemed like a nice man. It's just so sad, such a waste."

"And you never even got any thanks from the Infanta for saving her life."

"As a matter of fact, we heard from her just yesterday." Annie laughed at Nick's look of astonishment. "She placed an order for ten of the carriages. Silas is already daydreaming about having hundreds of them zooming around the Spanish countryside."

Once again, the crowd surged ahead. Nick grinned, and his smile made him look like an eager little boy. "Well, here's your chance to forget about all of that. It's our turn." He guided Annie across the platform and through the door at the end of the waiting car.

Annie eyed the long, narrow compartment, and her steps dragged. "Nick, this is almost as big as a Pullman car. It must weigh tons! How can it possibly operate safely?"

Nick chuckled. "Haven't you been watching it do just that for the hour we stood in line?" He prodded her forward gently. "Would you like to sit down?"

Annie looked at the double row of padded, circular seats and shook her head. "I'd rather be close to you."

Nick's eyes gleamed. "I won't argue with that. Let's move over here so we can have a good view out the window." He stood behind her, cradling her shoulders in both his hands.

He leaned forward and whispered, "I'm right here. You're going to be fine." His breath felt warm against her ear. If she turned her head the slightest bit, his lips would graze her cheek.

When the last passenger entered the car, the attendant

locked the door and stood in front of it. All was still for one long, breathless moment; then a collective gasp went up as Ferris's great wheel began to turn.

Annie clamped her eyelids shut and leaned back against Nick. A tingling sensation buzzed in the pit of her stomach, and she wondered if Nick could feel her tremble. Up they soared, until it seemed as if they were about to shoot off to the stars.

"Look down there."

Annie eased her eyelids open and caught her breath at the sight before her. She caught Nick's hand and gripped it tight.

Below them lay the White City in all its splendor, illumined by a myriad of white lights. Annie could pick out the mighty sprawl of the Manufactures Building with ease. Beyond it, the waters of Lake Michigan spread to the far horizon.

Swinging her gaze back to the west, she saw the Wild West Show encampment, where lines of people waited at the gate.

"Nick, the show's going to start soon. Why aren't you over there?"

He gave her a quick squeeze. "It isn't a problem. This is where I want to be right now."

She twisted around to look at him, but his gaze was fixed on the view beyond the broad expanse of glass. She let herself relax and stared out at the dazzling display, trying to imprint it all on her mind so she could hold on to the memory forever: the Midway and the fairgrounds below; the people standing on the ground, gaping up at them; and Nick behind her, his presence giving her a sense of belonging she never thought she would feel again.

Her mind ran in circles as the wheel moved in its arc against the sky. The moment felt so perfect she wished it would never end, that she could stay here in this city of wonder and light forever with Nick beside her. She smiled at the fancy, knowing she wished for something that could never happen but longing for it all the same. Tomorrow, she would be leaving this enchanted place behind. . .and Nick with it.

Even as the bittersweet reminder crossed her mind, the wheel came to rest. It was time to disembark.

Nick helped her down the platform steps. "There now. Wasn't that worth waiting for?"

"Absolutely." She studied his face. Was he having the same wistful feelings after their magical ride?

Nick sighed. "You've had a long week, between all those meetings and getting ready to leave. I suppose I should get you back to Mrs. Purvis's."

Annie nodded, not trusting herself to speak.

Their footsteps made a steady rhythm along the walk, like a clock ticking off the minutes they had left together. Streetlamps marked their way, and they moved through pockets of darkness from one pool of light to the next.

Nick didn't speak until they turned onto Blackstone Avenue. "I wish you didn't have to leave."

"Me, too." *I'd stay, if only you would ask.* She would pack Silas onto the train and send him on his way in the morning. She'd stay in Chicago or go on to New York or travel to the ends of the earth if only Nick wanted her beside him.

All he had to do was ask.

The porch lamp spilled light over Mrs. Purvis's front steps, a welcoming circle of warmth. Nick stopped before they reached its edge and gently took her hands.

Annie threaded her fingers through his and stared up at him. Would he say anything now? Voice the question she longed to hear?

The shadows veiled his face. She longed to know what she might see in his eyes but was glad the same darkness kept him from reading her expression. All her yearning must be evident in her gaze.

Nick slipped his fingers from her grasp and trailed his hands up her arms. A shiver ran through her. Without conscious thought, she let her arms reach out and wrap around his waist. His arms tightened around her shoulders, and he drew her close.

Annie tilted her face to meet his and put all her longing into her kiss. She felt Nick's heart quicken, keeping time with her own. After a long moment, he drew away and cradled her face in his hands.

"I'll see you in the morning." His voice came out in a husky whisper.

Annie nodded and laid her palm against his cheek. Tears burned her eyes. At any moment, they would spill over and betray her. She nodded again, not daring to speak, and turned to go up the steps.

At the door, she stopped to look back. Through her unshed tears, the streetlamp's glow formed a halo of light around the man she loved.

CHAPTER 30

I'm going to miss you." Mrs. Purvis held Annie's reticule while Annie pinned her straw skimmer firmly in place. "Is there anything else that needs to be done?"

Annie ticked off a mental list: "Our rooms are cleared out, the drayman took our luggage to the station before breakfast, and the cab should be here any moment." She reclaimed her reticule. "I think that's everything."

Silas stepped out the front door and joined them on the porch. Mrs. Purvis fluttered her eyelashes. "I don't suppose you'd consider opening your factory here in Chicago?"

Silas's eyes widened like a horse ready to bolt. "No, no. We have everything well in hand, thank you."

Mrs. Purvis's shoulders drooped. "Ah, well." She looked over at the front door and began tapping in a line along its frame.

Silas gathered up his satchel. "Madam, there is one thing I must know before we take our leave. What *is* the purpose of all that tapping?"

"Oh, that? It's Randolph, my late husband." The landlady giggled when she saw Silas's start. "Not him personally, you understand. He promised me he would find a way to provide for me if anything ever happened to him. I'm sure he left something right here in this house, but he died before he could tell me where it was. He always did have a habit of putting things off."

Her momentary gloom faded, and her sunny demeanor returned. "I'm sure I'll find it someday. God has taken care of me so far. In the meantime, I'll just keep looking."

Silas gave her a sidelong glance and edged past the two women. "I believe I'll wait down on the walk."

Mrs. Purvis drew near to Annie. "Where is Nicholas? I expected to see him this morning."

"So did I." Annie tried to smile. "He was probably delayed. I'm sure we'll see him at the station."

"Annie, our ride is here."

She turned and gasped when she saw Silas standing proudly beside a gleaming carriage. "What on earth?" She hurried down the steps.

Silas caught his lapels in his hands. "I'm feeling rather expansive after our agreement with Mr. Hilliard, so I decided we could afford to ride to the station in style." He opened the door and handed her up with a gallantry she had never suspected he possessed.

Annie stepped inside, admiring the rich interior. *How much did this cost?* They weren't in the dire straits they might have experienced if the Trentons' plan had gone through, they would still have to watch their spending until profits from the carriage started rolling in. But she wasn't about to spoil Silas's surprise by appearing unappreciative. They could splurge just this once.

310

"Good-bye!" Mrs. Purvis waved vigorously with both hands. "Send me a letter every now and again."

Annie leaned out the window and waved until they were out of sight. When they rounded the corner, she settled back into the leather seat. "It was a lovely place to stay. I'm glad we got to know Mrs. Purvis."

Silas pulled out his handkerchief. "But did you hear that comment about opening a factory here?" He mopped his forehead with the snowy cloth. "The woman simply does not give up. I feel I've had a narrow escape, Annie. A very narrow escape."

He tucked the handkerchief back into his pocket, and a wistful expression crossed his face. "But she does make a marvelous pot roast."

At the station, Annie made sure their luggage had been delivered and put the claim checks in her reticule. Silas hooked his thumbs in his vest pockets and looked around the depot. "Quite a lot of water has passed under the bridge since we first set foot in Chicago, eh? It's been an adventure, but I'll admit I'm ready to go home."

He followed Annie to the platform. "Do you suppose they will have heard about our triumph already? I wonder if they'll have a 'Welcome Home' banner at the station? A brass band, maybe. . ."

Lost in her own thoughts, Annie murmured a noncommital answer. It wouldn't feel like home anymore. A home meant more than a collection of rooms. It was a place where lives were joined and hearts connected.

She found a spot on the crowded platform. Where could Nick be? After last night, she had expected. . . Well, maybe she didn't know what to expect, after all. Maybe the connection had only existed in her mind.

Her thoughts whirled like the crowd around them as people got off a train that had just pulled in. More people were coming to the fair now than at the beginning. Maybe Silas was right; it was a good time to leave.

Her practical side asserted itself. *What did you want? For Nick to smother you with kisses and beg you to stay?* Well. . .yes. *That isn't going to happen, and you'll just have to face it.* A film of tears blurred the scene on the platform.

Annie blinked them away and craned her neck, trying to see through the crowd and trying even more not to look like she was doing just that.

Silas leaned over to her. "I don't know why he isn't here, my dear. I was sure he'd come to see us off."

"Oh, I wasn't. . . All right, I was." She gave him a faint smile.

The outbound passengers shuffled impatiently, looking every bit as tired as Annie felt. She hugged her reticule to her side and felt her new Bible press against her ribs. She held it tighter, treasuring the reminder of God's Word. He, at least, would never leave her.

Pull yourself together, Annie. This was no time to be maudlin. She had a life to live and a purpose to fulfill. . .though she didn't have the slightest idea at the moment what that purpose might be.

"All aboard!" At the conductor's loud cry, the restless crowd swarmed toward the train. Annie waited until Silas's attention was directed elsewhere, then stood on tiptoe, looking in vain for chestnut hair and broad, buckskin-clad shoulders. She toyed with the idea of waiting until the other passengers boarded the train and the platform emptied but knew she might find it hard to locate two seats together.

No. The moment for daydreams had passed, and it was time to get back to the business of life. Her summer idyll was over.

With a determined tilt to her chin, she squared her shoulders and picked up her valise, then ushered Silas up the steps and into the car. Halfway along the aisle, she spotted two seats side by side. *Thank You, Lord.* Annie settled herself by the window while Silas took the aisle seat. She pressed her forehead against the glass and scanned the platform.

"There you are."

Annie glanced toward the aisle and saw a man dressed in a black broadcloth jacket. She looked again. "Nick?"

He smiled, assuring her she hadn't lost her senses. There he stood, the width of him filling the aisle, his presence filling her soul with happiness.

Her heart slowed, then picked up speed. A smile parted her lips. "You came."

"I brought you a gift." He held out a paper-wrapped parcel.

"Another one?"

Nick leaned over Silas and pressed it into her hands. Her fingers closed around it. "This one isn't from me."

Mystified, Annie pulled away the paper to find a soft buckskin jacket fringed along the sleeves and bottom edge. Beaded American flags decorated both sides of the front.

She stared at the lovely garment. "It's beautiful. But who—"

"Look underneath. There's a card."

Annie felt beneath the jacket and pulled out a small piece of pasteboard:

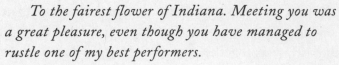

To the fairest flower of Indiana. Meeting you was a great pleasure, even though you have managed to rustle one of my best performers.

Fondest regards,
Col. Wm. F. Cody

Annie stared at the note, trying to make sense of the words. "I don't understand."

Nick smiled and put his hand on Silas's shoulder. "Uncle, there's an empty seat in the row just behind. Would you mind moving back there?"

"Eh? Oh, not at all. I'd be happy to." Silas gathered up his satchel and stepped into the aisle.

Nick slid into the seat next to Annie. His presence seemed to take up all the available air. She found it difficult to breathe.

"That's better," he said. "Now I don't feel like I'm looming over you."

Annie finally found her voice. "I was afraid I wouldn't get a chance to say good-bye."

Nick returned her gaze with equal intensity. "I would have been here sooner, but I had a little trouble with Ranger."

The train car jolted slightly as the couplings took up the slack. The wheels began to turn, and the train inched forward. Nick didn't seem the least bit concerned.

Annie put her hand on his sleeve. "Nick, the train is moving."

"So it is." He settled back as if he planned to enjoy the ride.

Annie smiled and let herself relax. So he hadn't come just to say a brief farewell. He was going to ride with them to the next stop. She floundered for something to talk about. "You said you had some trouble with your horse. Is he all right?"

"He'll be fine as soon as we pick up speed. It's just that he hates being cooped up in a freight car."

"Freight car?" Annie swiveled around and shot a glance at the door at the end of the aisle. "You mean he's on the train?"

"Yep." Nick stretched out his legs. "He kicked up such a fuss I thought we'd never get him loaded."

Annie brightened. "What a wonderful idea! You're going to ride him back to the encampment after you get off the train."

Nick shook his head. "He's gotten a little spoiled just doing two shows a day. I don't think he'd be any too pleased about having to carry me all the way back from Indiana."

Annie's mouth dropped open. A wild hope stirred in her chest.

Nick straightened and leaned toward her. "I talked to Colonel Cody a couple of days ago. I told him I was quitting."

She pressed her fingers against her temple. "You're leaving the show? But, Nick, you love it."

"I did. But it just isn't for me anymore. It's time for me to move on. I've traded in my buckskin for broadcloth." He slid his thumb along his lapel and grinned.

Annie twisted in her seat so she could face him directly. "How did Colonel Cody take it?"

Laughter rumbled from Nick's chest. "At first, I think he figured I was angling for a raise. Once I convinced him I was serious, he gave me his blessing and sent you that jacket."

"But what about all the excitement? The adventure?"

The corners of his mouth curled up. "I have a feeling I'll find plenty of that."

Annie gave a soft laugh. "In Indiana?"

He ran his finger along her cheek. "I've had more adventures

315

trying to keep up with you than anything I've ever done in the arena."

Annie's eyes misted. "But what are you going to do now?"

Nick tapped his fingers together. "I figure I need to spend more time with Uncle Silas. You never know. I might ask him for a job as a foreman in the new factory." A grin split his face. "Maybe learning to crack that bullwhip will still come in handy."

The grin faded. He leaned closer and took her right hand in his. "What Bill Cody said in his note is true, Annie. You've stolen my heart. I don't know if it's too soon for you to be sure of how you feel, but I'll be waiting whenever you are ready."

Annie caught her breath. Was she ready? Her reticule lay in her lap. She could feel the weight of the new Bible pressing against her knees. She traced its outline with the fingers of her left hand. Already, she had to remind herself it wasn't the same one she had carried with her for more than a year. After only a week, it fit into her reticule as though it belonged.

Could it be the same with her heart? Would it make room for Nick as readily?

She looked back up at him and gazed into dark brown eyes filled with love, admiration, and an unspoken desire that made her shiver. She reached up and touched his face. Already, its planes were becoming familiar to her fingers.

Her words came out as the barest whisper. "Are you proposing?"

He pulled her nearer. His thumbs stroked slow circles on the back on her hand. "I don't want to rush you, but yes, I am. I'm offering you myself, my love, and all that my heart holds."

Annie traced the outline of his chin with a feather touch. "I never thought I could love again." A sigh escaped her lips. "But it seems I was wrong."

Nick's fingers tightened on her hand. "Is that a yes?"

She looked into his eyes, and in that instant, she felt the last of her doubts and fears dissolve. Will would always be a part of her, and she would treasure his memory forever. But those memories belonged to the past. The future lay before her, and she was ready to embrace it.

Her lips curved into a tremulous smile. "Yes."

Nick captured both her hands in his and pressed them to his lips. His eyes stared into hers with an intensity that shook her to the core. He leaned so close his breath brushed across her ear when he spoke. "If we only had some privacy, we could seal this with a proper kiss."

Annie pulled away long enough to glance around the car. Everywhere she looked, exhausted passengers dozed, sated from their time at the fair. In the seat behind her, Silas scribbled away in his notebook.

She turned back to Nick, the man to whom she had pledged her heart. The one with whom she would share her tomorrows.

"I don't think anyone will notice." With a sigh of surrender, she melted into his arms and lifted her face as his lips sought hers.

About the Author

Author of nine novels and eleven novellas, Carol Cox's love of history, mystery, and romance is evident in the books she writes. A pastor's wife, Carol has a passion for fiction and is a firm believer in the power of story to convey spiritual truths. She makes her home with her husband and young daughter in northern Arizona, where the deer and the antelope really do play—often within view of the family's front porch. To learn more about Carol and her books, visit her Web site at www.CarolCoxBooks.com. She'd love to hear from you!

WATCH FOR

FAIR GAME

BOOK 2

in the series

SPRING 2007

AVAILABLE WHEREVER GREAT
CHRISTIAN FICTION IS SOLD